Jordan's Sister

BRANDI EASTERLING COLLINS

LUMINESCE
•PUBLISHING•

Luminesce Publishing books may be ordered through booksellers or by contacting:

Luminesce Publishing
www.luminescepublishing.com

LUMINESCE
•PUBLISHING•

Cover image © Brandi Easterling Collins
Illustrations designed by Freepik
Cover design © Luminesce Publishing and Felisha Weaver
Interior design © Luminesce Publishing
Author photos © Felisha Weaver Photography

ISBN: 978-1-7322289-8-6 (hardcover)
ISBN: 978-1-7322289-0-0 (paperback)
ISBN: 978-1-7322289-1-7 (ebook)
Library of Congress Control Number: 2021933111

This novel is dedicated to all the people who have been "Laynes" in my life at different points in time—those who have loved me at my best, loved me even more at my worst, supported me when I was broken, and encouraged me to always let my light shine.

Acknowledgements:

Thank you to my husband, Jonathan, for listening to me babble about this book for almost two years and offering opinions from a male perspective when needed. Thank you to my children, Drew and Meredith, for allowing me time to write and telling their teachers about their mom, the author.

Thank you to my wonderful friends and beta readers, Alisha, Felisha, Liz, and Melissa for their valuable feedback and support of this story.

Thank you to Felisha Weaver for photography and graphic design consultation to help my book cover look its best.

Thank you for the continued support of the Campbell, Collins, Easterling and Russell families as I pursue my writing dreams.

Thank you to the #amwriting and #writingcommunity Twitter communities for the continuous support and encouragement of independent authors and to authors Brad Carl, Devin Cutting, and Sarah Krewis for their willingness to help and answer questions during my writing journey.

Thank you to my favorite mutts, the late Buddy, Peanut, and Roscoe for being a captive audience during my read-aloud editing sessions.

Chapter 1

Sunday, May 22, 2016

Dressed in her standard work uniform of black pants and a long-sleeved white shirt, Taylor unbuttoned her cuffs and rolled the sleeves past her elbows, exposing the small four-leaf clover tattoo on the inside of her forearm. Her long hair was pulled into a tight bun to appease the bar owner, who had strict rules about hair but was more lenient about piercings and tattoos.

After she had dyed her hair black at eighteen, Taylor added two additional earrings to each ear and a tiny green-stoned stud to her nose to help disguise herself. She preferred her new look to being just another pretty, blue-eyed blond in California. Taylor wished she'd inherited her father's green eyes—the only thing she wanted from him—but instead she looked like her mother.

She had worked at the Mocking Bird bar three nights a week for the past four months since leasing an apartment upstairs. She loved the atmosphere more than anything and adored her tiny one-bedroom apartment, a vast contrast to her huge childhood home. It was her last night working at the bar because her four-week temporary job would begin the next day. Taylor didn't have to work at all; she chose to work to be around normal people who didn't know her past. Her extensive trust fund could last the rest of her life if she lived modestly and managed the money responsibly. She didn't have many friends, but the superficial relationships she'd developed with the regular customers and the more meaningful ones with her neighbors helped quell her loneliness.

It was Sunday night, live-band karaoke night. As the band finished setting up, the regular performers filtered in and waited patiently, all ready to take the stage and imagine their own fame for the evening. Sundays were great, but Taylor's favorite nights at the Mocking Bird were the last Fridays of every month because of the showcase for songwriters. Several up-and-coming artists had received record deals after performing there. The owner, Marcus Cosney, joked all the time with customers that Songbird was taken, so he had to be creative with the name.

Taylor glanced at the television in the corner as she wiped off the well-worn counter, always careful with its delicate mother-of-pearl details. Mr. Cosney preferred showing celebrity gossip in his bar because he said politics or sports caused angry customers. It was easy enough to ignore; Taylor rarely watched anything. But something on TV that evening caught her attention. The show came back from a commercial break boasting an exclusive interview with the actress Jordan Hoffman.

"And we're back with Jordan Hoffman, star of the *Awake* trilogy and former child star of *The Spectacular Smiths*," the host said. "Jordan, it's so great to have you here with us."

Jordan smiled sweetly at the camera. She looked perfect. Her blue eyes sparkled, and her golden hair fell in loose curls around her shoulders. She wore a form-fitting red dress like she always did for interviews. Red looked radiant on her, showcasing a classic beauty no one could deny. "I am thrilled to be here," she said. "*Awake* is such an amazing story. I am so honored to be able to portray Helena and offer readers of the books a true visual of the character."

"What is your favorite thing about Helena?" the host asked.

"Oh, there are too many things," Jordan said. "Helena is so sure of herself in the wake of such disastrous conditions. I have truly enjoyed watching her change and grow as the story progressed. I think fans will really enjoy the final installment this fall."

"How is this different from your role as Laken on the sitcom?"

"Oh, I couldn't even begin to compare the two characters. Laken was just a regular girl, and Helena is a hero in the face of disaster. The two couldn't be more different except for the fact they look alike." Jordan giggled and fussed with her hair.

"Which character do you identify with the most, Laken or Helena?"

"Oh, definitely Laken. Everyone knows my name after the *Awake* movies, but I would like to think I'm still just a regular person."

"I hear there will be a lot more music in this installment," the host said. "Can you tell us anything?"

"Oh, I'm sworn to secrecy, but I will say the hot new guitarist is someone I'm looking forward to working with." Jordan laughed, holding her hand against her chest.

Taylor rolled her eyes and turned off the TV so the band could start their soundcheck. *What a load of bullshit*, she thought. Someone else had written Jordan's comments. There was no way Jordan could have come up with them herself. No one knew her the way Taylor did. People knew her name and thought they knew all about her because Jordan was America's sweetheart on the cover of every magazine, but only Taylor knew her dark past—the drugs, the mental breakdown, and her subsequent suicide attempt—things that if leaked to the press would knock her off her pedestal. But Taylor would never say anything bad about Jordan publicly; she would rather pretend she didn't know her at all. It had been at least six months since Taylor had seen her in person.

Willow, a part-time bartender, slipped in through the employee entrance in the back. She lived upstairs with her girlfriend, Kayla, the owner's daughter, which gave her free rein of the whole establishment. Dressed in her usual workout clothes, there was nothing extraordinary about Willow's appearance.

"Hey girl, that was some good music last night," Willow said as she sat at the counter in front of Taylor. "I'm glad the revolving door at your place seems to have stopped." Her mousy-brown hair, which was the same shade as her eyes, was pulled back in a ponytail. If the color beige could have been a person, it would have been Willow, which worked well for her because she preferred to blend in.

Taylor laughed. "Yeah, I'm trying the celibate lifestyle like you suggested. I hope my guitar wasn't too loud."

"I prefer that to other noises," Willow said with a smirk. "But I didn't say be celibate; I said to consider dating someone and not sleeping around. There's no sense in being lonely."

Lonely didn't even begin to cover what Taylor felt during her late nights writing songs. "You not working tonight?"

"No, I'm off the schedule till Tuesday. I have to go with Marcus to a doctor's appointment tomorrow afternoon."

"Is he okay?" Taylor asked, scanning Willow's face for the truth. She cared a lot for soft-spoken Mr. Cosney, who kept his greying black hair in a buzz cut as he had since his tour in Vietnam during the late 60s. On especially warm days, he would roll up his sleeves, allowing the employees a rare glimpse of the handmade military tattoos barely visible on his dark brown skin.

"He's fine," Willow said. "Just an outpatient foot thing."

"Good." Taylor smiled at Willow and breathed a sigh of relief.

"It won't be the same here without you working. Will you be in class tomorrow?"

"No," Taylor said. "I got my schedule, and it overlaps with your morning class. I promise I'll keep practicing on the weekends."

"You still need a lot of practice."

"I'll come back to class when the recording's over. And I'll come back here to sing when I have something good enough finished. What can I get you?"

"Whatever's cheapest is fine."

"It's not like you're paying anyway."

"True," Willow said with a shrug.

Taylor looked up as the bell on the front door dinged. A couple walked in and took seats at one of the tables at the front near the small stage. The place was big enough for the customers, but not so large it wasn't still cozy and intimate with its 1920s tin ceilings and original woodwork.

Through the window, Taylor noticed a guy standing outside with a black guitar case on his shoulder. He had long, wavy light brown hair and colorful geometric tattoos on both forearms. He looked at his own reflection in the window as if he didn't realize he could be seen from inside while he talked on his phone.

Willow followed Taylor's gaze, then looked back at her. "Taylor!" she exclaimed. "The beer!"

"Shit," Taylor muttered. She quickly turned off the tap and mopped up the beer from the countertop.

Willow shook her head. "Think of your music," she said. "You need to release some of your songs."

"He's hot, and he has a guitar," Taylor whispered, trying not to drool. "I got distracted."

"Think dating—not one-night stands. I think he's coming in here. Ask him out. You're a liberated woman. Maybe he could help you with your music."

Outside the Mocking Bird, Layne finished his call with his sister. No matter how many times he'd told Christina he was fine with his ex-girlfriend getting married, she didn't believe him.

5

"You were with her for more than two years; are you sure you're okay?" his sister asked.

"Yes, Christina, I'm fine," he said with a sigh. "And it's been another two years since I broke up with her. I really need to go pick up my key now."

"I just wonder why you signed a six-month lease for a four-week job and don't consider that running away? What about your house?"

"Sis, I love you, but you already have a husband and kids to deal with. Stop worrying about me. My house is fine. I've rented it out for the next six months anyway. I'll decide later if I want to sell it or live there again. I'm happy Amanda got married."

"Then why haven't you had another relationship since you ended things with her?"

Layne looked through the window at a beautiful dark-haired woman watching him from behind the mirrored counter at the back. "Because I haven't met the right person. I'm hanging up now." He ended the call, rolling his eyes. Christina had tried to set him up on no less than four blind dates in the last six months.

It wasn't that Layne didn't want another relationship, he just needed to find someone who wanted the same things he did. Settling down with kids and a boring job wasn't his dream. He walked into the bar and watched the woman clean up a mess on the counter.

Layne approached the bar and read the woman's nametag. "Hi, Taylor, I'm looking for Marcus Cosney," he said. "He was supposed to leave a key for me. I'm Layne." He extended his hand.

"Oh." Taylor shook his hand and held it just a moment longer than necessary before letting go, which made Layne's skin tingle. "You're the new tenant. I saw the movers delivering your stuff earlier today. Sorry, Mr. Cosney hasn't left the key with me yet, but he'll probably check in soon if you want to hang out."

Layne looked at Taylor's body and stopped when he got back to her eyes. "Sure," he said. He sat down and stood his guitar case against the counter. She was the hottest woman he'd ever seen and looked familiar, but Layne couldn't think of where he might have seen her before. "The bartenders weren't so pretty at the last place I went."

Taylor smiled. "You know how to use that thing?" she asked, pointing to the guitar. "Or do you just carry it around for show?"

"What do you think?" he asked with a grin. He watched as Taylor blushed. She was more than just beautiful, she was cute and seemed sweet as well.

"Well, open mic night isn't until Friday, so all we have going tonight is live-band karaoke, 90s night," Taylor said. "You can hear our regulars. Some of them are pretty good...others not so much."

Layne laughed. "I guess I'll have to wait until Friday. I'm a songwriter."

"Another one?" Willow asked, shaking her head. "God, you people love this place."

"Huh?" Layne asked. "What other one?"

"Taylor here is one of the best singers I've heard," Willow said. "Just wait, she always has to start off the karaoke to get the regulars inspired."

Layne turned to face Taylor. "A singer? Do you play too? Write?" It was too good to be true that Taylor shared his passion for music.

Taylor glared at Willow. "A little," she said.

"Well," Layne said. "I'm looking forward to hearing you."

"What'll you have?" Taylor asked. "You can't sit at the counter without a drink."

"Beer's fine."

"What kind?"

"Surprise me," he said as he stood up. "Will you watch my guitar for a minute?"

"Sure," Taylor said.

Layne reminded Taylor of a guy named Brandon she'd met as a teenager, who was also a singer. They'd shared a brief moment but hadn't kept in touch, much to her disappointment. Brandon had the most stunning emerald green eyes—Taylor's birthstone and favorite color. Intrigued, she turned to Willow as Layne went into the restroom. "Oh, my God, is he not the sexiest guy you've ever seen?"

Willow flashed her a confused look. "You do remember I'm dating a woman, right?"

"Sorry. He reminds me of a guy I met once. Do you remember that boy band Backdraft?" Taylor grabbed a glass and filled it with their most popular German beer, placing it in front of Layne's stool.

"Yeah, they released a couple of good songs I guess."

"Brandon Stallings. I met him once when we were kids. Layne resembles him."

Willow laughed. "All those boys looked the same to me. I have Layne's key. Marcus left it with me. I didn't want to interrupt all the flirting. You want it?"

"Sure," Taylor said. "I guess we can't keep it from him."

"Why don't you just ask him out instead of standing there lusting? Think potential relationship."

"I've told you, I'm not good at those. I don't even know if he's single, or straight." Taylor rested her head against her hands.

"Considering he just undressed you with his eyes, I'd say he's both. Plus, he looks to be about your age. He can't be past twenty-five—not that you checked his ID like you're supposed to."

Taylor threw her hands in the air. "Give me a break! I haven't served him yet."

"Oh, I imagine you'll be serving him in other ways," Willow said, her eyebrows raised.

"Hey," Taylor said, playfully tossing peanuts at Willow. "If you're so concerned, you can check his ID when he gets back."

Willow introduced herself as another bartender and asked to see Layne's ID when he came back to the counter. She grinned at him as she looked at it. "He's good," she told Taylor. "All legal at twenty-four." She left to sit with some friends who were calling her over to a corner table near the front windows.

When Taylor gave Layne his key, he thanked her but didn't get up. She studied his face, which looked like it hadn't been shaved in a couple of days. She figured he'd only recently progressed from cute to handsome. "You really staying for karaoke?" she asked.

"I'm staying to hear you," he said. "You look so familiar. Where might I have seen you before?"

Taylor wondered if he recognized her but figured a guy like him wouldn't have seen her on *The Spectacular Smiths*, something she desperately wanted to leave behind. "I just have a common face," she said. "I guess you do, too, because I was thinking the same thing about you."

"Oh, I was somebody once, but you'd never guess who," he said.

"Who are you?" Taylor asked. She wondered again if he could be Brandon using a different name.

"I can't tell you everything all at once. What fun would that be?" Layne stared at Taylor's clover tattoo.

"You like clovers?" she asked, running her fingers across her tattoo.

"Yeah, something like that," he said, locking eyes with her. Taylor looked away to break the intensity of his stare.

The bar was getting more crowded, and three other bartenders had arrived for their shifts. Taylor looked at the clock and took a deep breath. She usually wasn't nervous about kicking off the singing, but it was different with Layne watching her. She walked over to the microphone and put on her biggest smile.

"It's great to see you all back here," she said. "I'm Taylor Lee, and tonight's my last night working at this fine establishment for a little while. I'll miss you all so much. I'll get us started, but then you guys have to jump in, okay?" Taylor studied the list of available songs for the evening. She could sing anything, really, but picked "Four-Leaf Clover" because she felt it best showcased her voice. She scanned the crowd while singing and made a point to look at Layne a couple of times to see if he was watching her, and he always was.

Layne was awestruck. Taylor had the most exquisite voice he'd heard in a long time, and she knew how to perform. The only person he could recall who sounded similar was Taylor Hoffman, who had played Sierra on *The Spectacular Smiths*. He'd met her briefly once on the set of the show when his band guest-starred but wasn't able to talk with her as long as he'd hoped to, something he'd always regretted. He remembered Taylor blushing when he complimented her that day. Was she the same Taylor or was it a coincidence? Her eyes and voice seemed to match. Add ten years, tattoos, the pierced nose and some black hair dye. Could it be?

It is her, he thought, *it has to be her.* According to the tabloids, she'd left the business entirely. Layne felt like part of Taylor's soul shined through as she sang, just like Taylor Hoffman's had during the show.

Taylor finished her song and received cheers from everyone in the bar. She left the stage, and others went up and performed, but none came close to being as good as her. Layne sat at the bar, slowly sipping his beer, waiting for Taylor to return from her rounds chatting with the customers.

"You did great," he said as Taylor stepped behind the counter. "You should sing all the time."

"Thank you," she said as she blushed. "I think I was born in the wrong generation. The music I love the most was released around the same time I was born. Will I get to hear you sing tonight?"

"Maybe," Layne said with a sly smile. He was now certain Taylor Lee was Taylor Hoffman. The tattoo on her arm felt like fate since he had his own clover tattoo on his chest—symbolic of having survived teenage stardom relatively unscathed. "It depends on if they can play my favorite song, which happens to be from the 90s."

"Which one?" Taylor asked. "I love 90s music, so I bet I know it."

Layne shook his head as he stood up. "You'll have to wait and see," he teased. He spoke with the band for a few seconds before he walked over to the microphone and moved the stool out of the way so he could stand.

As the band began to play "I'll Be," Layne watched Taylor's face light up. He sang with more emotion than any of the other performers had and felt like he was singing only to Taylor. When the song ended, the other customers stood up and cheered for him like they had for everyone else, only louder. He humbly thanked them and walked back to his seat at the counter.

Taylor smiled at him. "You should sing all the time too," she said.

"Thank you. I guess I passed your singing standards?"

"Your voice is amazing."

"I'm much better if I rehearse first," Layne said. "Maybe you could give me some pointers sometime."

"I'm actually off work soon," Taylor said. "I live upstairs, too, if you want to hang out and work on those pointers tonight."

Layne stretched his arms over his head and popped his fingers. "Yeah, I think I could fit it into my schedule," he said. "So, you're done working here for a bit?"

"Just four weeks. I have a temporary voice-over job, and then I'll come back I guess."

Layne figured Taylor's temporary job probably involved the final *Awake* movie with her sister. He knew he'd be working with a voice-over artist. If he was right, he was certain it would be the best job he'd ever had. Either way, the opportunity to reconnect with Taylor thrilled him.

Chapter 2

Taylor unlocked her apartment and let Layne follow her inside. After she had closed and locked the door, she plopped down on her old yellow couch and invited Layne to join her. He sat on the opposite end, one cushion away from her, and looked around the apartment.

"This place looks like mine," he said.

Last renovated in the 1950s, except for the updated appliances, the apartment had a large living area with no clear place for a dining table and a mostly-white kitchen at the back accented with cobalt-blue tiles on the countertops and backsplash. Thin-planked hardwood floors ran throughout the space into the tiny bedroom. It had all the quaint charm Taylor enjoyed.

"They all look the same," Taylor said. "Willow's apartment is a little bigger."

Layne leaned forward. "Do you always invite strange men you've just met into your apartment?" he asked. "Isn't that dangerous?"

Taylor looked at his eyes. They were emerald green with a sparkle in them she hadn't seen in anyone in years. "You look trustworthy," she said. She took off her shoes and pulled her legs underneath herself. "Plus, Mr. Cosney does extensive background checks, so you can't be hiding too much. Are you saying I should be afraid of you?"

"Terrified," he said, raising his eyebrows. "No. My friends tell me I'm a nice guy."

"I don't have many friends." Taylor took down her hair and let it fall over her shoulders. Willow was the first exception since her high school boyfriend. Before that, Jordan was her best and only friend, which hindered Taylor.

"I find that hard to believe," Layne said. "You seem nice enough that you should have a lot of friends."

"I have acquaintances because I'm friendly. It doesn't mean they're true friends." It was true because friendships required a level of intimacy she rarely allowed.

"Doesn't that get lonely?"

"Sometimes."

Layne tilted his head to the side and looked at Taylor for a moment before speaking again. "You don't seem lonely right now; you seem happy. The crowd loved you tonight."

"Music makes me happy, but they don't know me. You don't know me."

"But I think I'd like to."

"Are you going to tell me who you are?"

"Maybe," Layne said as he moved to the center cushion. "It depends on if you'll tell me who you are. I think I already know."

"Do you?" Taylor asked, using her hand to hide the slight smirk she felt spreading across her lips. "I seriously doubt it."

"Well, let me see if I can guess," he said. "But first, how old are you?"

"You already know I'm not jailbait since I'm a bartender."

Layne laughed. "Just answer the question."

"Fine. I'm almost twenty-three."

"See, that wasn't so bad. Now, something tells me you're a natural blond. Am I right?"

"Maybe…" Taylor watched as Layne's inquisitive look changed to a huge smile.

"Does the expression 'sweet puppies' mean anything to you?"

"Oh shit!" Taylor said as she covered her face with her hands, desperately trying to hide the redness. He was Brandon!

"I knew it!" Layne said. "You're Taylor Hoffman!"

"I can never escape the show or that damn catchphrase. Sweet puppies, you're right, Brandon Stallings!"

He laughed so much his whole body shook. "Yep, Layne's my middle name."

"That's why Willow had that look on her face after she checked your ID. I told her who I thought you resembled, and she said all you Backdraft boys looked the same."

"That modest boy band changed my life."

"Modest? Hardly. Holy shit! Brandon!" She immediately hugged him and backed away when he seemed surprised by her gesture. "It's so good to see you again. I thought I was going crazy because I felt like I'd met you before. Your eyes—those haven't changed like the rest of you."

Layne grinned. "Well, aging ten years has that effect. Plus, I don't bleach my hair blond anymore."

"Why didn't you just tell me?"

"I wasn't sure you remembered me. I was disappointed we didn't keep in touch."

"Which mask did you wear, green or red? You wouldn't tell me that day."

"Green."

Backdraft had been a huge sensation for a few years. Each of the four boys in the group had worn a mask across his eyes in either red, blue, green, or yellow during performances as a gimmick to set them apart from the other boy bands that had paved the way for their success. Two boys had green eyes, and two had brown. The boys also had similar hairstyles and body types, so fangirls always tried to guess which boy wore which mask. The band's trademark was singing beautifully together in perfect harmony.

Taylor remembered their meeting well.

2007

As Taylor walked into her dressing room, thinking she was alone, she began humming the song she would have to sing later. Heavy breathing coming from the back of the room startled her, and she found a blond teenage boy sitting on the floor near her makeup table. "Hey, what are you doing in here?" she asked. She watched him jump from where he sat, still struggling to catch his breath.

"I—I'm...sorry," he stammered.

She dumped out a paper sack from her vanity and rolled it down as she knelt in front of him. Taylor gently touched the boy's shoulder, and he pulled away. She handed him the bag. "Here, breathe in this. It'll help, I promise." She stayed beside him while he calmed down. He looked at her with the most beautiful green eyes she'd ever seen in her thirteen years.

"You're Taylor," he said. "God, I'm so embarrassed."

"Are you okay?" she asked.

His breathing was normal, and his face was no longer pale. "I'm okay," he said. "It's been a while since that's happened. I guess I got nervous about performing. Thanks for helping me."

Taylor realized who he was. "Oh, my God, you're Brandon Stallings! I didn't know Backdraft was here already."

"Yeah, the other guys went off to talk to Jordan I think."

Taylor stood up and grabbed a hair tie from her vanity, putting her long blond hair into a ponytail. She sat on the floor beside Brandon, leaving a few inches in between them. "Figures. Most people want to meet her right away."

Brandon looked at Taylor and smiled. "Not everyone."

"So, which mask do you wear?"

He laughed nervously. "I can't tell you; my manager would kill me. She'd also kill me if she knew I freaked out in your dressing room. I'm sorry. Please, don't tell anyone."

"It's okay," Taylor said. "I won't tell anyone, I promise, even if you won't tell me about the mask."

"What song you were humming before? You have a pretty voice."

16

She shrugged her shoulders. *"Just something silly I have to sing for the show in a couple of weeks. It's no big deal."*

"I wondered if it was really you singing when I watched the show a couple of weeks ago. I thought you were awesome."

"It's really me. You know, you're pretty awesome too. You're part of the most famous group around right now. It's like it happened overnight."

Brandon took a couple of shaky breaths. *"I know. I don't think I'll ever get used to being in front of a camera. How do you do it?"*

"I didn't know there was any other thing to do until I was already into it."

"So, you sing, but do you really play the piano?"

"Yeah. I'm also learning guitar, but the producers don't think it's right for Sierra, so they won't let me play it on the show."

"That's cool. I play guitar, too, but it's not right for Backdraft. I want to write my own songs someday."

Brandon's statement caught Taylor's attention. She'd already written a song. *"Why wait for someday?"*

He smiled and looked down at his hands. *"Do you ever wish you could run away from it all—the fame?"*

Taylor laughed. *"I did all the time until they let me sing. Now, I want to do that more than anything else,"* she said. *"I don't think I want to keep acting after the show's over."*

Brandon ran his fingers through his hair. *"At least there's an end in sight. I think I'm stuck."*

"But not forever, Brandon," Taylor said as she placed her hand on his arm. *"Backdraft doesn't have to last forever if you don't want it to. Start writing your own stuff."*

He brushed away a strand of hair from Taylor's face. *"You're so nice,"* he said. *"Not at all how I thought you'd be."*

Taylor blushed. *"How did you think I would be?"* she asked as the door burst open. Brandon jumped up, and Jordan came in, followed by the other three Backdraft members. *"Jordan! You scared me!"*

One of the Backdraft guys dragged Brandon out of the room and said, "Come on, dude, we have to rehearse."

Another said, "You can hook up with her later."

Brandon gave a slight wave to Taylor, who still sat against the wall with her legs stretched out in front of her. She waved back and then looked up at her sister.

Jordan scoffed as she turned to leave the room. "Like you have a chance with him," she said, slamming the door behind her.

"Do you remember what we talked about that day?" Layne asked.

"Of course, I do," Taylor said. She'd always thought of their conversation as one of the best of her teenage years. "After you calmed down, we talked about music. You asked me if I really sang and played the piano, and I told you I was learning guitar."

"Uh huh, and when I told you I could play, too, you were impressed. Maybe even a little bit star-struck. I know I was."

"Mildly impressed," Taylor said with a smirk.

"You told me you preferred singing to acting and hoped to take a break when the show ended."

"You were overwhelmed by the fame. Then the other guys came back in and dragged you off somewhere."

"Yeah, I could have killed them," Layne said. "I always regretted not getting your number."

"Did you ever have any more panic attacks?"

Layne pressed his lips together and nodded. "Several times, mostly before big concerts. It's funny, I did the same thing you taught me each time and always wondered what you were doing. The guys teased me about trying to hook up with you, but that wasn't what I was thinking. They're all at least a year older than me, so they gave me all kinds of hell."

"I always wondered about you after I heard Backdraft broke up," Taylor said, absentmindedly twirling her hair around her fingers. "After that, though, I stopped following the tabloids. Sounds like you're as screwed up as I am."

Layne leaned his head against the back of the couch and covered his eyes with his arms. "Totally. You know, your sister made out with Chase in between takes that day. He kept bragging about it. I guess you know they hooked up for a while afterward."

Taylor ignored Layne's reference to Jordan. She knew her sister dated Chase on and off for years. "You changed your name and appearance to get away from it all," she said. "You used to be so preppy."

"Yep, just like you. People still recognize me sometimes, but no one bothers me too much. You've done a better job of it. You can't hide forever, though. People will recognize you if they look closely enough. Plus, Jordan still seems to be chasing fame and finding it."

Taylor was close enough to smell the beer on Layne's breath when he sat up and faced her. "So, is it true you broke up the band to go solo?" she asked.

"Ah, so you were a fangirl," he said with a chuckle. "It's the only way you'd know which eye colors went with which masks."

Taylor was caught—she had been a huge fan. "Maybe I recall one of the songs. 'Heart to Face' was so damn catchy."

"I wrote it a couple of weeks after we talked."

"Yeah, it seemed different than the others." Taylor sang the lines she remembered from his song. *"With my heart to face, I can't escape this place…"*

Layne moved closer to Taylor. "Just admit you were a fangirl," he said. "Which one of us did you think was the cutest? All the girls had a favorite."

"I'm not answering," she said. This man, who was extremely famous before, now seemed so normal and silly—drunk maybe. And his lips, despite smelling like beer, were deliciously kissable.

"Oh, that means it was me," he said, pointing to himself. "You had my poster hanging above your bed and went to sleep dreaming about me every night. Now, you think the dream has come true because I'm here on your couch."

Taylor locked eyes with Layne. "Wow, you are modest, aren't you? And slightly drunk." She'd seen that look before from more guys than she could count. They'd all been different in their own ways, but each served the same purpose—a temporary escape from the life she felt dragging her down all the time.

As they spoke, Layne kept moving closer—way too close for ordinary conversation. "I'm not drunk at all," he said. "Not even buzzed."

"Really?" Taylor wasn't sure she believed him since his cheeks were flushed, and he couldn't seem to sit still. Maybe he was just nervous. Either way, she wanted to kiss him.

"Didn't even finish my beer. I watched you and listened to you sing. You have the most amazing voice."

"I bet you say that to a lot of women."

"No, I've actually never said that to a woman before. But there may or may not have been a poster of you above my bed." He winked at her.

"Oh, a fanboy?"

"I couldn't help it. You were so talented, and so nice when we met," Layne said as he brushed Taylor's hair out of her face and moved closer. "I had the biggest crush on you those last two seasons. And your voice. Wow. It's how I knew for sure who you were when you were singing earlier."

Instantly, Taylor was transported back to the first time he touched her face, and all the butterflies she'd felt at thirteen came fluttering back. She gasped loudly enough to startle Layne into moving back a bit.

"What song best describes how you feel?" he asked.

Taylor laughed at the absurdity of his question, releasing some of her nervous energy. "Like, right now, or in general?"

"Whatever you want. Just pick one."

She thought about it. "Well, there's this Sia song…"

"Sia?" Layne asked, raising one eyebrow. "Like 'Chandelier' Sia?"

"Yeah, but not that song. This one's older, not as popular. It's called 'Breathe Me.' It came out about ten years before 'Chandelier.' Pre-wig."

"I've never heard it."

"You want to hear it?"

"Yeah." He moved closer, but not as close as before. "Will you sing it for me?"

"I can't do it justice." Taylor found the song on her phone and played it for Layne. He took the phone from her to listen. Taylor closed her eyes and listened to the raw emotion in the lyrics. No one could have written a better song to describe how she felt about her life in general. Layne's shoulder brushed against hers as the song ended. "Did you like it?" she asked without opening her eyes.

"I did," he said. "I think you could sing it and do it justice. Even without the lyrics, the music is incredible and full of raw emotion."

Taylor opened her eyes the instant she felt Layne's hand caress her cheek. He seemed to be using his eyes to ask permission to kiss her as he inched closer.

"You know," Layne continued, now inches away from her face. "The day we met, I wanted to kiss you, but we were interrupted. Since I had never kissed anyone, I wouldn't have known what to do, anyway."

"What about now?" Taylor asked, suddenly desperate for him to touch her again. She didn't realize how lonely she'd been until Layne moved in the last few inches to gently kiss her. She kissed him back more passionately than either of them expected, as though she'd been starved for his affection her entire life.

"Wow," Layne whispered as they broke for air. He pulled Taylor closer and kissed her again.

He had guessed right about the Backdraft poster above Taylor's bed when she was a teenager. Plus, she'd just had the best conversation she could remember for the longest time and didn't want to stop kissing Layne. Although she'd promised Willow she would try dating, Taylor already knew how her evening would end.

After he let Taylor pull his shirt over his head, Layne hesitated before touching the buttons on her shirt. "Do you want to do this?" he asked, kissing her collarbone and working his way up her neck. "We can stop."

Suddenly hurt, Taylor pulled away. It had been several weeks since anyone touched her. "Do you want to stop?"

"No." Layne pulled Taylor back into his arms.

"Then don't." Without further hesitation, they made their way to the bedroom where Taylor made her intentions clear by pulling a condom out of her nightstand drawer.

Afterward, Taylor's heart and mind were racing, and her hands felt clammy. Panic was setting in, which surprised her. In the past, she felt relaxed and indifferent about kicking guys out of her apartment after they'd exhausted themselves. Embarrassed and exposed, Taylor quickly dressed in shorts and a t-shirt while she waited for Layne to come out of her bathroom.

When Layne got out, he bent down and touched Taylor's face, sending her already pounding heart into a frenzy. Looking at his eyes made her lightheaded.

"Hey, are you okay?" Layne asked.

"I'm fine," Taylor said, but she could tell by the look on his face that Layne wasn't any more convinced than she was. She tried to calm herself by taking a few deep breaths.

Layne sat and put his arm around Taylor. "You're not fine; you're shaking. I didn't hurt you, did I?"

Taylor shook her head. "No, I'm just tired."

He gently touched a large bruise on her knee. "Taylor, what's with all these bruises on your legs? Did someone else hurt you?"

"It's nothing and not what you think." She pushed his hand away, gripping his fingers tightly enough to control the shaking in her own hand. "You should go. I have to get up early for work." Despite the connection she felt to Layne, she'd never let anyone sleep in her bed with her since her high school boyfriend, Michael. After their painful breakup, she hadn't wanted another serious relationship.

"I want to see you again," Layne said.

"I'm sure we'll see each other around."

"I don't want to leave it up to chance this time. Could I get your number? I want to take you out sometime soon."

Taylor went back to her living room and picked up her phone, her hands still shaking.

Layne took the phone, sent himself a message, and handed it back to Taylor. "You're still shaking," he said.

"You're staring at me."

"Because you're incredibly beautiful." He hugged Taylor and pressed his lips to her forehead. "Goodnight. Get some rest."

Taylor had to get up early for work the next day, but she couldn't shut off her mind. After trying for more than an hour to go to sleep, she grabbed a notebook and began scribbling random thoughts as they came to her, unsure if she was writing poetry or a song until a melody lingered on the tip of her tongue as she mouthed the words. While writing, Taylor preferred the old-school pen and paper approach rather than getting out her laptop. According to her creative writing professor in college, coherency could happen later. She just wanted to get everything out of her head.

She had taken online classes to earn her degree in general studies with an emphasis in writing. Fear of recognition had kept her from the traditional route, but she wanted to accomplish something for which Jordan had no interest.

After writing awhile, Taylor felt more at peace and stretched out on her bed again. Her phone buzzed beside her with a text from Layne. He'd saved his number as a new contact.

Taylor, I really enjoyed our evening. Talking to you mainly. Not that I didn't enjoy the rest of it. I hope to see you again soon.

She read the message he'd sent to himself earlier: **The beautiful and amazing Taylor Lee.**

Taylor replied. **Goodnight, Layne.**

I can't believe Brandon Stallings is my neighbor, and I had sex with him, she thought before she drifted off to sleep.

chapter 3

Jordan wondered who the new guy was at the Mocking Bird as she watched him from behind her dark glasses and auburn wig—her standard disguise for spying on her sister. The guy was handsome but not in an obvious way. He'd be downright sexy if he'd get a haircut. Even so, he was a musician, apparent by the guitar beside him, and that alone made him Jordan's type.

She sat in the back corner, out of view of the stage where she always sat while Taylor sang. Her sister was up on stage using her first and middle names. It was ridiculous for Taylor to not capitalize on her former fame. Jordan hated to admit it, but Taylor was good. Really good. Better than any of the vocalists Jordan had encountered in the Hollywood scene—all without any vocal training. Sure, she'd had music lessons in guitar and piano, but neither took much effort. Nothing seemed to require much effort from Taylor. Acting, dancing, singing, playing music—Taylor was rubbing her perfection in Jordan's face all the time.

But it's me who's famous, not her, Jordan reminded herself as her sister finished the song. It was Jordan who'd had the television interview air earlier in the evening, taped more than a week ago. Over two months had passed since she'd last watched Taylor. Studio scenes for *Awake* were finished, and Jordan wanted to see what her sister was doing. The crowd still loved Taylor, but Jordan thought karaoke was lame.

She glanced at the long-haired guy, who was practically giving Taylor a standing ovation. *He's not that attractive,* Jordan thought. She slipped out the entrance before Taylor could make her rounds through the tables. Taylor was a creature of habit and worked her way through the bar in the same pattern from the last time Jordan was there. Several times and she'd never once discovered Jordan in the crowd.

Later, from Taylor's fire escape, Jordan peered through the slats of the blinds and watched her sister fall into bed with the long-haired guy from the bar. She'd seen her sister do the same thing with several guys since moving into the apartment. It was laughable. Her sister, who made her high school boyfriend beg for sex for a year before she finally gave it up, was now a slut. Taylor spent too much time screwing guys and not enough time furthering her career—something which could bring more positive publicity Jordan's way.

It was hard work staying in the headlines, and Taylor wasn't making it any easier. Jordan hated all the speculation and questions about what had happened to her baby sister. Just once, she wanted to get through an entire interview without being asked about adorable "sweet puppies" Taylor.

As Jordan left the parking lot, she took a knife out of her purse and stabbed it repeatedly into Taylor's tire. Miss Perfect would never make it to work on time. Jordan scowled as she walked back to her car.

Chapter 4

Monday, May 23, 2016

Layne hurriedly showered and dressed for his first day on set. He went to his kitchen, where the only thing unpacked was his coffee maker. His thoughts kept wandering back to Taylor. He used the same excuse the night before about needing to get up early for work and left her apartment feeling like his head was spinning. Taylor Hoffman—the actress and singer he had admired so much while he was in Backdraft. She was as beautiful and kind as he remembered. He could never have predicted how his evening would go when he arrived at the bar the night before.

Taylor was strong and confident, for the most part, but there was something else going on. Layne had never seen another woman react that way after sex—scared almost—like someone had hurt her before. The bruises on her legs were more than what could be attributed to clumsiness. He'd been with a lot of women during Backdraft's last tour, but none he'd felt a connection with. His one serious relationship in college had ended badly, and the handful of hookups since then left him feeling empty. Had he let himself be used because he was lonely? Layne wanted something more and decided he would ask Taylor out to see if she could be the one he'd been searching for.

When Layne got to the parking lot, Taylor was standing beside her car. "Damn it!" she said as she pounded the hood. "I don't have time for this!"

"Problems?" he asked.

Taylor jumped and turned around. "Yes," she said with an exasperated sigh. "My tire's flat. I'm going to be late to the *Awake* set. I'm supposed to be there in half an hour to record with the hot new guitarist the PA told me about."

Apparently, Layne's reputation had preceded him. "You won't be late. Come on, just ride with me," he said, laughing as he held up his guitar case. "Who do you think the hot new guitarist is?"

"Of course, he is," Taylor muttered, closing her eyes.

"What's that?" Layne asked, even though he'd heard her. Taylor was adorable in her flustered state.

"Nothing."

Layne walked over to inspect Taylor's tire. "That's messed up." He kneeled to look at it more closely and touched what looked like a puncture. A cold sweat broke out on his forehead as he looked up at Taylor, and he felt the strongest urge to protect her. "Looks like somebody slashed your tire. Do you know who could've done this?"

Taylor shrugged her shoulders, her expression a strange combination of irritation and indifference. "Who knows? You don't owe me a ride. I can call a cab."

"I definitely owe you something after last night…"

"Last night was fun, but that's it," Taylor said, her face turning bright red as she looked at the ground. "Just one night. I'm not really looking for anything more right now."

"You know, it really hurts you took advantage of me since I was lonely and drunk," Layne said with a smirk. He wanted to know if their humor and chemistry continued when they weren't on the verge of making out.

"Hardly," Taylor said, her mouth dropping open as she leaned against her car. "You didn't ask me to stop."

And there it was. This beautiful woman wasn't easily offended and could take some light-hearted flirting in the form of good-natured teasing—Layne's specialty. "Well, you know what the real cure for loneliness is?" he asked.

Taylor sighed and walked with Layne to his SUV. "I have a feeling you're going to tell me."

"Friendship," Layne said as he opened the passenger door. "I can be an awesome friend if you'll let me, and I'm available for rides of all kinds if you ever do want to revisit the fun of last night."

"No, thank you," Taylor said as she climbed into the seat. "But thanks for the ride to the set." She took a deep breath and kept eye contact with Layne as he walked around the front of the SUV. He knew he made her nervous but wasn't sure why.

"How long have you lived above the bar?" Layne asked as he drove out of the parking lot.

"About four months," Taylor said. "I couldn't stand living with my dad and his girlfriend anymore. I stayed with them while I went to college."

"Oh cool, you went to college? I did, too, after the band broke up."

"Yeah, online. I just finished. I studied writing mainly."

"That's awesome. Do you sing your own songs on Friday nights?"

"No, I haven't yet. The songwriter's showcase is only the last Friday of every month," Taylor said. "I don't really have anything finished, just a bunch of random lines that don't fit together. I think I'll have to wait until next time."

"Maybe I could help. I'm exceptionally good at fitting things together."

Taylor cut her eyes at him. "Half the things you say come out sounding dirty," she said. "Are you sure you're not still fourteen?"

Layne laughed. "I'm being serious here," he said. "I want to be your friend. Am I really so sexy you can't handle that?"

"I can handle a lot of things," Taylor said as she looked out the window.

"Now who's talking dirty? You want to handle me? Did you just realize I'm irresistible?" He nudged her shoulder.

"No."

"So, you don't find me attractive?"

"No…wait, yes."

"Which is it?"

"Shut up!" Taylor said, covering her face with her hands.

Layne started laughing again. "I'm attracted to you," he said. "It's okay that you find me attractive. I was voted the hottest guy in Backdraft by two different teen magazines—much to the other guys' disappointment."

"You're so full of yourself, I'm surprised there's enough room for me in your car!"

"Do you think you could you scream 'sweet puppies' for me next time we have sex?"

Taylor turned toward Layne, who was snickering again. "Oh, my God!"

"That works too."

"I cannot believe you just said that! You're seriously disturbed. There isn't going to be a next time."

"Couldn't hurt to ask," Layne said. He glanced at Taylor again, who was smiling and shaking her head, her cheeks flushed. She was exactly the type of woman he wanted to be with long-term, someone who could joke around with him. *There's more beauty in you than could ever be true*, he thought.

They arrived at the set just in time to keep their schedule running smoothly. The man at the front gate checked them in and allowed them to drive inside the gates to park. Taylor was glad Jordan wasn't due to arrive for two weeks. The producers and director were working on crowd shots with extras and some of the musical score but had already completed the indoor work with the lead actors in a studio. The outdoor shots would be the last things filmed.

The guitarist from the previous two installments of the trilogy had quit after an encounter with Jordan. Taylor overheard one of the producers at the end of the second installment saying she would have fired Jordan if she wasn't such a talented actress once the cameras started rolling. It was true. Jordan came alive when the director called "Action." Everyone on set was sworn to secrecy about Jordan's true nature. The studio had so much money tied up in the trilogy, they wanted to complete it without a scandal. They had trouble keeping personal assistants for Jordan, too, so it was a role Taylor would fill again for the last time. She was accustomed to Jordan's level of bullshit and didn't feel like anyone else should be subjected to it.

It was a long day on the set with a lot of rehearsal, but no recording of the music. Layne's natural ability on the guitar impressed Taylor, especially how adaptable he was to the ever-changing whim of the composer. The music director and composer kept arguing over the lyrics, so Taylor and Layne had downtime to continue talking. He teased her throughout the day, but never in a mean way—funny and friendly. Taylor studied Layne when he wasn't looking as he tuned his guitar. He was sexy and confident, but not in a stuck-up way. Something about Layne made Taylor anxious, yet more comfortable than with anyone else. She liked how he treated the janitor with the same level of respect as the director, even when there was no one else around to witness it. He was a genuinely nice guy.

Taylor watched the child actors running around the set while they waited for their next scene. They reminded her of herself and Jordan on the *Smiths* set.

Layne sat down beside her. "Cute kids," he said.

"Yeah, they're adorable. If they only knew what was up ahead for them."

"You like kids?"

"I do," Taylor said dreamily. "As long as they belong to other people. I don't want any of my own."

"Yeah, I feel the same way," Layne said, much to Taylor's surprise. "I love my niece and nephew, but I'm always ready to give them back to my sister at the end of the visit."

"Yeah." She looked at the kids, who squealed as their mother ran after them. "I can't imagine having to be responsible for someone else's life like that."

"Me neither. Hey, earlier in the car, I wasn't trying to be a jerk. I like to joke around and wanted to make you laugh and see your beautiful smile. I didn't mean to embarrass you or hurt your feelings."

"I know."

"Taylor, I like you, and I meant what I said about us being friends if you're up for it. We do have to work together for the next few weeks, and we're neighbors."

Taylor looked at him. *Damn,* she thought, *he is incredibly sexy, but I do need friends.* "Sure," she said. "Friends would be nice."

"Of course, more than friends would be great, too, but that's up to you."

"Layne!" It was too soon for Taylor to be thinking of anything like that. Sure, they'd slept together, but it was a one-time lapse in judgment, right?

Layne smiled and bumped Taylor's shoulder. "You and Jordan pretty much grew up on set, huh?"

"I feel like I was raised by the tutors. I was five when the show began and fifteen when it ended."

"Did you enjoy it?"

"Parts of it," Taylor said. "The last two seasons were the best for me. One of the producers heard me singing one day during some downtime between rehearsals, so they rewrote one of the episodes to showcase my singing. It took off after that, and they let me drop the stupid catchphrase for the most part. I think I was relieved more than anything when it ended. When I was a little girl, I thought every kid's life was like mine. It was my normal— as screwed up as it was."

"What were you singing the day the producer heard you?"

Taylor smiled as she reminisced, "Most likely something of Avril's, I was always singing her stuff. I don't remember which song."

"I actually bought the *Smiths* soundtrack," Layne said. "Did you get to help write any of the songs?"

"No. I just sang what they told me. By the time the show ended, I was so exhausted I just wanted to hide out. I was sick of it all, you know—the magazines and paparazzi all the time. I enrolled in a private high school, and after I graduated, I cut off all my hair and dyed it. I liked the color so much, I just kept it that way as it grew out."

"You look good with dark hair," Layne said, taking a strand of Taylor's hair. "But you looked good before too."

"What about you?" Taylor asked. "Did you enjoy the fame and the touring?"

"Parts of it. I don't know what the hell possessed me to go to the audition for singers, but the record execs liked my voice, so I was recording with Backdraft before I knew what was happening. I got pulled out of school, got a private tutor, and bleached my hair to match the other guys."

"You do have a good voice," Taylor said.

"I sold myself out, though," Layne said. "What we did with Backdraft wasn't the kind of music I wanted to make. I wanted actual songwriting and playing my guitar, something a bit edgier and deeper than bubble-gum pop. The paparazzi were suffocating us at the end. The attention was flattering from the fans, but it got kind of crazy sometimes. Girls mailed us their panties." He grinned at Taylor.

"Ha ha," Taylor said as she nudged his shoulder. "I'll admit I had your albums, and I looked at some of the articles online, but I never mailed you any panties."

"It's okay," Layne said with a wink. "As you recall, I've already seen yours."

Taylor shook her head. "It won't be happening again," she said. Or maybe it would, but not yet.

"You're breaking my heart." Layne sighed. "All those articles were mostly bullshit put out by our publicist. Stupid quizzes to see which Backdraft guy you were most compatible with."

"I never took those."

"What's funny is, one time, I took a quiz about myself and failed it."

"That is funny," Taylor said. "I think there were some about me too. I try not to look anymore. Who knows what else is out there about me…"

"I thought you wanted to sing again?"

"I do, but not as Sierra from the show. I want my music to speak for itself. Isn't that what you want too?"

"Yeah. I'm not sure about the record exec route, though. I might release something myself online instead and see how it goes. I'd have to count on residue from the Backdraft fan base. With social media, it could work."

"The bane of my father's existence," Taylor said. "He's one of those record execs. Miles Hoffman." Maybe she shouldn't have mentioned her father. The last thing she wanted to do was talk about him, considering he didn't seem to care enough to be part of Taylor's life short of throwing money at her.

"Why don't you release an album through him?"

"Because I don't want to owe him anything. I'd rather do it on my own or not do it at all. I've considered the indie route, too, but then I would have to start social media accounts. Right now, I don't do anything, and Jordan goes out of her way to post crap all the time. I just don't want to come out of hiding quite yet. I've enjoyed the solitude and anonymity."

"But then people like me figure out who you are."

"Yep, there's always some pain in the ass who wants to be my friend," Taylor said as she grinned at Layne. She could tease him like he teased her; it was only fair. "I don't have many friends, so I should probably take what I can get, right?"

Layne grabbed his chest dramatically. "Don't be mean to me," he said. "My heart can't take it. I'm a good friend to have."

Layne stole glances at Taylor any chance he could while they listened to the arguing coming from the music producers' table. Even when she smiled or laughed, there was still something painful locked inside her. Someone or something had hurt her so deeply hints of it showed on the surface through the sadness in her eyes.

Late in the day, the music producers dismissed the crew, having decided to wait until the next day to finalize their lyric changes. Layne wasn't ready for their time together to end; he could have talked to Taylor all night.

"You ready to go home?" Layne offered his hand to help Taylor stand. She took his hand and paused long enough to look into Layne's eyes before she let go. Being just her friend would be difficult because Layne wanted nothing more than to kiss her and hold her again.

chapter 5

The sun was beginning to set as Taylor and Layne left work for the day. It was the best first day Taylor could have expected for an *Awake* movie. Jordan not being there made the whole energy level on the set more positive. Another key factor was Layne. Taylor had known she might bump into him in the hallway on occasion. But working with him so closely meant she could not be spared from the embarrassment of the night before. Her reasons for shaking after their encounter left her stumped.

"We should get something to eat," Layne said when they were almost back to the apartment building. "We could pick up something and take it back to your place or go out somewhere if you'd rather do that. My place is still a mess."

Taylor had to admit she was starving. "I don't really want to go out anywhere," she said. "I'm so tired, but I'm okay with picking up something and eating at my place."

"What do you want? Pizza? Chinese?"

"Hey, there's a great pizza place a few blocks from our building. It takes longer, though, if you can wait."

"That depends," Layne said as they pulled into the parking lot. "Can we talk more while we wait?"

"Well, that's part of being friends, right?"

"Yes, and another part is helping each other out. Why don't you call in the order while I put the spare on your car?"

"You don't have to do that." Seriously, was he a boy scout too?

"I insist; now give me your keys."

Taylor placed her keys in Layne's outstretched hand. "What kind of pizza do you like?"

"It doesn't matter to me. I like all kinds as long as you're not one of those weirdos who gets anchovies on yours."

"That's not my favorite meat." Blood rushed to Taylor's cheeks. Why was she so nervous around him? "Don't—"

"I can't even go there."

Layne laughed so hard that Taylor started laughing too. She had to wait to regain her composure before she could call the pizza parlor. While she made the call, Layne changed the tire. Someone had definitely slashed it—apparent by the punctures he showed Taylor. She didn't want to believe it and insisted she must have run over something.

"Minotti's isn't too busy tonight," Taylor said. "About half an hour, so we can wait around here for a bit and then walk to get it. It's just a small place. They don't deliver."

"You sure you want to walk? I thought you were tired?"

"I still need some exercise since I missed my class this morning," Taylor said, stretching her arms and legs.

"It won't take me too much longer to get this done. What kind of class are you taking?"

"Kickboxing. Willow teaches it. She pretty much insisted I join her a couple of months ago."

"That explains the bruises I noticed on your legs last night. I'm impressed, but now I'm a little scared of you." He struggled with the last lug nut on the tire, finally getting it loose.

Taylor laughed. "Yeah, I suck at it, but I'm getting better," she said. "You should see Willow; she can kick a grown man's ass. She helped me out once." Immediately, Taylor knew she'd said too much because Layne looked confused as he removed the damaged tire.

"Helped you?" he asked, picking up the spare and placing it on the car. "What happened?"

"It's not a big deal," Taylor said as she handed him the lug nuts.

"Then tell me. We're friends now."

After one look at Layne, Taylor knew she could trust him with her secret. "About two months ago, there was a guy who hit me. He was the last guy I brought up to my apartment before you. Willow stopped him from hurting me more and kicked him out of the building. Her girlfriend, Kayla—Mr. Cosney's daughter—just finished med school, so she looked at my cheekbone the next morning to make sure nothing was broken. Afterward, Willow practically dragged me to class with her to learn to defend myself."

"He hit you in the face?" Layne reacted as if someone had just punched him in the gut.

Taylor nodded. "He started being too rough with me, so I told him I didn't want to anymore and asked him to leave. He grabbed me and wouldn't let go, so I kneed him in the groin, and then he punched me."

"What an asshole," Layne said, disgusted. "He didn't..."

"No, he didn't get the chance after Willow came in," Taylor said, shaking her head. "It was my fault for bringing him into my apartment."

"Do you think he did this to your tire?"

"He wouldn't have known which car, and he was from out of town, anyway. He was so drunk and probably doesn't even remember what he did. Willow put him in a cab. He'll never come back here."

"You should still report this to the police," Layne said. He put the damaged tire in the trunk and slammed the lid closed. "It could be a stalker or something—someone who's figured out who you are and has been watching you."

"I doubt it. I'm not that interesting."

Layne walked over to Taylor and leaned down to look into her eyes. "You're definitely that interesting," he said. "I need to go wash my hands, and then I'll be ready to walk with you. Will you come upstairs with me so you're not out here alone?"

Taylor followed Layne to his apartment. It was a mirror image of her place. She looked around and thought about how she'd never been to a guy's apartment before. She watched Layne at the sink, noticing the green shade of his hair under the fluorescent lighting. As Taylor's eyes drifted down his back, Layne turned around and caught her gaze as she looked up.

He grinned. "I caught you. You were checking out my ass."

"Ugh, you're so wrong." Taylor sat on a bar stool and leaned her arms on the counter. Layne did have a cute ass, though.

Layne walked behind Taylor and put his hands on her shoulders. "You're wrong, you know," he said. "It was his fault he hit you, not yours. I would never do that. Ever. I can't stand the thought of any man mistreating a woman or forcing himself on her. It's not right. I'm so sorry."

Taylor turned to face Layne. "Willow said the same thing, but she also told me to stop sleeping around. It may come as a shock to you, but that night wasn't the first time I'd brought home someone I just met."

He sat on the other stool. "Been there," he said. "If you won't listen to me, then listen to Willow. She sounds like a good friend."

"She is a good friend, more like a big sister," Taylor said. "I'm trying to be better. As good as she thinks I can be, I guess. She thinks I should try dating and actually find someone."

"Oh yeah?"

"Yeah, but I don't think I'm ready for that yet."

"Why not?"

"With so much going on in my life, I probably shouldn't be with anyone right now. Maybe I'm a lost cause since I fell back into old habits with you. I'm not sure what I was thinking last night. I guess I was lonely. You're a nice guy. I'm sorry."

"Don't apologize," Layne said. "I've had my share of hookups too. I'm not perfect. But remember, we're not strangers anymore.

We're friends, so whatever you were thinking or not thinking last night, I'm not sorry about us getting to know each other. And honestly, I'm not sorry we hooked up. I try not to have any regrets, and you shouldn't either. Think about right now. Forgive yourself."

"Come on, let's go get our food," Taylor said as she stood up.

Layne stood up too. "If you promise to protect me," he said. "It's dark now."

"You look like you can protect yourself."

"I'm all about protection," he said with a laugh.

Taylor rolled her eyes at him. "You're hopeless."

"Yeah, but you know you like me."

Willow and Kayla were in the hallway when Taylor and Layne stepped out of his apartment. The couple seemed mismatched—tiny, plain Willow with beautiful, tall Kayla, with her perfectly-styled black hair and honey-colored skin. The two were undeniably in love, apparent to everyone they encountered.

"I heard you last night," Willow whispered to Taylor while Kayla introduced herself to Layne.

Taylor shook her head at Willow and said goodbye to Kayla. The last thing she wanted was another lecture.

Layne opened the main door for Taylor and waited for her to walk through. He found it odd that Taylor seemed surprised by his gesture. They walked in silence for the first block, so close together their arms brushed several times. He fought the urge to take her hand. "What was Willow saying to you in the hallway?" he asked. "She made you smile."

"She was teasing me about the thin walls," Taylor said.

Layne stopped walking. "Wait," he said. "She could hear us last night?"

Taylor stopped to allow him to catch up. "She prefers to hear me play my guitar."

"I'd like to hear that too. Maybe we can play with each other later."

"There you go talking dirty again." Taylor stopped walking and crossed her arms as she looked up at Layne.

"You're the one who keeps turning everything I say into something dirty," Layne said as he nudged her shoulder. *Shit*, he thought, *I shouldn't have touched her.* All he wanted to do was touch her.

They arrived at the pizza parlor, and Layne opened the door, once again. Taylor walked inside and greeted the staff behind the counter.

"Taylor!" the owner—a plump, balding man—yelled as he walked around to the front of the counter.

"Hey, Mr. Minotti," Taylor said as she hugged him. "I'm so glad you're feeling better. Your wife told me about your surgery."

"Yeah," he said. "Damn appendix, who needs it, you know? Well, aren't you going to introduce me to your boyfriend?" Mr. Minotti glared at Layne, sizing him up.

Taylor turned to Layne and didn't bother correcting the old man. "This is Layne. Layne, this is Mr. Minotti, the best pizza chef I've ever met," she said.

Layne shook his hand. "Good to meet you, sir," he said.

"You take care of this one," Mr. Minotti said to Layne, softening his stance. "She's a good girl."

"Don't worry," Layne said as he looked at Taylor. "I will."

Taylor looked uncomfortable, so Layne took a step back to give her some space. "Is my order ready?" she asked.

"Of course," Mr. Minotti said. "But your money is no good here tonight, young lady. I appreciate the gift basket you sent to the hospital for me. Thank you."

"You're welcome," Taylor said as she hugged him again. "Just take care of yourself, okay?" She dropped her cash into the tip jar on the counter, getting Mr. Minotti's disapproving glance as they left.

As Layne held the door open for Taylor, Mr. Minotti locked eyes with him and gestured that he'd be watching. Layne nodded in agreement and waved at the old man.

Taylor was silent most of the way back. Seeing Mr. Minotti always made her long for a normal family. A family who looked out for each other. A family who loved each other.

"You're a good person, Taylor," Layne said as they reached the halfway point.

"Why do you say that?"

"You sent a gift to that old man while he was in the hospital. You treat him like family when you haven't known him very long."

"He's a legend. I never knew my grandfathers, so I'd like to think they would have been like him in some alternate universe where I grew up with a normal family. I kind of let him keep the illusion that I'm a good girl."

"I only knew one of my grandfathers. He taught me how to play the guitar."

Taylor laughed. "Until you played at rehearsal today, I seriously wondered if you could or if you just carried around a guitar to get girls," she said. "You've proven yourself, though. You're definitely talented. I'm glad to know you can do more than just sing in harmony and do cheesy dance moves."

"I seem to recall some pretty cheesy dance moves from you on the show," Layne said. "Especially the ones you and Jordan did together. Are you two still close?"

Taylor avoided his question.

Back at her apartment, Taylor grabbed paper towels from her kitchen and a couple of cans of root beer. Root beer, skim milk and ketchup were pretty much the only things in her refrigerator. Layne was sitting on the couch with the pizza box opened on the coffee table when she walked back in the living room.

"I hope root beer is okay," Taylor said. "I know it's odd coming from a bartender, but I don't drink."

"It's fine," Layne said as he handed Taylor a slice of pizza. "I don't really drink anymore. There were several times in the last few years when I drank too much and didn't like who I was or what I did. I've seen what it can do to people."

"Yeah, I know what you mean." Taylor took a bite of the pizza, glad it was cool enough to not burn her mouth. "I figured it out by the time I was twelve. My childhood was pretty chaotic. I could make martinis for my mom's friends before I could make Kool-Aid. My mom drank a lot. I think it's part of what broke up my parents' marriage. She's in a rehab center now, and Dad's shacking up with his girlfriend who's just a few years older than me."

"Maybe your mom will get better with rehab."

"I don't think so…"

"Why not?"

"It was more than just alcohol, Layne. She had a stroke." Taylor couldn't believe she was telling him about her mother. She hadn't told anyone.

"I'm sorry." Layne hesitated for a moment, then put his pizza down and caressed Taylor's cheek, moving away quickly.

"It's just another thing on the long list of things I can't change." Taylor went back to eating, and they sat in silence for a couple of minutes.

"It wasn't just me who broke up Backdraft," Layne said, wiping his mouth. "Chase went into treatment."

"Alcohol or drugs?" Taylor asked. Layne looked away. "Sorry, it's really none of my business."

"No," Layne said. "It's okay to ask me questions. Treatment for both. We were all scared for him. Chase almost died from a heroin overdose at the end of our last tour. I took the fall for breaking up the band to keep his name out of the headlines. Kyle, Noah, and I just drank but never touched other drugs—nothing hard anyway. Sleeping pills or caffeine pills on occasion, but no real abuse of anything. Are you surprised?"

Relieved, Taylor thought. "No," she said. "You look like you take care of yourself, and I can tell you don't smoke—at least I don't smell it on you."

"Oh, so you were already checking me out, and now you're smelling me?" He grinned and moved closer. "Now you can sniff me easier."

"Layne, you were doing well there for a bit." She playfully punched him in the arm, and he pretended to be hurt, laughing the whole time.

"No, I don't smoke," Layne said as he caressed Taylor's neck. "Never have. It's really bad for the vocal cords, but you know that already because you don't either."

Taylor closed her eyes. "What song speaks to you most right now?" she asked.

"That's a tough question."

"You made me answer it last night."

Layne took out his phone and flipped through the songs in his collection. "Probably this one," he said. He played "One Thing" by Finger Eleven.

"What do you think they're singing about?" Taylor asked.

"I'm not sure what they intended, but I think it's about love. The best songs are." Layne looked like he wanted to kiss her again.

Things were moving too fast because the whole evening felt like a date, and Taylor wasn't ready. "You should probably go home now."

Reluctantly, Layne agreed and got up. "I've enjoyed spending the day with you," he said. "As awesome as last night was, today was better, just hanging out."

Taylor thought guys would say almost anything if they thought it would get them laid, but Layne seemed different. She felt like she could trust him. "You sound like you mean that," she said.

Layne smiled at Taylor and reached out to brush her hair behind her ear. "I do," he said. "And I think Willow's right; you should try dating."

"I'm not good at dating."

"You were good at it tonight." He kissed Taylor's forehead, holding his lips there as he hugged her. "You should consider going out on a real date with me. I'd pick you up, bring you flowers, take you to dinner, kiss you goodnight—all that stuff."

All of it with him sounded perfect. Maybe it wasn't too soon to date someone like him. "I'll think about it."

Layne's face lit up. "You will?"

"Goodnight, Layne," Taylor said as she pushed him into the hallway. After she closed her door, her apartment was cold and lonely.

chapter 6

Tuesday, May 24, 2016

The next morning, Layne let Taylor drive him to work to thank him for driving the previous day. The day was so busy, they had little time to talk in between recordings and rehearsals. They'd barely spoken on the way to the set that morning and did the same thing during the drive home, just listening to music, occasionally commenting on a song. Layne had told Taylor he wanted to date her and was waiting for her to make the next move. He didn't want to pressure her and wanted to be cautious with her feelings—and his own.

When they arrived home, Layne opened the door for Taylor and followed her upstairs. He watched as she hesitated before opening her door. He unlocked his door as slowly as possible, debating whether he should ask Taylor to come over. He sighed with relief when she spoke to him.

"Layne?"

"Yeah?" He avoided turning around to hide his huge smile from her.

"I was planning to eat leftover pizza and watch something tonight if you want to hang out."

"Sure. I can do that."

Layne couldn't focus at all on the show streaming on Taylor's laptop. All he could think about was how badly he wanted to kiss her again. He covered his face with his hands. "It's been a long day," he said. "At least we got a lot of work done. I don't think the recording will take very long since we nailed everything in one take today."

"Yep, we nailed it all day," she said with a laugh.

"And you say I'm dirty-minded…"

Taylor sighed. "I'll be right back."

Layne got up when he heard the bathroom door close and went to Taylor's bedroom to look out the window. He picked up an open notebook on the bed and looked at the messy scribbles, almost hearing the melody of Taylor's song as he read. She wrote like he did—raw emotion and lack of punctuation.

Taylor washed her face with cold water in her tiny bathroom and sighed again as she looked in the mirror. Without the heavy eye makeup, she could still pass for a teenager. She felt like a teenager, nervous about a cute boy waiting for her in the living room. She looked at the dizzying pattern of black and white hexagon tiles scattered sporadically on the floor while trying to calm her nerves. When she came out of the bathroom, Layne was sitting on the bed looking at her songwriting notebook.

He smiled at her. "Ah, I can see your face now."

"It's probably pretty scary," she said as she sat down beside him.

"Nope, you're beautiful," Layne said. He pushed Taylor's hair behind her ear and left his hand on her face, running his thumb down her cheek. "Just more natural now."

Taylor grabbed Layne's wrist and pushed his hand away. "Layne," she said. "Enough! That tickles!"

"I'm sorry," he said. "I'll try to keep my hands to myself. Taylor, you should be singing and writing songs all the time."

"Why are you looking at my writing?"

Layne held up the notebook. "It was just laying here open. These words are more than just poetry, Taylor. These words are lyrics for songs you should sing."

"Sometimes I think the best songs have already been written." Taylor wasn't convinced she had what it took to write a truly great song.

"That's not true. Look at this one, 'If you're nice, I'll let you come inside, into my secret place where I go to hide.' It's good stuff. With a little polishing, a couple of stanzas and the right melody."

Taylor frowned. "You shouldn't be in here," she said. "You have to go now." She took his hands and pulled him off the bed, causing him to bump into her. She couldn't deny the attraction she felt any longer and pushed Layne back on the bed. She brushed her fingers against his cheek, feeling the stubble. Her heart started pounding as she looked into his eyes. There had never been anyone she'd wanted to be with more than once. She wanted to kiss him but thought about her own rule of not letting anyone get close enough to hurt her. *Oh God*, Taylor thought, *what should I do?* She was going to break her own rule.

Layne looked up at Taylor and wondered what she was thinking. He wanted to pull her onto the bed with him but hesitated. "Hey, this is starting to feel more than friendly," he said, clearing his throat.

"Damn it," Taylor said as she started to pull away.

"Taylor, it's okay." Layne hooked his fingers in the belt loops on Taylor's jeans and drew her closer, resting his hands on her hips. His pulse started racing as she sat on his leg and pushed his hair behind his shoulders. Inches away from his face, she stopped again and shared his shallow breathing. Layne kept his eyes locked with Taylor's and kept a small distance between their lips as he draped his arms around her. "Do you still want me to leave?" he asked.

"I don't know what I want anymore," she whispered, her eyes showing her confliction. "It's just...you..." She pressed her forehead against his. "I'm sorry."

Layne thought his heart might jump out of his chest and was sure Taylor could feel it too. "I want to kiss you now. Is that okay?"

Taylor answered by slamming her lips into his so aggressively that their teeth clashed together.

"Whoa, slow down." Layne grabbed Taylor's face and guided her to a slower pace.

"Just shut up," Taylor said, shoving him against the bed.

Layne kicked off his shoes as Taylor pulled off his shirt. She stopped kissing him one last time to reach for his belt buckle. Layne wasted no time undressing Taylor; he'd wanted her all day.

Afterward, Taylor felt like she had betrayed herself. *Just because I'm hot for him doesn't mean he won't hurt me*, she thought. Her motto had been to kick them out as soon as the condom came off. No cuddling, no sleeping over, just sex, and then they left without expectations. It was better that way. They couldn't hurt her if she didn't let them.

Her arrangement worked fine for a couple of months. Then, Willow had to run to assist her with getting the drunk, abusive guy out of her apartment. Up until then, through their small-talk at the bar, Taylor thought the most interesting thing about Willow was that she was a lesbian. After, it was that tiny Willow was a hardcore kickboxer who literally kicked the guy's ass. Later, Willow took Taylor to her own apartment and put frozen peas on Taylor's cheekbone to reduce the swelling. She had also given Taylor a piece of her mind.

March 2016

"*You've got to stop this self-destructive behavior,*" Willow said. "*I've been watching you with your revolving door of dudes since you moved in here. It's not healthy. You're better than this.*"

"*You don't know me.*"

"*I know who you were, and I know the type. I recognized you when we first met the day you moved in. I know you're going by Taylor Lee now, but you're Taylor Hoffman. I read that your sister's going to be in town soon for filming the final installment of that movie.*"

"*God,*" Taylor said. "*I didn't think anyone would recognize me.*"

"*It'll take a lot more than hair dye and a pierced nose to hide your identity. Those blue eyes of yours and your voice…they're very distinctive.*"

"*Unfortunately.*"

"*Taylor, why are you working in a bar and living in this dump? Why aren't you out there with your sister chasing fame? I always thought you were the more talented one.*"

"*I guess I like the atmosphere here,*" Taylor said, shifting the peas on her face. "*Or at least the music when people sing their own songs.*"

"*Then why aren't you singing your own? These walls are paper-thin, so in addition to hearing you with the dudes, I also hear you singing songs I've never heard before.*"

"*And why are you living here? In this dump? Is it just because your girlfriend's dad owns the building?*"

Willow sat down beside Taylor and removed the peas to check the swelling. "*We lived here for free while Kayla was in med school. Now she's interning at the hospital, so we've decided to awhile longer to work on her student loans. I teach ten classes a week at the gym three blocks away. It pays the bills and keeps me in shape. We're planning to get married next spring.*"

"*That's great. Congratulations. Thanks for your help, but I need to sleep this off so I can work tomorrow.*"

"*No problem.*" Willow grabbed Taylor's shoulders and looked her in the eyes. "*Girl, you're too special to be slutting it up in here. Have more respect for yourself and stop using casual sex as a drug. Do something productive, and then find a real man who loves you."*

Taylor broke Willow's gaze and stared at the floor. "I tried once, and it didn't work out so well for me."

"Well, try again," she said, shaking her head. "And let me know if the swelling gets worse. Kayla can look at it for you in the morning. I expect to see you in my beginner's class next Monday morning. And Saturday, you're coming to my place for dinner. We're celebrating my thirtieth birthday."

"Fine, I'll be there."

"Good. From what I can see, you need a friend. I could use another one too."

As Taylor caught her breath, she noticed she was tracing her fingers over the outline of the large four-leaf clover tattoo on Layne's chest. She got up and pulled her shirt back over her head. Layne stretched before he rolled over and went into Taylor's bathroom. While he was out of the room, Taylor put on the rest of her clothes and sat on her bed to wait for him. She glanced at her own clover tattoo and traced its outline. What were the odds? It was her first tattoo on her eighteenth birthday. She'd gotten a few more since then: two yellow roses on her shoulder, a collection of musical notes on her hip, and her zodiac sign—Gemini—on her bicep. Each one had meant something to her at the time, but none were planned too far in advance.

The same thing happened with the tiny stud in her nose—an addition to her change in appearance after she had dyed her platinum-blond hair black.

Layne came out of the bathroom and stood naked in front of Taylor before he put on his underwear. He sat on the bed beside her. "So, that happened again," he said, nudging Taylor. "You keep taking advantage of me."

"Please go home now," she said. "We both have to get up early."

Layne got up and finished dressing. "Can I still drive you to the set tomorrow?"

"No, not tomorrow. I've got somewhere to be right after work, but I'll see you there." Taylor followed Layne to the door to lock it behind him.

Right before he stepped into the hallway, Layne pulled Taylor close. "I'm excellent at goodnight kisses," he said with a grin as he leaned in to kiss her.

Never wanting to stop, Taylor forced herself to pull away before she could get completely lost in his kiss. "Goodnight."

"See you tomorrow," Layne said as Taylor closed her door.

In the hallway, Layne leaned against the wall and closed his eyes. Willow startled him when she spoke. "You better not hurt her," she said. "I'll kick your ass. I don't care how famous you were."

"I'm not trying to hurt her," he said, turning to Willow. "I'd be more worried about her hurting me. She told me you're teaching her kickboxing."

"She's getting good at it. She's the best student in my class."

"What?" Layne laughed. "Now you're just lying. Taylor told me she sucks at it and has the bruises to show for it. We met about ten years ago when my band played on her show. Did she tell you? She and I understand each other since we both grew up in the spotlight."

Willow looked up and down at Layne. "So, is it true you're trying to go solo? I bet you're here to try your hand at open mic night for the record execs."

"You caught me," Layne said with a shrug. "Goodnight, I have work tomorrow." He opened his apartment door and walked inside.

Taylor leaned against her door while she listened to the exchange between Layne and Willow in the hallway. She wondered what Layne meant by being more worried about her hurting him. She rested her head in her hands and asked herself, "What am I doing?"

chapter 7

Wednesday, May 25, 2016

After a quick wave to Layne at the end of their workday, Taylor began the hour-long drive to Victorville where her mother, Janice, lived in a private rehab center. It was her first evening visit, as she usually went on Wednesday mornings. When she walked into the room, her mother appeared as she always did: pale, thin, and still except for her slow, rhythmic breathing. Janice's greying blond hair was spread out on the pillow as if it had been recently brushed.

"Hi, Mom," Taylor said. She put her guitar beside the bed and took her mother's cold hand. "It's Taylor. I'm here to check on you again."

There was no response in Janice's facial expression or in her hand.

"Mom," Taylor continued. "Are you awake? Can you squeeze my hand?"

Again, there was no response. Taylor looked around the room at the mint green walls and old-fashioned wallpaper border. Her eyes stopped on the IV bags hanging above her mother—the only nutrition keeping her alive.

Janice had been a good mother until she suddenly wasn't anymore. Her alcohol problem began several years before Taylor's father left when she was fifteen. Janice was a high-functioning alcoholic for two years until Jordan came back from filming the last of three horror flicks with a cocaine habit. Everything fell apart after Jordan shared the drugs with their mother. Within six months, Janice had overdosed on cocaine and suffered a massive stroke with little hope for recovery.

Nothing significant had changed in years. Janice would occasionally open her eyes when Taylor spoke, but Taylor didn't think her mother could understand anything. She seemed to be in limbo between life and death and had little movement except for opening her eyes to stare blankly into space or grimacing on occasion. Taylor wasn't religious, but sometimes she prayed for her mother's death to put an end to the suffering. She always felt guilty about it because she wasn't sure if she wanted her mother's suffering to end or her own. It was no way to live—existing, but not really being alive.

Taylor pulled out her guitar and played "Landslide" for her mother. She'd sung it at each visit since it was Janice's favorite song. It was the one song Taylor could remember singing with her mother as a child. During the days Janice seemed agitated, Taylor's singing always seemed to calm her.

After putting away her guitar, Taylor took her mother's hand. "Mom, I met someone. His name is Layne. I think you'd like him. He's tall and handsome. Kind. He's a singer and songwriter like me. I like spending time with him, and I think he likes me too."

"He sounds wonderful, Miss Hoffman," a female voice said from behind Taylor, causing her to jump before she turned around. "Sorry to startle you." It was Rhonda, a nurse in her fifties who usually worked the day shift when Taylor would visit. Her brown hair was pulled into a ponytail, and she had dark circles under her eyes.

"Hi, Rhonda," Taylor said. "I didn't expect to see you here tonight."

"They put me on nights this week to fill in, and it's busting my old butt." Rhonda put her hand on Taylor's shoulder. "No change during the last week. No responses. She hasn't opened her eyes at all, that I know of, in over a month."

"Do you think she's getting worse?"

"That's not for me to determine."

"Rhonda, you see this all the time. Please tell me so I can prepare myself." Taylor watched as Rhonda walked toward the door and was surprised when she closed it and came back to sit in the other chair beside the bed.

"Sweetheart," Rhonda said, taking Taylor's hand. "You should prepare yourself. I don't think your mother has long left in this world."

Taylor looked at the tears in the woman's eyes and wondered how someone with so much compassion could stand to work in a profession that often dealt with death. "Thank you for your honesty," she said. "Do you think she's in pain?"

"No, honey," Rhonda said. "Not anymore. We're keeping her comfortable with morphine. I think the administrator will be calling you soon about signing a DNR. Do you know what that is?"

Taylor sighed. "I do. If you don't mind, I'd like some more time alone with her."

"Of course." Rhonda gave Taylor's hand a squeeze and left the room, closing the door behind her.

Tears filled Taylor's eyes as she continued to hold her mother's hand. "Mom, I love you and don't want you to suffer anymore, but I can't keep coming here like this. It hurts too much." She kissed her on the forehead. As she began to let go of her mother's hand, Taylor felt a bit of pressure on her fingers. "Mom? Squeeze my hand if you can hear me." She looked for signs of life other than the shallow breathing, but there were none. Determined that she'd imagined her mother's movement, Taylor looked at her one last time before leaving the room. "Goodbye," she whispered, wiping her eyes.

During the drive back, Taylor rolled down her windows and let the wind blow her hair while she sang along to the radio. Several miles away from her apartment, her car began shaking. By the time she could pull into a store parking lot, the shaking was so violent, she knew she had another flat. Taylor checked the time and took out her phone. Willow would be working at the bar, but she figured Layne might be around, so she called him.

"Hey," he answered after the first ring. "What's up? Do you miss me already?"

"Hey," Taylor said. "I'm actually stranded. Another flat." She heard keys jingling.

"I'm on my way," Layne said. "Where are you? Are you in a safe place?"

"A store parking lot. I'm fine."

"I'll be right there. Text me the address."

Taylor sat in her car and listened to the radio while she waited for Layne. The previous evening with him was even better than the first. It was like he'd already memorized every inch of her body and knew all the right places to touch. He wanted a real date, and Taylor decided she would agree, especially since he hadn't hesitated to drop everything to come get her.

Layne was there within fifteen minutes, although the drive should have taken at least twenty. He pulled up beside Taylor's car and jumped out to open the door for her. "I got here as fast as I could," he said. "Are you okay?"

"Fine, but I think I bent the rim on the spare. At least it happened here and not half an hour ago on the way out of Victorville."

"Wow, that's a pretty good drive. What's out there?"

"The rehab center. I visit my mother every Wednesday."

"Oh. How is she?"

"She's not doing very well. The nurse doesn't think she'll live much longer."

Layne gave Taylor a half-hearted smile. "I'm sorry, Taylor," he said as he hugged her.

Taylor pulled away. "It is what it is. Can you take me home now? I'll call a tow for my car on our way back. I don't think anyone will bother it. Would you mind grabbing my guitar out of the back seat?"

After Taylor called the tow truck, she turned to Layne, who was softly singing along with the radio as he drove. "Okay, I'll go out on a date with you—one date—but I don't know what will come of it," she said. "That is, if your offer still stands."

"Of course, it does," Layne said. "Tomorrow night after work? Dinner?"

"Yes, but my life's crazy right now, and I wasn't looking for anything. I've told you that."

"Neither was I, but you kind of fell into my lap, didn't you? Twice now."

What have I gotten myself into? Taylor thought. *He thinks he's charming. Who am I kidding? He is charming.*

They practiced one of the songs for the *Awake* movie as Layne drove them back to the apartment building. Earlier in the day, there was a part that had given them trouble, but now they had it timed perfectly.

"I'm glad you called me," Layne said at Taylor's apartment door.

"Thank you for helping me."

"Told you I'm an awesome friend. I guess you'll have to let me drive you to work tomorrow."

"Pick me up at seven?"

"That's a bit early for an eight o'clock start time." Layne handed Taylor her guitar.

"The least I can do is buy you breakfast on the way since you came to my rescue tonight."

Layne kissed Taylor on the cheek. "I can't say no to a pre-date breakfast. See you at seven." He unlocked his door and went inside.

Inside her apartment, Taylor took out her guitar and lightly strummed a few notes while she ate a bowl of cereal for dinner. Having worked on a song for several weeks unable to piece things together, Taylor gave up on it and began working on the new one—the one she'd started the night she first hooked up with Layne. It was a love song. She couldn't think of exactly how to begin it, so she just jotted down a few lines to go with the melody in her mind.

I think I'd run away
I never thought that I would feel this way again

There's nowhere left to hide,
In this place of mine.
I never knew exactly what I'd find.

I'm so afraid with every breath I take
There's no one else who makes me feel this way, like you.

After conceding that she was stuck, Taylor put away her notebook and guitar and stretched out on her couch. She could hear faint guitar sounds coming from across the hall. It would be nice having another songwriter nearby if she wouldn't let the fact she'd slept with him twice get in the way. The time she'd spent with him when they weren't naked was more telling. Even Taylor couldn't deny their chemistry and genuine like for each other. There was also the fact she'd agreed to go out with him—a thought that made her uneasy.

chapter 8

Thursday, May 26, 2016

Just after midnight, Layne smiled when the soft music coming from Taylor's apartment stopped. He wanted to text her a goodnight message but knew better than to disrupt the creative process. Plus, he didn't want to seem too aggressive. *Tomorrow,* he thought, *I'll get to show her how good dating me could be.*

He'd mulled over a soft ballad in his head since Sunday. A love song, going back to his songwriting roots from his biggest hit with Backdraft. He debated using the word "insane" in a soft love song and figured he could get away with it since his favorite song used the word "suicide."

There's more beauty in you
Than could ever be true
I've spent all of my life
Waiting for you

I'll take all your pain
And lock it away
If I don't kiss your lips
I might go insane

He felt insane. No matter what else he tried to think about, his thoughts wandered back to Taylor. The cute way she blushed when he teased her, and the way she wrinkled her brow a bit when she was frustrated. The lavender scent of her hair and how her lips tasted like cherries. He couldn't get her out of his mind as he tried to go to sleep.

Layne woke up on his own long before his alarm would go off. He hadn't slept much and was still exhausted. After tossing and turning for a few minutes, he got up and showered to get ready for his breakfast date with Taylor. It was a date, wasn't it? Layne didn't usually eat breakfast so early. Five minutes before seven, there was a light knocking on his door. Taylor was standing in the hallway with a white bag and two cups of coffee.

"I realized I didn't ask if you were much of a breakfast person," she said. "I couldn't sleep, so I walked to the coffee shop and got muffins and bagels."

Layne stepped aside to let her in. "This is great, actually." She looked more awake than he felt, her hair and makeup perfect. "You look amazing. I'm not much of a morning person."

"That's what the coffee's for. It'll be my second cup."

"I don't have any milk for the coffee…"

Taylor put everything down on the counter and sat on the bar stool. "Black's fine," she said. "Thanks again for coming to my rescue last night."

"You don't have to thank me for that."

"I got an email from the repair shop. My wheel got damaged, so my car won't be ready until Saturday."

"I guess you'll have to let me drive you to work until it's ready." Layne felt slightly guilty being happy about the damage.

"Guess so," Taylor said. "I appreciate it."

By the time Layne and Taylor arrived home after work, his stomach was in knots as about their first real date. "I'm going to get cleaned up and change," he said. "I'll pick you up in twenty minutes. Wear comfortable shoes."

"Why? Are we going dancing?"

Layne grinned. "Maybe…"

"Where are we going?"

"It's a cute little restaurant by the beach. I think you'll love it."

"Make it thirty minutes," Taylor said as she walked into her apartment.

Layne quickly showered, then attempted to shave with his shaking hands. "Get it together, man," he said to himself in the mirror. "She's already seen you naked." He took a calming breath and dried his hair again with a towel and used it to stop the bleeding on a couple of nicks on his chin. He pulled his anxiety meds out of the cabinet and took one of the pills, chasing it with two chewable antacids. After pulling his hair into a ponytail, he thought he looked presentable enough in a green button-up shirt and loose khaki pants. A quick glance at his phone told him he still had fifteen minutes before he was due to pick up Taylor. He went to his couch and stretched out to relax before he would need to leave.

"Shit," Layne said as he jumped up. "Flowers..." He ran downstairs and around the corner to the bar. He remembered real roses in the vases from the night he'd moved in.

Mr. Cosney was behind the counter when Layne walked in. "What can I get for you?" he asked.

"No drink," Layne said as he placed cash on the counter. "I just want to take one of those roses."

"Well, I'll have to say that's a first. Hot date?"

"First date. The first of many, I hope. It's for Taylor. Please?"

"Go ahead," Mr. Cosney said with a chuckle. "Watch yourself, son. If you hurt her, I'll snap you like a twig." He made the motion with his hands.

"Thank you," Layne said, too nervous to consider the death threat.

Taylor showered and put on makeup. She stood beside her closet considering her options with absolutely no idea what to wear. She didn't want to be too casual or overdressed. Finally settling on a black and white dress and flats, Taylor put on earrings to match and used her flat-iron to smooth her hair. She wondered why she was making such a big fuss for a guy who had already seen her naked, and instantly realized she was both nervous and excited about their date.

She had just finished with her hair when Layne knocked on her door. She was surprised to find him standing there holding a yellow rose like the ones Mr. Cosney kept in the vases downstairs.

Layne smiled and handed her the rose. "You look amazing," he said. "Are you ready?"

"Almost," Taylor said. She took the rose to her kitchen and put it in a glass of water before returning to Layne. "Now I'm ready. Thank you. Surprised Mr. Cosney parted with one of his roses…"

"I can be persuasive, as you know," he said. "I promised you flowers."

She glanced up at him. *Persuasive and sexy as hell*, she thought. "You look nice. What all do you have planned for us?"

"Dinner…dancing…a walk on the beach. The night is just getting started. Just one rule, we leave our phones in the car. No distractions. I want you all to myself."

"Okay," Taylor said as he led her out of her apartment.

In the hallway, Layne stopped long enough to put his arm around Taylor and take a photo of them with his phone. "Just documenting our first date," he said. "I'm really glad we're doing this."

Layne took Taylor to a small restaurant with a dance floor and an open patio that overlooked the ocean. The candlelight and white tablecloths gave it a cozy, intimate feel he hoped Taylor would find romantic. They talked about work at first—a safe subject—while they enjoyed their meal. He had made the reservation based on his sister's review of the restaurant the last time he babysat for her. Now, as he looked at Taylor in the low light, he understood why the place was worth the drive.

After the waiter had cleared their plates, Layne took Taylor's hand and asked her to dance with him. "Come on," he said. "You can't be that out of practice." After three slow dances with her, holding her close, he didn't want the night to end.

Taylor pulled away first. "You said something about a walk…"

As they walked on the beach carrying their shoes, Layne took a chance by reaching for Taylor's free hand. She didn't pull away but cocked her head to the side as she looked at him. She didn't even have to try to be sexy because every step she took made Layne's heart race with anticipation of kissing her again.

"At this point in the date, I hold your hand so you won't trip in the sand," he said. "Safety first. All part of the total date experience, so just go with it."

"Does this experience end with you trying to get in my pants?"

"Never! I'm shocked you would think I'm the type of guy who would try to take advantage of you on our first date."

Taylor laughed. "Well, how am I supposed to spend the rest of my evening if I'm not defending my honor from your scandalous advances?"

Layne sat and patted the sand beside him. "By sitting with me and answering my scandalous questions. Or looking at the stars."

Taylor threw down her shoes and sat on the sand to look at the sky. Layne glanced up at the few stars visible between the clouds and the streetlights before looking at Taylor again.

"It's so pretty," she said.

"Beautiful." Layne didn't take his eyes off Taylor. She was stunning.

"You're not even looking," she said as she lay back on the sand.

"Why don't you have many friends?" he asked as he stretched out beside her.

"You, of all people, should understand. Didn't you ever wonder if someone wanted to be your friend because of who you actually were or because of who they thought you were? Or in my case, who Jordan was."

Layne's best friends were the Backdraft guys. "You're right," he said. "I don't have many either. I know a lot of people, but it's all on the surface. True friends, I can count on one hand."

"Lots of acquaintances."

"What are we?" he asked. When Taylor didn't answer, Layne took her hand and linked their pinkies together.

"What are you doing?" she asked.

"Seeing if you fit in with my other people," he said. "I have an opening. You fit."

Taylor started laughing and sat up. "You're using up all your good lines for a guy not trying to get me into bed." She shivered as she unlinked her pinkie from his.

Layne sat up and wrapped his arms around Taylor. "I'm not much on lines," he said. "I like you. A lot. I don't think one date will be enough. I want to see you again. I want to know you."

"Do you?" Taylor asked, leaning her head back on his shoulder. "Or do you think I'm a challenge or just another conquest for you?"

Layne laughed and leaned forward to see if Taylor was joking, but she just stared at him, trying to read him in the low light from the lampposts. "Oh, you're serious," he said. "Yeah, I think you're challenging, but I don't play games either. I meant what I said."

"Why do you like me?"

Layne wanted to give Taylor the best reassurance he could. She needed a good answer; she needed the truth. "Because you're sweet, only you don't know it. Because you love music. You're talented, funny, and sexy. And you're smart…"

"I wouldn't call what I've been doing lately smart."

"Why? Because you've slept around a bit? I don't care about that. Stop beating yourself up."

"I promised Willow I wouldn't do that anymore…" Taylor took Layne's hand, surprising him.

"Don't worry about Willow," he said, kissing Taylor's hand. "You say you care about what you promised her, but then tell me you're not good at dating. I'm telling you, you're wrong. But, really, none of that matters more than what you actually want. What do you want, Taylor?"

"I don't want to do what I've been doing anymore. It stopped being fun. I feel so…" She looked at him for a moment before looking out at the ocean.

"Empty?" Layne suggested. "Scared sometimes? Lonely even when you're surrounded by people?" He hoped to make her understand he knew how she felt.

Taylor's mouth dropped open as she turned to him. "Why would you say that?" she asked.

"It's how I feel. Well, how I felt…until you came back into my life. When I'm with you, I don't feel that way anymore. I already know you're different."

"I think I might be a lost cause," she said.

"You're not lost because I found you." He stood up and helped Taylor to her feet, pulling her close. She trembled in his arms. "We should go, though, since the wind's picking up, and you're cold. I think it might rain."

"I'm not cold," Taylor said, her lip quivering. "I just can't stop..." She crossed her arms and rubbed them from her shoulders to her elbows.

Layne moved closer to her. "Maybe it's because you're scared to admit you like me too."

Taylor laughed through her tight smile. "Maybe I am a little cold."

Layne held Taylor as tightly as he could, her heart pounding against his chest. Time stood still for a moment as he held her, closed his eyes, and breathed her in, hoping she felt the same connection. Layne looked at Taylor's lips to see if she would speak, and when she didn't, he kissed her and felt her arms tighten around him as she kissed him back.

When they separated to catch their breath, Layne took Taylor's hand again. "Come on," he said.

Taylor glanced at her phone as Layne helped her into his SUV. One missed call from Jordan, but no messages or texts. She slipped it back into the glove box.

"No phones, remember?" Layne teased as he got in.

"Just checking to make sure there's not a call from the rehab center."

"Anything?"

"No, just Jordan. There's no message or text, so I'll call her back later," Taylor said. "Or not."

"It's still early. What do you want to do now?"

"Thursdays are duet nights at the Mocking Bird..."

Layne laughed. "You want to?"

"It's completely crazy, but I do," Taylor said. The night wasn't over, but it was the most amazing date. She still felt the echo of Layne's words in her head and the ghost of his pinkie linked with hers. His soft lips tasted like peppermint, likely from the tube of lip balm she'd seen him slip into his pocket before their walk. She wanted to kiss him again.

At the Mocking Bird, Layne flipped through the available songs. There were a few songs on the list he knew well, but one stood out he thought Taylor would know. "Hey," he said. "Do you know 'Leather and Lace,' or should I keep looking?"

"That's perfect," Taylor said, smiling again. "I seriously love Stevie Nicks. She's amazing."

Everyone stopped what they were doing to listen as soon as Taylor's voice filled the space. Layne watched her with admiration as he waited for his verse. She seemed to enjoy the attention and lack of pressure singing someone else's song. Layne wanted to reach out and touch Taylor while he sang with her but fought the urge. Willow and Kayla were at a table in the back with some friends. They jumped to their feet and cheered as Layne helped Taylor step off the stage. Just as her feet hit the ground, a short man in a suit approached them. He'd watched Taylor and Layne closely during their performance—a record exec waiting to pounce.

"I think I could sell you two as a couple act," the man said. "Think about it and give me a call." He shook Layne's hand and handed Taylor a business card. He left before they could respond.

Layne looked at Taylor and shrugged. "Maybe we should call him?"

She glanced at the card and handed it to Layne. "It's getting late. Aren't you supposed to walk me to my door?" She led him through the employee exit to the stairs.

At Taylor's door, Layne took her hands. "I had a really great time with you tonight," he said. "We should do this again."

"I did too," Taylor said with a sly grin. "But I only agreed to one date."

Layne stepped closer to Taylor until she backed up against her door. "I hope you'll change your mind," he said. "Now, can I kiss you goodnight? It's my specialty kiss. You'll definitely want to see me again after it."

She rested her arms on his chest. "So confident."

"So beautiful." He pulled her close and kissed her with all the passion that had built up inside him from the moment they had taken the stage. Taylor draped her arms around his neck, both getting lost in the moment until Willow and Kayla coming up the stairs interrupted them.

Layne continued to hold Taylor in his arms, their lips inches apart. He didn't care who might find them. "Goodnight," he said. "I'll see you tomorrow." He kissed her again.

Breathless, Taylor pulled away, barely acknowledging her neighbors as they shuffled past them to their own apartment. "You want to come in?" she whispered.

"More than you can imagine," Layne said before kissing Taylor on the forehead. He cradled her head in his arms, resting his chin on top. "But that's not what tonight was about. We'll talk more tomorrow."

"Goodnight," she said. She gave Layne one last kiss on the lips before letting go of him and retreating into her apartment.

Layne stood in the middle of the hallway for a moment, wishing he'd joined Taylor in her apartment. Ultimately, he decided there would be other opportunities because he was now certain she liked him as much as he liked her.

chapter 9

Jordan arrived at the rehab center late in the evening as she usually did for her monthly visits to her mother. She always worried someone might recognize her if she visited any earlier. Even so, she still wore her standard traveling disguise of dark sunglasses to hide her bright blue eyes and a navy baseball cap over her long blond hair, which was pulled into a bun. It wouldn't have mattered; the private facility catered to other high-maintenance clients like Jordan who desired the utmost discretion.

"Miss Hoffman, come in," the night nurse said as Jordan entered her mother's room. Emanuel was a friendly, short Hispanic man with a goatee. "Your mother has been agitated today. We're giving her some extra pain medication through her central line to make her more comfortable."

Jordan turned on her sweetest smile. "Thank you so much, Emanuel," she said. "I am so glad my mother has someone so kind to take care of her." She eyed an empty syringe on the bedside table while Emanuel checked the IV lines. She quickly picked it up inside her hat and backed away to sit in a chair. Emanuel smiled at Jordan as he disposed of the syringe packaging and medicine vile from the table. "Hey, Manny?"

"Yes, Miss Hoffman?"

"Could you bring my mother an extra blanket? She looks cold."

"Yes, ma'am. I will put one in the dryer for a few minutes and bring it right away."

"You're such a dear," Jordan said.

As soon as Emanuel was out of sight, Jordan rolled her eyes and shut the door. She looked down at her mother's frail, atrophied arms. Janice didn't move, but Jordan could see her chest rising and falling as she breathed.

"Mother!" she said.

No response. Taylor claimed their mother had opened her eyes a few times, but Jordan never witnessed it.

"Open your eyes, you stupid bitch!" Jordan squeezed her mother's hand as hard as she could and waited for some sign her mother was still in there somewhere.

Still no response. Jordan took the syringe from under her hat and filled it with air. She checked to make sure she was still alone and injected the air into the IV line. After three times, there was no change on the monitors. Jordan swiftly dropped the syringe into the box on the wall and sat on the side of the bed, scowling at her mother.

"Things would be so much easier for me if you were dead," she said. "This place is expensive, and you're just wasting away. How could you have been so stupid, Mom? I needed you."

Emanuel came back in with a blanket. "Here you go, Mrs. Hoffman," he said as he placed the blanket on top of her. "This should keep you nice and warm."

At that moment, the heart monitor alarm began shrieking. Emanuel gasped and slammed his hand against a blue button on the wall. "I need some help in here!" he screamed as he lowered the bed. "She's coding!"

Jordan gave the performance of her lifetime, crying beside her mother's bedside as doctors and nurses rushed in. A few minutes later, a volunteer led Jordan to a private area. As soon as she was alone, Jordan dried her eyes and pulled out her phone. She called Taylor but hung up without leaving a message when voicemail picked up. She posted the same message on all her social media accounts.

Fans, please pray for my mother. She's suffered a stroke and is not doing well.

As the responses came rolling in, Jordan smiled and leaned back in her chair to wait for news from the doctors. About an hour later, her mother's doctor came in. Jordan immediately turned on her tears for the man.

"Please, what happened to my mother?" she asked.

The doctor sat down beside her. "Miss Hoffman, I'm sorry, but we think she suffered another stroke," he said. "We have her intubated, and her heart is beating again, but we don't think she has enough brain function left to breathe on her own. We should know more by morning."

Jordan sobbed and fell into the doctor's arms. "Doctor, please, can I stay in her room with her tonight? I know it's against the rules, but will you make an exception for me?" she asked. She had to sell her sadness; no one would suspect her.

"Of course. Do you want us to call your sister? Taylor has power of attorney, so she'll need to be here tomorrow to discuss end of life care if it comes to that."

"No, thank you. I'll call my sister and tell her what's going on. Thank you for being so kind to us."

The doctor led Jordan back to her mother's room. Janice looked much worse with a ventilator breathing for her and another monitor attached to her head. *It's almost over,* Jordan thought as she sat beside her mother's bed and rested her head on it, pretending to cry.

Throughout the night, Jordan updated her fans on social media, enjoying their attention, but she didn't call Taylor again. Different doctors and nurses came in to look at the readout of the monitors and expressed their sympathy to Jordan. She turned on tears instantly for each of them and asked if her mother was in any pain. The doctors didn't think Janice could feel anything at all, but they were running tests to confirm their suspicions.

chapter 10

Friday, May 27, 2016

Taylor woke to the sounds of thunder and rain falling outside her window. As she reached for her phone to check the time, it rang in her hand. The production assistant on the line let her know the set was closed until Tuesday. She wondered what it would mean for her and Layne. She'd had trouble falling asleep because she couldn't stop thinking about their date. Taylor crawled back into bed and heard a text message alert.

Layne: **Sucks no recording today.**
Taylor: **Good day to stay in bed.**
Layne: **I'll be right over.**
Taylor: **No. That's not what I meant!**
Layne: **Kidding. Stuff to do today anyway. Prepping to sing tonight. You should come with me.**
Taylor: **Maybe...**
Layne: **I think we had an awesome first date. The songwriter's thing could be a good second date.**
Taylor: **Maybe we should slow down.**
Layne: **Slow is fine. I just want to see you again.**
Taylor: **I'm going back to sleep. I'll talk to you later.**

Taylor put her phone down beside her and tried to go back to sleep. When she had almost drifted off, she received another text alert.

Jordan: **Tay, you need to come see Mom. She's bad.**
Taylor: **How bad?**

Jordan: **Doc thinks another stroke. They want to talk to you.**

Taylor: **I'll get there as soon as I can.**

Jordan: **Glad you care so much. Do you have something better to do? You didn't call me back last night.**

Taylor: **You didn't leave a message. I was busy. I'm off work, but my car's in the shop. I'll have to see if I can borrow my friend's car.**

Jordan: **I can't wait here for you. I have another interview today.**

Taylor: **Don't bother. You've never been there the other times I've visited.**

Taylor saw that Jordan had read her last message, but she didn't reply. "Shit!" She threw her phone on her bed.

She pulled her hair into a loose bun and wiped the tears off her face. Taylor didn't cry often, but when she did, she preferred to do so in the shower to wash away the evidence. She splashed cold water on her face and looked in the mirror. With all the rain, there was no point putting on any makeup.

Taylor grabbed her purse and stepped into the hallway, locking her apartment as she closed the door. She knew Willow had classes every morning and would have driven to the gym due to the rain. A cab ride to the rehab center would be ridiculous since she couldn't predict how long she'd have to stay. She hesitated for a moment before knocking on Layne's door. It was too soon to need him so much when everything felt confusing.

"Just a minute!" Layne called.

Taylor heard Layne looking through the peephole before he opened the door. He was wearing jeans and had no shirt or shoes on. He had a huge smile on his face as he dried his hair with a towel.

"Change your mind about…" His smile disappeared as soon as he looked at Taylor more closely. He touched her cheek. "Taylor, what's wrong? You've been crying."

"I hate to ask," she said as she turned away from Layne's hand.

"What is it?" He pulled her into his arms.

Taylor looked up at him, feeling defeated. "I need to go to the rehab center to see my mom," she said. "It's not looking good. They think she had another stroke. I'll pay for the gas if you'll let me borrow your SUV."

"Come in." Layne put his hand on Taylor's back and led her into his apartment. "Just give me a sec to finish getting dressed. I'll drive you there, and you're not paying me for anything."

"You don't have to do that."

"Taylor, you shouldn't drive when you're upset. It's not safe. I'm taking you."

"Okay," she said reluctantly as Layne walked back to his bedroom.

She sat on his couch beside a few boxes stacked on the floor and looked at an open notebook with a pen on top. Taylor read the writing on the top page. "There's more beauty in you than could ever be true," she whispered to herself. "I've spent all of my life waiting for you." It was the perfect opening verse for a love song. Taylor jumped as Layne came back into the room carrying his shoes.

"Now who's spying?" he asked.

"It's pretty," Taylor said. "You don't type things either?"

"I like to write with a pen to scratch things out if I need to. I'm not sure where I'm going with it, so I just have the one verse so far."

She was too busy thinking about her mother to give the song any further thought. She'd last seen her mother only two days ago. Everything was fine—not great—but stable. An uneasy sensation settled in Taylor's gut. Nurse Rhonda was right. This time, her mother's body was dying, but her soul had been gone since the first stroke.

"Hey," Layne said. "Are you ready to go?"

Taylor stood up and followed him outside. When they got downstairs, Layne asked Taylor to wait inside while he drove close to the door to pick her up. He got out of the SUV in the rain to open the door for her. He was already drenched from getting the vehicle in the first place, so a little more water didn't seem to make a difference to him.

During the drive to the rehab center, Layne asked Taylor questions about her mother, and she answered like someone reciting words from a script. She spoke distantly about her mother's drug and alcohol abuse. Everything had contributed to the first stroke—the result of a cocaine overdose and excessive drinking.

After a while, when Taylor stopped talking, Layne discovered she was asleep. When they were almost to the rehab center, Taylor's phone rang, jolting her awake. Layne listened to her side of the conversation.

"I'm actually on my way now," she said. "I should be there in about ten minutes."

Taylor paused to listen.

"Okay, I'll check in first thing," she said before putting her phone back in her purse.

"Everything okay?" Layne asked.

"I don't think so," Taylor said. "They wouldn't tell me anything. They just want me to come right away. I have power of attorney."

Layne had a bad feeling about the whole situation as he let Taylor out at the front door of the facility. He found a place to park and went inside. Taylor wasn't around, so he sat near the front door to wait for her. Feeling helpless, Layne prayed for peace for Taylor and wisdom for himself to be able to help her through whatever would happen next.

Taylor went straight to the nurses' station. "I'm Taylor Lee," she said. "Sorry, Taylor Hoffman. My mother's doctor wants to see me."

A tall, handsome black man with greying hair came out to speak with Taylor. "Miss Hoffman," the doctor said. "Are you here alone?"

"Wasn't my sister here earlier?"

"Yes, she stayed the night here, but your mother's condition wasn't confirmed until after she left this morning."

"I'm not alone," she said. "A friend drove me here." He was going to tell her bad news; Taylor was sure of it. Why else would he be concerned about her being alone?

"Okay," the doctor said. "Let's go to my office. Do you want to get your friend?"

"No." Taylor had only told Layne an abbreviated version of her mother's history. She'd left out the part about Jordan having introduced their mother to cocaine in the first place. It wasn't something she'd told anyone, nor had she told anyone about Jordan's drug rehab stint or suicide attempt. The press believed the scars on Jordan's wrists were the result of surgery for broken bones from an on-set injury. Taylor wasn't ready to share everything with Layne. It was difficult enough to let him drive her to the rehab center.

She followed the doctor to his office and studied the photos on his wall made up of people who were likely his children and grandchildren. Adorable little boys with missing teeth and girls with braided pigtails. The kind of family Taylor could never imagine for herself someday.

The doctor sat in a chair close to Taylor and spoke softly to her. "Miss Hoffman, while your sister was here yesterday evening, we believe your mother suffered another stroke. Her heart stopped. Because there was no DNR in place, we resuscitated her, but we've now discovered she is no longer breathing on her own. The ventilator is doing all of the work for her."

"What does that mean?"

The doctor explained what it meant for a person to be brain dead. He described all the tests they had run throughout the night to make their determination. Taylor listened, trying to comprehend everything.

"Okay. So, you're telling me she's dead—but not dead until I authorize you to pull the plug?"

"I'm so sorry. As power of attorney, it is your decision on whether or not you want us to continue life support."

Taylor looked at the photos of the doctor's family again. "What would you do if it were one of them?" she asked, pointing to the frames on the wall.

"I can't make the decision for you," he said. "But hypothetically, if it were someone for whom I had to make the decision, I would choose to end life support if there was no chance for recovery."

"I'll sign the paperwork," Taylor said.

"Would you like to see her first?"

"No." Having only seen her two days ago, Taylor didn't want to see her with all the extra tubes.

The doctor left and came back with a friendly looking white-haired woman, Rita, who went over the paperwork Taylor had to sign. Methodically, she signed everything placed in front of her. After the doctor informed Taylor her mother had passed away, she allowed Rita to help arrange cremation services.

Taylor tried several times to reach her sister before giving up and sending a text for Jordan to call her. She knew leaving a message was pointless because Jordan never checked her voicemail. She called her dad's house and left a message with his girlfriend about her mother's death. Rita kept asking Taylor if she was okay, and Taylor kept assuring her she was fine. Her mother had been dead for years; the rest was just a formality. It was really over. Finally.

Layne stood up as Taylor walked in the lobby. He started to speak, but Taylor just shook her head. He ran his hand through his hair and approached her. He tried to hug her, but she pulled away and walked out the front door.

A white-haired woman with rapid footsteps approached Layne. "Are you here with Taylor Hoffman?" she asked.

"Yes, ma'am," Layne said. "I'm about to drive her home."

"Good," she said, handing him an envelope. "Please make sure she gets this. Tell her to call Rita if she has any questions."

"I will. Thank you."

Layne went outside and found Taylor standing on the covered sidewalk, staring off into the rain. He put his hand on her shoulder.

"Please take me home," she said.

"Taylor, are you okay?" She didn't answer; she just walked toward the parking lot, getting drenched in the downpour.

chapter 11

L ayne hoped Taylor would talk to him during the drive back, but she stayed silent and stared out the window. He put his radio on a station he thought she might like and tried to concentrate on driving in the rain. Layne had checked the weather on his phone at the rehab center, and rain was predicted for the whole area into the evening.

He wanted to do something to help Taylor but didn't feel he knew her well enough yet to know what she needed. What he did know was he already cared about her more than he cared about anyone else at that moment.

As they pulled into the parking lot for their building, Taylor's phone rang. She glanced down at it and exhaled deeply before answering. "Hey, Jordan, where are you?"

Pause.

"Screw you! I got there as soon as I could, but I—"

Pause.

"Jordan, stop! She's gone. She died!"

Layne looked at Taylor, who had closed her eyes as she continued to speak to her sister.

"It's already done," Taylor continued. "Cremation. We can do a memorial later, but none of her friends ever visited."

Jordan's yelling echoed through the phone.

"It wouldn't have made a difference, Jordan. Goodbye."

Taylor ended the call and turned off her phone, silencing Jordan's voice. "Thank you for the ride," she said as she stepped out into the rain.

Layne locked his SUV and ran up the stairs after her. When he got to the hallway, Taylor stood between their apartment doors with her arms hung loosely at her sides, lost and unable to decide which way to go. He walked around to see her face. She wasn't crying; she had no expression at all when she looked up at him. Layne wrapped his arms around Taylor, holding her tightly for a moment as he cradled her head. Even though she didn't hug him back, Layne didn't want to let her go. This broken soul before him was the same beautiful woman he'd kissed in the hallway not even twenty-four hours before. Now, she was hurting and needed him.

"Why don't you come inside with me?" Layne asked as he let go of her.

Taylor still didn't speak; she nodded and followed Layne into his apartment. He started moving some boxes, but Taylor had already sat on the floor and propped herself against the arm of the couch. Layne stopped what he was doing and kneeled in front of her. He still wasn't sure what to say or do. Taylor acted like she was in shock.

"Taylor, I'm so sorry."

She looked down at the floor. "Don't be," she said flatly. "She's been mentally gone for years."

"What was Jordan yelling at you about?"

"She's just making it all about her, as usual. She's probably already put out a statement to reap the sympathy. She never cares how I might feel."

"It's okay to be sad. It's normal to feel a lot of emotions when someone you love dies."

"Normal? I'm not normal!" Taylor cried.

"Don't say that."

She laughed until tears formed in her eyes. "I wanted her dead."

"Taylor..." He had never seen someone in so much pain.

"But now she's gone, and I'm all alone, and I'm not even sad—I'm relieved—it's finally over. I've been praying for her death for years! What kind of person does that?" Taylor started breathing faster and massaging her temples, pressing harder than she should.

"You're not alone," Layne said, pulling Taylor's hands away from her head. "You're safe here with me." He pulled Taylor into his arms and held her tightly as she tried to push him away. No longer able to hold everything inside, she stopped struggling and broke down sobbing. Layne kissed the top of Taylor's head and breathed slow and steady while he held her and tried to help her calm down. The longer she cried, the more heartache he felt for her.

After several minutes, Taylor pulled away and dried her face with her shirt. Layne's shirt, already damp from the rain, was now soaked from her tears. "I'm sorry," she said as she touched his chest.

"It's fine." Layne pulled off his shirt and tossed it on the couch. "Are you okay?" Taylor fell back into his arms and kissed him hard. Surprised, he pushed her away by her shoulders. "Whoa, what are you doing?"

"Please," Taylor begged as she moved closer to him. "Just one more time."

He wiped the tears from Taylor's cheeks. "I don't want just one more time with you," he said. "I want more, but you're not in the best place to think about that right now."

"Please," she said as another tear rolled down her cheek. "I can't…I don't want to feel this anymore. Make it stop."

Layne swallowed the lump in his throat and softly kissed Taylor, feeling her tears on his face. He wanted to help her but felt guilty as he carried her to his bed and began undressing her. Attraction wasn't the problem because even with Taylor's face red and puffy from crying, she was still the most beautiful woman he had ever seen. It might have been too soon, but his feelings for her were strong. Layne liked to be needed but wondered if Taylor was using him to escape her pain just because he was there or if she had any feelings for him at all. Relieved she was no longer crying by the time he finished undressing her, Layne took Taylor into his arms and kissed her again, taking great care to be slow and gentle with her.

Later, when he came out of his bathroom, Layne found Taylor asleep on his bed looking small and exposed, wearing nothing but her panties and one of his shirts that was so twisted up, it barely hid her breasts. He covered her with a blanket and bent down to kiss her on the forehead.

After he got dressed, Layne realized he hadn't eaten all day and figured Taylor hadn't either. There was no food in his apartment, but he didn't want to leave Taylor alone. He didn't know if she liked Chinese food, and her favorite pizza place didn't deliver. As he stood in his living room debating what to do, Layne heard keys jingling in the hallway. When he opened the door, he startled Willow, who almost dropped her gym bag and dripping umbrella.

"Hey," she said as she started to unlock her apartment.

Layne walked over to her. "I need a favor."

Willow tilted her head to the side. "What kind of favor?"

"For Taylor," Layne said. "I don't want to leave her alone. She's asleep in my apartment."

"What's going on?" Willow opened her door and threw her stuff inside. She closed the door and glared at Layne with her arms crossed. "What the hell did you give her?"

"Nothing."

"What's she on? Or did you get her drunk?" Willow backed him into the wall.

"She's sober," Layne said. "So am I. She's upset because her mom died this afternoon."

"Oh God!" Willow said, covering her mouth as she backed away. "Poor thing! Is she okay?"

"Taylor's exhausted from crying and finally fell asleep. I'm worried about her. She hasn't eaten all day, so I want to go get her favorite pizza. They don't deliver, and she doesn't need to be left alone."

"Wait, she cried in front of you?"

"Yeah, in front of me, on me. Why is that such a big deal?"

"Because she doesn't do that," Willow said. "Something's hurt her so badly, she keeps everyone at a safe distance. She's told me a little about her life, and I love her like a sister, but I still feel like she's keeping me at arm's length. Something happened I would expect anyone to cry about, but she didn't. There are a lot of things she won't talk about, and she shuts down when I ask her."

"She told me you're like a sister to her," Layne said. "And she told me about you helping her with a guy who hit her. Is that what you expected her to cry about?"

Willow nodded. "I'm glad she's opening up to you."

"Look, I'm not so stupid I can't see she's hurting, even before today," Layne said, leaning against the wall. "She's not just some booty call to me. I care about her."

"I'm sorry for jumping to the wrong conclusion," Willow said. "I'll call Mr. Minotti and order her favorite, and I'll wait with her until you get back."

"Thank you."

As Layne drove to the pizza parlor, he wondered what he would say to Taylor when she woke up later and how he could convince her to stay the night with him so he could be there for her. He already thought she was incredibly strong, but it didn't exclude her from needing someone, and he wanted nothing more than to be that someone.

When Layne arrived at his destination, Mr. Minotti was standing behind the counter next to an older woman with dark, curly hair.

"Dear, this is Taylor's boyfriend," Mr. Minotti told the woman as Layne approached the counter. "Layne, right?"

"Yes, sir," he said.

"How's Taylor holding up?" the woman asked Layne. "Willow told us what happened. I'm Mrs. Minotti."

"Nice to meet you," Layne said as he shook her hand. "She'll be okay. She was resting when I left. Willow's with her."

"Well, be sure to give her our condolences," Mr. Minotti said as he tried to refuse Layne's money.

"I will, and I insist," Layne said as he put the cash on the counter.

"The order will be up in about ten minutes," Mr. Minotti said.

Layne's phone rang. It was Christina. "I'll take my call outside and come back," he told Mr. Minotti. Outside, under the awning to avoid the rain, he answered his phone. "Hey, sis."

"Brandon," she scolded. "I've been calling you and texting you for the past couple of days. What's going on with you? It's not like you to not respond."

"I'm sorry. I've been busy. I was working, then working on a song…"

"I'm just worried about you."

"Don't be."

"I don't want you to be lonely with everything going on. Amanda's wedding…"

"I don't want to talk about Amanda." Layne sat on the bench under the awning and rested his head in his hands.

"Because you're not over her?"

"No, because I am over her."

"Good, because there's someone I want to introduce you to from school."

Layne groaned. "Chris, no. I don't want to be set up."

"A former student-teacher," Christina said, ignoring him. "She's fresh out of college and completely adorable."

"Not interested."

"Come on, just meet her."

"No."

"One date."

"Chris, give it a rest," Layne said. He knew his sister wouldn't let it go if he didn't fess up. "I'm not interested because I'm seeing someone, and I really like her. I don't want to date anyone else."

"That's great, Brandon!"

"Sis, please, you know I'm going by Layne now."

"I'll never get used to it. *Well?*"

"Well, what?"

"Seriously?" she asked, exasperated. "Tell me about the woman you've met!"

Layne laughed. "She's a singer who lives in my building. She's smart, funny, and beautiful."

"Does she know who you are?"

"Of course."

"And did the revelation come before or after you'd asked her out?"

"She knows who I am, and it's not a problem. She acted when she was a kid, so she knows how it is." Layne started playing with a stray thread on the edge of his shirt, ready for the conversation to be over.

"Well, that's a positive. I'm looking forward to meeting her."

"Slow down, we're not to that point yet. Seriously, I've only really known Taylor for six days. We first met about ten years ago when Backdraft guest-starred on *The Spectacular Smiths.*"

"And I've known you your whole life, little brother. You just described her in three words, and the first two had nothing to do with her appearance. Six days in or not, you're falling for her. I can hear it in your voice. And wait, Taylor? You mean Taylor Hoffman? She was so adorable."

"Yes, and she still is. I have to go. I'm taking some food back to my apartment for Taylor. She's had a bad day."

"Fine. May I still bring the kids by to see your new place soon?"

"Yeah. I'll talk to you about that later," Layne said, ending the call. He went back inside and collected his order. On the way out, Layne heard Mrs. Minotti speak to her husband.

"Such a cute couple," she said.

"You should see them together," Mr. Minotti said. "He looks at her the way I see you, beautiful."

God, if they only knew, Layne thought as he walked back to his SUV. He thought about his last girlfriend, Amanda. They'd connected with their musical abilities but not necessarily with the love of music like Taylor. As they were breaking up, he'd learned all the spontaneity Amanda seemed to possess was calculated and manipulative. They had both accused the other of being a liar during their messy breakup. Afterward, there was no chance of them being friends. He was with her for a couple of years, but in the back of his mind, he'd always known it wouldn't last because they both wanted too many different things.

Layne hoped to have many more nights with Taylor. The more he learned about her, the more he wanted to know.

When Taylor woke up, she didn't know where she was at first. The bed was not her own; she was still in Layne's apartment. She leaned back against the pillow and closed her eyes for a moment to comfort her sore eyes and stop her throbbing head. Taylor grabbed the blanket that was draped over her legs and wrapped it around herself as she got up to look for Layne. She couldn't find her jeans and didn't recognize the shirt she was wearing.

"Layne?" she called. Taylor was surprised to find Willow in the living room.

Willow put down her phone and sat up on the end of the couch. "Hey, Taylor."

"What are you doing here? Where's Layne?"

"He asked me to stay while he went to get you something to eat. I'm so sorry about your mom. You never talked about her. Was she sick?"

Taylor wrapped the blanket around herself to better hide her bare legs. "It's okay," she said. "She had a stroke after a drug overdose several years ago and never really woke up. Her prognosis was never good."

"I had no idea."

"No one did before I told Layne."

Willow moved the boxes so Taylor could sit down. "Girl, what's going on between you and him? Is he your boyfriend?"

Taylor sighed. "We're friends."

"Looks like more than friends from where I'm sitting," Willow said. "What are you doing? Do you even know?"

"I don't need another lecture," Taylor said, resting her head in her hands. "He knows I'm not looking for anything serious right now. We've only been on one date. We're keeping it casual."

"You might be keeping it casual, but he's not."

Taylor looked up at her. "Why do you say that?"

"Open your eyes," Willow said, shaking her head. "I see the way he kisses you and saw how you kissed him last night—some serious passion going on there. Today, he's genuinely concerned about you. I thought he was going to cry when he asked me to stay with you. Sometimes we find something good when we're not looking. He's falling for you."

"No, he isn't," Taylor said. "It's too soon for that."

Willow picked up Layne's notebook and shoved it in Taylor's face. "Then what's this?"

Taylor put the notebook back on top of the boxes. "It's just a song he's writing," she said. "It is possible to write a love song that isn't about any one person. It can't be about me; we barely know each other."

"Yeah, and you've slept with him how many times now since you met him? I thought you might be starting a relationship with him. The way you two sang together last night was incredible. Several people were recording it. There's probably a video on YouTube already."

"We're just hanging out, and we happen to be attracted to each other. That's it." Taylor got up and went to the kitchen. She looked in all the cabinets until she found a glass to get some water and went back to the living room.

"That's generally how relationships start," Willow said as Taylor sat down. "Just wait, when Layne gets back, he'll find some reason to touch you."

"You don't know what you're talking about. We're just friends…"

"Yeah—with benefits. I'm gay, not blind, Taylor. Either you're using him, which is cruel, or you're in denial you feel something for him, which is sad. It's obvious he cares about you. Plus, he told me he does."

"Shh!" Taylor whispered as the door opened.

Layne walked in carrying a pizza box. He placed it on the counter, then immediately walked over to Taylor. "I'm glad you're awake. Are you feeling better after resting?" He wrapped his arm around Taylor as he sat beside her. "I was worried about you."

Willow raised her eyebrows at Taylor, her way of saying "I told you so."

"I am," Taylor said.

After Willow left, Taylor sat with Layne on his couch and ate without speaking until the music coming from the bar broke the silence. "Oh, Layne, you're missing the songwriter's showcase tonight. Why don't you go? I'll go home."

"No," Layne said, resting his hand on Taylor's arm. "I'll go next time. I don't have the song I want to sing finished yet anyway."

"I'm sorry I've kept you from it all day." Taylor covered Layne's hand with her own and wondered why she'd been compelled to do so as soon as her skin touched his.

Layne brushed Taylor's hair out of her face. "I care about you," he said, then quickly added, "You're my friend, and you needed me today. That's always more important than writing a song."

"About what you said earlier...you're good with us keeping things casual for now?"

Layne thought about it for a moment. "Like what, friends with benefits?"

"I guess..." she said. "Can you agree to that?"

He looked at the floor. "Casual, fine, for now, if you must label it as something. But exclusive."

"Exclusive?"

"It's the only way I'm okay with it. I can't do this if there might be someone else too. During our arrangement, we agree there's no sex with anyone else. And we promise to continue dating to get to know each other better and stay friends before anything else."

Taylor sighed with relief. It gave her more time to be with him without the boyfriend label that scared her so much. "I'm good with that," she said. "I need to go home. My head's killing me. Where are my clothes?"

Layne helped Taylor find her clothes under the mess of blankets in his room and watched her dress.

"Thank you for being here for me today," she said softly.

"Anytime."

"I have to go."

"I wish you would stay."

She couldn't stay. Too much had happened, and the day needed to end. Taylor followed Layne to his living room, where he opened the door but stood in the way. "Goodnight, Layne," she said as she tried to go around him.

Layne put his arm out in front of Taylor, stopping her. "Wait," he pleaded.

Casual or not, Taylor knew Layne was about to touch her again, and she wanted him to. He hugged Taylor so tightly new tears escaped the corners of her eyes. She immediately felt dizzy and clung to him to steady herself. *Damn it,* Taylor thought, *Willow's right.*

"Come get me if you need anything," Layne said as he loosened his grip on Taylor. He wiped the tears from her cheeks and slowly kissed her on the forehead. "You should drink some more water since you've cried so much. I'll talk to you tomorrow."

"Okay. Goodnight." Taylor walked across the hall to her apartment.

After she grabbed a bottle of water from her refrigerator, Taylor sat on her couch and turned on her phone. There were three messages, one from Jordan and two from her dad. She didn't feel like calling them back, so she stretched out on the couch to rest and fell asleep within minutes.

When Taylor woke up a couple of hours later, she checked the time on her phone. Just past midnight. It was her birthday, and she couldn't go back to sleep.

chapter 12

Sitting on her patio in Los Angeles, Jordan stared at the stars before she pulled out her phone to read the comments from fans expressing their condolences. Several thousand new comments had posted since she'd announced her mother's death. The posts that infuriated her the most were ones with condolences to both her and Taylor together. Taylor wasn't supportive of Jordan's career at all. Taylor didn't bother trying to be famous, but there were still articles popping up with theories about her disappearance from the Hollywood scene. Jordan's sister was more popular than ever now and didn't even care.

Jordan looked at the headlines that came up when she searched her own name. There were already posts about the death of her mother, complete with pictures of the entire Hoffman family with their late 90s hairstyles and clothing. The last paragraph mentioned Jordan's continued movie success with the *Awake* trilogy and stated Taylor Hoffman had moved away from Hollywood, her exact occupation unknown.

Not for long, Jordan thought. She posted an anonymous comment on the article.

I hear Taylor Hoffman is working at some low-class karaoke bar outside of LA.

Now, I just sit back and wait, Jordan thought. *That'll teach her to abandon and ignore me.* Taylor had stolen Michael away from her. The little bitch must have known Jordan liked Michael first.

Jordan had tried for weeks to get Michael back from Taylor before she gave up and left for filming. When she came back, Michael was still dating Taylor and continued to push Jordan away. He said he loved Taylor and wasn't interested. Drugging him had been a stroke of genius. Jordan told Michael that Taylor planned to dump him and provided a drink and a shoulder to cry on. Jordan didn't want Michael anymore after they'd had sex, especially since he'd whispered Taylor's name.

Michael couldn't remember anything, but the satisfaction of having gotten him away from Taylor was enough for Jordan at the time. It was perfect that Taylor dumped Michael afterward and refused to forgive him. She'd also refused to forgive Jordan but still came crawling back for the opportunity to sing for *Awake*.

Jordan looked at her phone again. Taylor hadn't responded to her voicemail from earlier. It was just past midnight on Taylor's twenty-third birthday. Jordan sent her sister another text.

Happy Birthday, Tay. Sorry it's a shitty one.

Jordan watched as the message went from delivered to read, but Taylor didn't respond.

chapter 13

Saturday, May 28, 2016

Layne spent most of Friday evening looking at Jordan's social media accounts. Taylor was right about her sister being an attention whore. She'd posted the same announcement on every account Layne could find. He figured Jordan loved all the attention and heartfelt prayers from fans. Layne didn't care about Jordan; it was Taylor he cared about. Layne wasn't completely comfortable with the arrangement he'd agreed to but acknowledged he would have agreed to almost anything for the chance to stay close to her.

He pulled up Taylor's IMDB profile. Her date of birth was listed as May 28, 1993. It was Taylor's birthday. He immediately got up, grabbed his keys and wallet, and headed to the parking lot. He drove to the supermarket a couple of miles away. He had to acknowledge Taylor's birthday.

At the store, he bought a two-pack of cupcakes with both chocolate and vanilla, birthday candles, and a lighter. After his day with Taylor, Layne wanted more and knew she'd need some convincing over time to take the casual label out of their relationship, but it wasn't the best time for that. All he could do now was prove to her that he cared and could be an attentive boyfriend.

The cashier made a comment about his purchase. "Aww, for someone special?" the middle-aged woman asked.

"Yeah," Layne said with a grin. He paid for his items and headed back to his apartment. When he got home, Layne pulled out his phone and sent Taylor a message. He figured she'd still be awake.

Happy Birthday

Layne waited while Taylor typed back to him.

Thank you. You're up late.

Layne opened the cupcakes and placed candles in each of them. After dropping the lighter into his pocket, he went to Taylor's door and sent her another text.

Knock knock

Gentle knocking on her door startled Taylor as she read Layne's text. She looked out the peephole at Layne standing there with his hands behind his back. When she opened the door, Layne grinned and held out a vanilla cupcake with a candle stuck in the top.

"You know, I might have let you in if you'd brought chocolate," Taylor joked as she started to close the door.

Layne stuck out his foot to stop the door and held out a chocolate cupcake. "I came prepared," he said.

Taylor smirked and let him in. Layne placed the cupcakes on Taylor's countertop and took out a lighter.

"You have to make a wish." He lit the candle and held out the cupcake for Taylor.

"How did you know it was my birthday?" she asked, taking the cupcake.

"There's all sorts of information on the internet."

Taylor blew out the candle and unwrapped the cupcake. "Haven't you seen enough of me? Especially since I fell apart and cried on you."

"You had every reason to fall apart." Layne took the other cupcake and sat on Taylor's couch. "I'll leave if you want me to, but I didn't think you should be alone after what happened, especially on your birthday."

Taylor looked at Layne. He was wearing a ratty old t-shirt and jeans with his hair pulled back. Clean-shaven, he looked like a little boy sitting there with his cupcake. She didn't want him to leave but was scared to let him stay. "You want to watch a movie or something?" she asked as she sat down beside him. "I can't promise I'll stay awake through the whole thing, but you can wake me when it's over if I fall asleep, right?"

"Sure."

"We can watch something on the television in my bedroom, or we can stream something on my laptop in here."

"Whatever you want is fine."

Taylor stood up and walked to her bedroom door. "The screen is bigger on the TV if you promise to behave yourself."

"I can if you can." Layne followed Taylor and sat on the bed while she signed in to her Netflix account.

"What kind of movie do you want?" she asked, hoping Layne would make the decision for them.

"After the day you've had, we should watch a comedy."

"Which one?"

"Go to the comedy category and click over to the twenty-third title in honor of your birthday and then hit play."

Taylor did what Layne suggested while he stacked the pillows against the wall. She wondered where she should sit.

"Come on," Layne said as he held out his arms. "I promise, I won't bite you. Not on your birthday. I'm not your sex-slave right now, just your adorable friend."

Taylor laughed and crawled over to Layne. She pressed her ear against his chest and let him wrap his arms around her.

"Thank you," she said. "I think you're the nicest person I've ever met."

Layne held her close. "Are you okay, really? You've dealt with a lot over the last twenty-four hours."

"I will be." Taylor felt safe in Layne's arms and was so exhausted, she closed her eyes as the movie started, letting her sadness fade away.

Within minutes of the movie starting, Layne noticed Taylor wasn't laughing or moving at all. He suspected she was asleep. "Taylor?"

When she didn't respond, Layne moved a few of the pillows and leaned back to make her more comfortable. None of his movements had woken her; Taylor's breathing was still slow and relaxed. Layne thought about the conversation with his sister. Falling for someone in barely a week. It sounded crazy, but it was exactly how he felt because Taylor was enchanting like no one else in his life.

"Taylor," he whispered. "I don't think I can keep this casual because I'm in danger of falling in love with you." Layne knew Taylor hadn't heard him because she didn't move at all. He kissed the top of her head and closed his eyes.

When Taylor woke up, the movie was over, and a couple of hours had passed. Layne slept peacefully with his arm draped over her. She hated to wake him but sleeping over was outside the rules of their arrangement. She gently shook his shoulder.

Layne opened his eyes and smiled at Taylor. "Hey," he said, stretching with a groan. "You didn't even make it past the opening credits."

"Looks like you fell asleep too," Taylor said. "You need to go home now. I have to get up early to go get my car."

Layne stretched again and sat up. "I wish you'd let me stay."

"That's against the rules."

"We haven't defined all the rules."

"Thank you for the cupcake," Taylor said, wanting to change the subject. "It was nice. Maybe we can talk some more or play some music after I pick up my car and go to the gym."

"Definitely." Layne stood up and walked to the door, followed by Taylor. He smoothed Taylor's messed up hair and touched the pillow creases on her face. "How do you manage to look so beautiful all the time?"

"Saying that's against the rules too," Taylor said as she pushed him out the door.

"I've never liked rules, anyway," Layne said. He kissed Taylor on the forehead. "I want to go with you to the gym since I've been meaning to check it out, and I'll drive you to pick up your car."

"Alright," she said with a sigh.

Layne took Taylor's face in his hands and quickly kissed her on the lips. "Happy Birthday," he said before walking across the hall to his apartment.

Taylor shut her door and locked it. She leaned her head against it and closed her eyes. *I still don't know what I'm doing*, she thought as she went back to her room and stretched out on her bed. She wrapped her arms around her pillow, which smelled like Layne, grabbed her notebook off the nightstand, and started writing.

I don't think you're the same. I don't think you'll hurt me. If you leave, I'm to blame. There is danger with you. Danger of falling in love? Sometimes when I look at you, I think you already are. If I could just let you love me, because I'm already in too far.

Taylor picked up her phone and listened to the three voicemails she'd ignored earlier. The first one was from Jordan.

"Taylor, I think you're right about not having a memorial. Do whatever you want with the ashes. I don't care."

The next two messages were from her dad. When had he last called her back? Taylor couldn't remember.

"Taylor, I'm sorry to hear of Janice's death. Let me know if you need money to pay for anything."

Taylor deleted her dad's message and listened to his next one.

"Taylor, I'll be out of town for a week, so take care. Oh...I think I missed your birthday last week. Happy Birthday."

"You don't care about my birthday if you can't even remember the date," Taylor said. She threw her phone back on her bed.

But Layne cares, Taylor thought. She picked up her phone again and sent him a text.

> Taylor: **We should talk about our rules.**
> Layne: **Rules are made to be broken.**
> Taylor: **No more sleeping over.**
> Layne: **That was an accident.**
> Taylor: **I need time.**
> Layne: **Time to realize how awesome I am? You agreed we could date and be friends.**
> Taylor: **You agreed to keep things casual for now.**

Layne: **For now. You agreed we could get to know each other better. Tell me all your secrets. Imagine a maniacal laugh in the background…**

Taylor: **My secrets are scary.**

Layne: **I'm not scared.**

Taylor: **You probably should be. I'm pretty messed up.**

Layne: **I know you're going through a lot of shit right now. I want to know everything about you, including the messed-up parts.**

Taylor: **That's definitely against the rules. You're being bold via text.**

Layne: **I'll say it to your face. Let me come back over. Or you can come over here.**

Taylor: **Against the rules.**

Layne: **We should be willing to change our rules as we go.**

Taylor: **I'll see you tomorrow. Goodnight.**

Layne: **It's already tomorrow. See you in a few hours.**

Taylor collapsed on her bed and covered her face with her hands. Layne was basically perfect, but the thought of a serious relationship with him or anyone else made her want to run away.

chapter 14

After a couple of hours of sleep, Taylor got up and dressed for her workout. She hadn't taken very good care of herself for the past few days, so exercise would do her good and help take her mind off the death of her mother. She knocked on Layne's door and was surprised to find him already dressed for the gym.

"It's weird seeing you in sweats." Taylor scanned his clothing. "It doesn't seem to be your style."

Layne laughed. "What's my style?"

"Jeans. Old t-shirts. No man-bun."

"Are you saying these pants make my ass look big?" Layne turned around for her opinion.

Heat rose to Taylor's cheeks. "I'm not looking at your ass."

"Well, looking at my ass isn't against the rules, so I guess it's okay," he said with a sigh. "Come on, let's go." He locked his door and took Taylor's hand.

Her hand tingled as she pulled it from his grip. "That's against the rules," she said.

"Sorry," Layne said. "I told you I'm not great with rules."

The mechanic came out to talk to Taylor after the cashier had handed her the keys.

"Miss, someone did a real number on your tire," the mechanic said.

"So, it was slashed," Layne said. "That's what I thought when I looked at it."

"More like stabbed," the mechanic said. "I lost count at twenty punctures. I saved the tire in case you want to report it to the police. There was a manufacturer's defect in your spare; that's what caused the problem with it, so no charge on that one."

"Twenty?" Taylor asked. "Who does that?" Then she knew. Jordan would do that. She suspected Jordan had done it to her boyfriend's car when they were in high school, even though her sister denied it at the time.

"You should report it," Layne said as he placed his hand on Taylor's shoulder. "Whoever did it could come back and hurt something else. Or hurt you."

"No, I don't want to report it," Taylor said. "Thank you. I'm sure it won't happen again."

Layne followed Taylor to her car. "Hey, why don't you want to report it?" he asked.

"Because I think I know who did it."

"Who?"

"It's not important," Taylor said.

Layne threw his hands up in the air. "Yeah, it is important. It's your safety we're talking about. Was it an ex?"

"No. I only have one ex-boyfriend, and I haven't heard from him in years. He wouldn't do it. He doesn't even know where I am."

"And you're absolutely certain it wasn't that asshole who hit you?"

"I'm sure," Taylor said. "I'll see you at the gym. Do you know where it is?"

"I'll follow you."

Once inside the gym, Taylor left Layne at the free weights while she went to a stationary bike for some cardio. She could almost feel her blood boiling as she thought about her sister. Why was Jordan bothering her again? It was one thing to have sister squabbles when they were kids resulting in torn clothing and broken cell phones, but the car tire was definitely an escalation.

Taylor wondered if Jordan was taking drugs again because she was always more paranoid and cruel with drugs in her system.

Taylor didn't want Layne exposed to Jordan at all but knew it was coming since Jordan would arrive on set soon. *Surely, he will see through her,* she thought. Either way, she hoped keeping Layne at a safe distance would protect him from Jordan's manipulation.

She glanced at Layne several times. Other women were looking at him, and a few would occasionally strike up brief conversations with him. One woman, a petite redhead with large breasts, seemed to be flirting heavily with Layne. Instantly, Taylor felt a twinge of nausea, which she tried to ignore.

Layne noticed Taylor watching him while he talked to a red-haired woman. He caught a glimpse of jealousy in her eyes before she turned away and pedaled faster on the bike. That alone gave Layne hope that Taylor might have feelings for him. He had no clue what the woman in front of him was saying as he turned back to her but didn't want to be rude. She was in good shape, pretty, and was probably in her early thirties.

"So, what do you think?" the woman asked.

"Um, sorry, could you say that again? The music is so loud in here."

"I was asking if you need a workout partner. Someone to push you and spot for you." She twirled the end of her ponytail around her finger and batted her eyelashes at him.

"I don't do a lot of lifting that would require a spotter, but thanks. I have to go now; I think my girlfriend is ready for me to help her with the punching bag," he said, gesturing toward Taylor. "It was nice meeting you."

Layne left the disappointed woman standing by the weights and walked over to Taylor, who was just getting off the bike. As he put his hand on her shoulder, "Heart to Face" started playing over the gym's speakers. Taylor started laughing as Layne covered his face.

"Takes you back in time, doesn't it?" she asked.

"Sweet puppies, it does!" he said.

"Ha," Taylor said as she glanced over Layne's shoulder. "Did you get her number?"

Layne turned to see who Taylor was looking at just in time to see the red-haired woman walk away. "You jealous?" He grinned.

"Of course not," Taylor said, her face still flushed from the bike. "I have no reason to be."

"You're right. You don't have a reason to be jealous, but it's adorable you are anyway." Layne quickly kissed Taylor before she could respond. "Oops, I think I broke those rules again. I'm not supposed to kiss you in public, am I?"

"I think you're breaking the rules on purpose."

"Are you going to show me those mad kickboxing skills or not?"

"Fine," Taylor said as she led Layne to the punching bags.

It wasn't long before Taylor got into a great rhythm while kicking the bag. She worked out her aggression with such force that Layne had trouble holding it steady. He moved slightly to ask her to take a break, but it was too late to stop her foot from slamming into the side of his head, right beside his eye. Pain radiated through his head as he dropped to his knees. Taylor gasped as she stopped the bag from swinging.

Layne had trouble catching his breath for a moment. "Fuck!" he muttered as he grabbed his head. He wasn't mad at Taylor, but he was in a lot of pain and felt stupid for having moved while she was kicking.

"Oh God, Layne!" Taylor said as she knelt beside him. "Are you okay?" She wrapped her arms around him and kissed the top of his head. "I'm so sorry!"

He leaned against Taylor and let her hold him for a moment. Getting kicked in the face was worth it for her reaction. "I'll be okay," he said.

One of the trainers rushed over and checked Layne's eyes with a small flashlight. "Man," he said as he looked at Taylor and shook his head. "You kicked the shit out of him. Remind me not to train with you. You're one of Willow's students; I remember seeing you in her class."

"Yes," Taylor said. "I'm not very good."

"That's obvious," the trainer said with a chuckle.

"I'm fine," Layne said. "I think I'm done working out for the day, though." He tried to stand, but the room was spinning, so he sat down again. "Shit…I'm not fine."

The trainer, who was bigger and taller than Layne, effortlessly helped him to his feet. "You probably have a mild concussion," he said. "You don't need to be driving, and someone needs to watch you for several hours."

"I'll drive him home," Taylor said. "We can come back for his car later."

"Okay," Layne said. He was glad Taylor would have to look after him for the day.

The trainer helped Layne out to Taylor's car. He closed the door and turned to Taylor. "Dude must be really into you," he said, loud enough for Layne to hear. "I'd be pretty pissed if someone kicked me like that."

"It was an accident," Taylor said. "My foot slipped."

"Is your foot okay?" the trainer asked.

"It's fine," she said. "Thanks for your help."

"Watch your boyfriend closely," the trainer called as he walked back toward the gym. "If he starts puking, get him to the hospital."

"I will."

Layne reclined in the passenger's seat as Taylor got in her car. His head was throbbing, and he could feel his eye swelling.

"Do I need to take you to the urgent care clinic?" she asked.

"No, I think I'll be fine. I doubt they can do anything more than what I can do at home."

"I'm so sorry. I just slipped and couldn't stop."

Layne reached out and patted Taylor's knee. "It's okay," he said. "At least it got me away from all those women throwing themselves at me."

Taylor laughed so hard she snorted. "All? Please...there were, like, three," she said.

"Which proves you were watching. And counting," Layne said as he looked at Taylor's red face. "I told them I had a girlfriend to make them back off."

As she drove, Taylor realized she was jealous when those women were flirting with Layne. She wondered if Layne had noticed the two different guys hitting on her. She'd told both guys she was there with her boyfriend, a lie that effortlessly passed through her lips.

"So, did you give those guys your number?" Layne asked as Taylor pulled into the parking lot behind their building. He had noticed.

"No, I did the same thing you did," Taylor said.

"You told them you had a girlfriend? That's pretty hot."

"Yeah, that's what I did," Taylor said, shaking her head. Layne's mind always went straight to the gutter. "Let's get you upstairs. I still have the package of peas in my freezer from my black eye. It's helped with all the bruises from kickboxing."

Once they were upstairs, Layne sprawled out on Taylor's couch while she retrieved the peas from the freezer. She wrapped a towel around the package and placed it on Layne's face. He rose long enough for Taylor to sit and rested his head on her lap.

"I've never been hit in the face," Layne said. "I guess I know what it feels like now. It hurts. A lot."

"Yeah, I know," Taylor said as she smoothed Layne's hair. "Can you forgive me, or does this end our friendship?"

"There's nothing to forgive." Layne winced as Taylor shifted the peas. "I'm sorry you have to take care of me."

"I don't mind. Besides, it's my fault." Taylor was used to taking care of everything. When her mother had drunk herself into a stupor, it was Taylor who cleaned up the vomit to spare the housekeepers and keep them from quitting. Her sister's drug-induced manic episodes were Taylor's responsibility, too, until Jordan went to rehab. Taylor remembered feeling relieved when Jordan moved back to their mother's home after rehab instead of their father's home with Taylor. At least for a little while, Taylor had only herself to care for because she rarely saw her father or his young girlfriend. Layne needed her help now, and at least he appreciated it.

"This is helping," Layne said. "I can't feel my face. My nose works, though, and I stink."

"Can you stand long enough to take a shower?"

Layne stood up slowly, and Taylor put her arms out, ready to catch him if needed. "I'm not as dizzy as before, but you should probably go in the shower with me just in case," he said, winking with his good eye.

Taylor smirked. "Uh huh."

"You want me to be safe, don't you?" Layne teased. "Come on, you could use a shower after working out, anyway, and we've already seen each other naked."

"Fine." Taylor took the peas from Layne and tossed them back in the freezer.

As many guys as Taylor had been with, she'd never showered with one. She warmed up the water while Layne undressed. She studied his body under the bright lights in her bathroom. He was fit but not overly muscular, and his body hair was sparse but not because he'd shaved it. As she looked at Layne, Taylor had to admit that even with his swollen eye, she still found him attractive.

Layne caught Taylor looking at him. "I know," he said. "I'm a fine specimen worthy of admiration."

"And yet so humble." Taylor helped Layne into the tub, then she undressed and joined him.

"This is already the best shower I've had all week," Layne said. He grinned at Taylor as he looked at her body under the bright light above the shower. When Taylor turned around, Layne ran his fingertips over the yellow roses tattoo on her shoulder and kissed it. "What does this one mean? The roses. It's the only one I don't get. It looks like one of them is wilted a bit."

"Roses mean different things based on their color. Red for love, pink for admiration, white for purity. Yellow roses are my favorite because they represent joy, friendship, and optimism. I needed that when I got it after my mom's first stroke. She always told Jordan and me that we were her 'beautiful yellow roses.' I wasn't feeling very beautiful when I got it, so the wilted one is for me. I felt like I didn't have any friends at all, or anyone to help me, so I had to be my own friend, make my own joy, and take care of myself." Taylor turned to face Layne and thought he pitied her. "Don't feel sorry for me."

"I feel something," he said as he hugged her and kissed her forehead. "But it's not pity. I know that's breaking the rules of friendship and our casual thing."

Taylor rested her head on Layne's shoulder. "I've never been great at friendships or relationships," she said.

Layne held her tighter. "Then practice with me," he said. "I've told you, I'm not very good with rules."

"You keep saying that, but you don't seem to break any rules except for ones with me."

"I promise, I won't kiss you again unless you look like you want me to."

"Here," she said, handing Layne her body wash.

He looked at the pink bottle. "I'll smell like you."

"It's not that bad."

After they had washed, Taylor turned off the water and stepped out of the tub. She handed Layne a towel and watched him dry his hair.

"I can feel you watching me," he said, grinning from underneath the towel.

"I'm just making sure you're okay," Taylor said. "You're not still dizzy?"

"Only when I look at you."

She rolled her eyes. "You're relentless."

Layne pulled the towel from his head and wrapped it around his waist as he stood in front of the mirror. "Damn. Do I look too rough for you to want to take advantage of me later?"

Taylor gently touched Layne's cheek underneath the swelling. "Not too bad," she said.

"I don't have any clean clothes here," Layne said as he hugged Taylor again. "Could you go get some for me?"

Taylor pulled away and looked at Layne. She wanted him to kiss her. As Layne's towel slipped, Taylor tried to catch it, her hand landing on his naked butt instead. "That was an accident," she said, too embarrassed to move her hand.

Layne grabbed the back of Taylor's head and kissed her. "I don't need clothes right now," he said as Taylor dragged him into her bedroom.

Cold with the air conditioner blowing directly on her, Taylor pulled the blanket back over herself and moved closer to feel Layne's warmth. Being naked with him felt completely natural, but in the back of her mind, she was still uneasy being so close to him. She had told him things no one else knew about her. No one else knew the reason behind the tattoo on her shoulder. Layne wrapped his arms around her and pulled her head onto his chest. His heart still pounded. Taylor closed her eyes for a moment and tried to overcome her clamminess and the feeling of terror spinning around in her head. When Layne's stomach growled, breaking the silence, Taylor was so relieved she giggled. "You hungry?" she asked.

"I would much rather stay naked in bed with you all day, but I'm starving. I didn't eat this morning. Could we have something delivered?"

Taylor reached for her phone. "Chinese is the only decent food we can get delivered in this neighborhood. Will that work?" she asked. "I could get enough for leftovers to last us the rest of the weekend."

"So, you're letting me stay?"

"An exception to the rules for the night since I have to watch you."

After Taylor called in their order, she got dressed and brushed her hair to look presentable before she crossed the hallway to get Layne's clothes.

It was strange being in Layne's apartment without him. Had she only just been there the day before? The last two days ran together with the death of her mother and now her birthday. Was it still Saturday? Taylor glanced at her phone to confirm the date as she walked into Layne's room. It was neater than she'd left it the evening before. The bed was made, and his clothes were put away in the dresser drawers. She dug through everything until she found his underwear, socks, jeans and a t-shirt. She figured shoes weren't important since he had his sneakers at her apartment. She went into his bathroom and grabbed his deodorant and toothbrush and took the things back to her apartment. She still felt some reluctance about him sleeping at her place.

Layne was still lying in her bed when Taylor placed his things beside him. "Thank you," he said as he got up to get dressed. When he got to the t-shirt, he started laughing. He turned it around and showed Taylor the image on the front. It was a picture of him when he was in Backdraft. "Nice choice."

Taylor laughed. "I didn't even look at it," she said. "But you should totally wear it. It's hilarious."

Layne slipped it over his head. "My sister gave it to me as a joke," he said. "It's my laundry day shirt."

"No one but me will see you anyway."

"I think I need those peas again. I'm not trying to make you feel bad, but my eye hurts."

Taylor left Layne with the frozen peas on his face while she went downstairs to get their food. Willow was in the stairwell on her way out as Taylor went back upstairs.

"That's a lot of food," Willow said.

"It's not like I cook," Taylor said. Willow gave her a half-hearted smile. "Please don't look at me like that."

"Like what?"

"Like I might break."

"How are you holding up, really? Have you talked to your dad or your sister?"

"They called, and Jordan sent me a happy birthday text early this morning. We'll probably do a memorial next week after the ashes are ready."

"I didn't know today was your birthday. Why don't you come to our place for dinner tonight? Kayla will be home, and her dad's planning to join us."

"Thank you, but no. I don't really feel like it tonight. Another time?"

Willow squeezed Taylor's shoulder. "You shouldn't be alone on your birthday," she said.

"I'm not. Layne's waiting for me."

"Oh," Willow said with a knowing smirk.

"I don't need a lecture."

"I can usually detect assholes pretty quickly, and he's not one. He's a good guy."

"I know." Taylor looked down at the floor.

"So, treat him like one is all I'm saying."

"I have to go." As Taylor reached the top of the stairs, she turned around and looked at Willow, who was still standing in the same spot watching her.

"Happy Birthday, Taylor," Willow said.

"Thanks."

As Taylor walked back into her apartment, Layne looked at her and smiled. She thought of him as a pet for a moment, loyal and always happy to see her, and she caught herself smiling back.

"We could work on our music this afternoon," Layne said. "I'd love to hear the songs you're working on if you're willing to share them with me."

"Sure." Having someone waiting for her was comforting. *But he isn't a pet,* Taylor thought. *He's real, and he has feelings. Feelings for me.*

Maybe she felt something, too, something more than fear.

chapter 15

Sunday, May 29, 2016

They stayed up most of the night and early morning talking in Taylor's bed. The subject of fame came up late in their conversation. As Taylor turned on her side to look out the window, Layne spooned with her, hoping she wouldn't pull away.

"You really don't want people to associate you with your character Sierra, do you?" he asked.

"I think I'm a lot less squeaky clean than her at this point," Taylor said. "I don't want to be seen as a has-been TV star who's trying to get famous again. I've done the fame thing once, and I was too young for it then."

"But don't you want some fame with your new music so people will hear it?"

"Recognition as an artist. Fame? Maybe more of an indie following…from people who never watched me on TV."

"I don't think you'll be able to separate it completely. I'm sure some people will fall in love with your music before they realize who you are, and others will only listen because of who you were. Does it matter as long as they hear you?"

"I guess I didn't think about it like that. I'm not sure yet if they'll like my songs."

Layne hugged Taylor tighter and moved her hair to kiss the back of her neck. "With your voice and lyrics like what I saw in your notebook, I know they will."

Taylor wiggled out of Layne's grip and turned to face him. "How can you have so much faith in me when you haven't heard any of my original stuff?"

"Because I am a good judge of character," Layne said before he kissed Taylor on the tip of her nose. "With all the passion you put into singing other people's songs, I can't wait to hear you sing something you wrote. So, let's hear it. Sing the lyrics I read in your notebook."

"That depends…do you think a song that uses the word 'baby' is too cheesy?"

"I'd have to hear it first. But you do realize half the songs I've written use that word."

"Fine," Taylor said. "What I have in mind is this: *'Baby, if you're nice, I'll let you come inside, into this secret place where I go to hide. I'm so afraid with every breath I take. There's no one else who makes me feel this way—like you.'* And then it goes into the next verse."

"I don't think using 'baby' is cheesy in your song. You needed another two-syllable word to get the rhythm right and make it sound like you're singing to one person. It seems to fit whether you're trying to make the song more about love or more about sex. The lyrics are suggestive and a little ambiguous. Is that how you meant them to be?"

"Everything always goes back to sex with you, doesn't it?" Taylor asked.

"We can talk about sex or have sex anytime you want," Layne said with a laugh. "But I did say the song was a love song first. You just heard the sex part and went back to all your dirty-minded thinking."

"Okay, your turn," Taylor said.

"My turn to be dirty? I'm totally up for that."

Taylor playfully punched him in the chest, causing contagious laughter from Layne. "No! Your turn to sing for me. Just enough so I can hear the melody. The song I saw on your notebook."

"I can do that." Layne took a deep breath. *"There's more beauty in you than could ever be true. I've spent all of my life waiting for you."* He didn't want to sing the rest of the first verse to avoid scaring

Taylor, but she'd eventually know the song was about her. Layne hoped her song was about him.

"Yours is less ambiguous. Straight-up love and admiration."

"Hope it's not too painfully generic."

"No," Taylor said. "It's pretty, and most songs are about love or sex anyway, right?" She touched Layne's cheek under his swollen eye. "Or drugs."

"It doesn't hurt so bad anymore. I'm tough."

"I'm really sorry."

"Stop apologizing. I'm fine." Layne gasped as Taylor traced his lips with her thumb, his whole body responding to her touch. He moved to kiss her and was thrilled when she pushed him back and climbed on top of him. Later, with his remaining energy spent, Layne fell asleep with Taylor in his arms.

After Taylor was sure Layne had fallen asleep, she studied his face in the light from the windows. The shadows hid his swollen eye, and he looked peaceful, his breathing slow and even. She kissed his brow and felt a jolt of energy pass through her body. She jumped out of bed and stumbled to her couch where she sat with her knees pulled up to her chest. It took several deep breaths to slow her pounding heart and labored breathing.

Later that morning, Taylor woke up, still on the couch with a blanket she didn't remember getting draped over her legs. Embarrassed by her panic earlier, she went back to her room to check on Layne. He looked like he belonged there in her bed. She wondered what it would be like to sleep with him every night and wake up next to him every morning. After Taylor had gathered her laundry to take down to the basement, she wrote Layne a note and left it beside him.

BRANDI EASTERLING COLLINS

A few minutes after starting the washer, Taylor heard footsteps behind her.

"There you are," Layne said, carrying his own laundry basket.

"Yeah, Sundays are my usual laundry days."

"Mine too."

They sat on top of a long table while they waited for their laundry. Taylor could feel Layne staring at the side of her face.

"What?" she asked. "You're staring at me."

"I was just wondering how you're doing. Everything with your mom…"

"I'm fine."

"What about last night?" he asked. "I found you asleep on the couch."

"You could have woken me if you needed something." In reality, him waking her would have made Taylor even more anxious than she was when she fell asleep.

"I didn't want to bother you. I didn't need anything, I was just worried when I woke up and you weren't there."

"Don't worry about me. I just had trouble going to sleep, and I didn't want to disturb you by tossing and turning."

"And I shouldn't be worried about that?" Layne asked, pinching Taylor's chin.

Taylor looked down at her hands. "Let's talk about something else."

Layne nudged her shoulder. "We could talk about sex," he said. "Last night was amazing."

"Layne!"

He laughed. "I'm just trying to lighten the mood. Tell me about your first time."

Taylor shook her head. "You first."

"I was seventeen, a late bloomer compared to the other guys. She was older—in her twenties at least—a bleach-blond with fake boobs. On a tour bus. It's all the times after I don't remember so well."

"Oh, a bad boy," Taylor said, raising her eyebrows.

"I thought I was. She was a little crazy."

"She must have been, going after a little boy like that."

"Funny," Layne said. "I was manly enough for the thirty seconds it lasted. So how about you? How old were you?"

"Sixteen, a couple of months before my seventeenth birthday," Taylor said. "With my boyfriend. Nothing spectacular. It sucked." But it hadn't sucked, not really. Her first time was sweet and romantic in the best possible way her seventeen-year-old boyfriend could plan. There were rose petals and candles in his bedroom while his parents were out of town. Taylor spent the night with Michael afterward because her mother was so plastered no one would have noticed if she had come home or not.

"Were you in love with him?"

Taylor wasn't sure she'd heard Layne correctly. "What?" she asked.

"Were you in love with him?" he asked again.

Taylor had been in love with Michael. So deeply in love that she still felt sick to her stomach any time she thought about him. "I don't want to talk about this anymore," she said. "Talk about something else."

"Like what? Laundry?"

"I don't know."

Layne shrugged. "Fine," he said as he got up to move his laundry to the dryer.

Taylor got up and moved her laundry, too, realizing she'd hurt Layne's feelings. She wanted to trust him more than anything and didn't want to doubt his sincerity about their friendship, but she still wasn't ready to tell him everything. Jordan had played a role in ending Taylor and Michael's relationship, not that he wasn't partly at fault. The tears, the apologies—nothing was enough to convince Taylor to trust him again. Forgiving Jordan was easier, strangely, but it came out of fear more than anything else. It was safer for Taylor to stay on Jordan's good side as much as possible. When Jordan was in a good mood and was getting her way, she could be an amazing sister, but then something would change in her that turned her mean and nasty.

Most other families didn't seem that way. Other families seemed better than hers, which was why Taylor always asked others about their own families and was genuinely interested in their responses. She looked at Layne, who sat quietly beside her. "Tell me about your family," she said.

He seemed surprised by her request. "We're pretty boring."

Taylor took Layne's hand, lacing her fingers with his, the boldest move she could manage at that point. "I like hearing about boring families."

Layne smiled. "My dad's an engineer, and my mom is a third-grade teacher. I have one sister, Christina, who's six years older than me. She's a high school math teacher. Her husband, Wade, does something in banking. They got married right out of college and have two kids, Cohen and Cecelia. I grew up in southern California and went to school there until Backdraft started—so your standard childhood. I'm really close to my sister, and I call my parents at least once every couple of days to keep them from worrying too much."

"It sounds wonderful," Taylor said, leaning her head on Layne's shoulder. "I grew up on the set from the time I was five. I don't really remember much before then. Dad was always gone working with artists, and Mom was the typical stage mother. I didn't go to an actual school until I enrolled in a private high school after the show ended. Jordan was there with me for a little while before she dropped out to film those horror movies. I can't say I wasn't glad she left. We're not close—at least, not anymore."

"I figured since you don't seem to want to talk about her. What happened?" Layne squeezed Taylor's hand.

"I went through high school always wondering if people really wanted to be my friend for who I was and not who I played on TV or if they only wanted to hang out with me with hopes of meeting Jordan."

"I doubt everyone was as into her as you think they were."

Taylor sighed. "You have no idea." Layne would be shocked if she told him everything Jordan had done. "I was close to my mom when I was a kid, but it's always been a struggle with my dad. I call him about once a month to check in, but he never calls me back. He left me messages on Friday, but I think it's only because I called his girlfriend instead of him. The second message was apologizing for missing my birthday earlier this month when it was actually the next day. Though, he never seems to forget those record release dates. I should probably stop calling."

"But you can't. You still love him." He was right. Taylor could only respond with a nod. Layne released Taylor's hand and put his arm around her shoulders. "I'll have to say, I've never enjoyed doing laundry so much or getting kicked in the face."

"You're never going to let me forget that, are you?" Taylor asked, smiling again.

"There's that smile I was wanting. And I promise to always wish you a happy birthday on the right day." Layne placed his hand on Taylor's cheek and moved in to kiss her.

"Layne…"

"Does our rule book say I can't kiss you when we're alone?" he asked without moving away, his lips brushing against hers as he spoke.

"I guess not, but—"

Layne interrupted Taylor with a kiss. As Taylor relaxed and kissed him back, she admitted that every time he touched her, she felt tiny strings tugging at her heart and tingles all over her body. *Damn it,* she thought, *why can't I just relax and let myself fall in love again?* Footsteps on the stairs caused Layne to jump and pull away.

"Don't mind me," Willow said as she dropped her laundry basket on the floor. "How long until a washer's free?"

"We're waiting on the dryer," Layne said. "Both washers are empty."

Willow squinted at Layne. "Damn, dude," she said. "Who'd you piss off?"

Layne looked at Taylor. "You told me it looked better today," he said, pointing to his eye.

Taylor laughed. "It does look better than last night," she said. "But it still looks terrible."

"Taylor kicked me in the face at the gym yesterday," Layne said. "She tells me it was an accident, but I'm beginning to wonder."

"I'm hopeless without your training, Willow," Taylor said.

Willow stared at them and grinned. "Both of you are hopeless," she said.

When the dryer timer sounded, Taylor jumped up and gathered Layne's clothes. She stopped the other dryer to get her clothes too. "Come on, Layne, we can fold these upstairs and get out of Willow's way."

"It's hard to get laundry done when you're too busy making out!" Willow called after them.

After they had folded laundry and eaten the last of the Chinese leftovers, Layne figured Taylor would kick him out soon. It had been a great weekend staying with her, and he hoped to get in at least one more decent conversation. He wanted to know what had hurt her so badly and figured it had something to do with her high school boyfriend.

"You're staring at me again," Taylor said.

"You shut down when I asked you if you loved your high school boyfriend. Why?"

"Why does it matter?"

"Because you matter."

Taylor closed her eyes as if looking at Layne were too painful. "Sometimes I think I'm one of those people who lets everything good in their life get sabotaged," she said. "It's happened every time I've started feeling happy. Things would be going so well, and then the universe would step in with a big 'fuck you' because I hadn't done anything to deserve it."

"That can't be true."

"But it is. My dad doesn't care. I don't think he ever wanted us—Jordan and me. After he left, my mom was so hammered all the time, she didn't care about us anymore either. I was so happy those last two seasons on the show because I got to sing, and there were adults paying attention to me. Then it got canceled, and there was nothing. I felt like no one in the world actually knew me or loved me. But then I met Michael, and we talked about so many things. I thought he loved me...but then I caught him cheating on me. I know I should have gotten over it by now because it was so long ago, but it broke my heart. It broke me."

Layne felt like Taylor was being completely honest with him for the first time. He took her hands and rested his thumbs on her wrists where he could feel her pulse. "Go on," he said. "You can talk to me."

A tear rolled down Taylor's cheek. "I loved him, Layne, and he hurt me so badly," she said. "I'm sorry. I haven't cried about this for years…"

"You can trust me," Layne said. "You already trust me with your body; why can't you trust me with the rest of you? You could have stayed in bed with me last night. You could have woken me up to talk if something was bothering you."

"It's hard for me to trust people." Taylor pressed her trembling lips together. "I guess I'm still broken, and I'm so afraid all my shit will be too much for anyone to deal with."

"I promise you it isn't—not for me. Just let me in."

"Are you supposed to be a saint or a knight in shining armor or something? I'm not sure if I still believe in the fairy tales I read when I was a kid."

"I'm no saint," Layne said as he put his hand on Taylor's shoulder. "I've hurt someone before, broken her heart. I don't ever want to do that again."

"What happened?" Taylor asked, her voice shaking.

"I met a girl in college who was sweet and innocent, and best of all, had no idea who I was at first. We were both studying music, and I took some writing classes too. Things got serious. She fell in love with me."

Taylor looked away. "But you didn't love her?"

Love was such strong word. What started out as mutual attraction and admiration between Layne and Amanda morphed into a physical relationship quickly—after she had said "I love you" but before Layne had. All their best conversations were late at night in the music labs long after everyone else had left. Everything seemed to have more meaning late at night when they should have been sleeping. Sometimes they would have sex in one of the labs because Amanda was unwilling to wait until they got back to her dorm room or his apartment.

Amanda was a virgin when they'd met and was probably a bit too anxious to lose that title along with her previous good-girl image. Layne had asked Amanda when they first started dating what she wanted out of life, and she said she wanted to live life to the fullest and live in the moment. Later, Layne realized she'd only said what she thought he wanted to hear because she had already fallen in love with him and would have done anything to be with him.

Layne acknowledged the irony in his current situation as he looked down at his hands. "I wanted to," he said. "No, I did...just not enough, you know? Not enough to change what I wanted out of life. I still wanted a career in music. She wanted to be a music teacher and to get married, have the house with the white picket fence and a couple of kids. It just wasn't what I wanted, and I knew she would never be happy if she gave up those wants to be with me. It wouldn't have been fair to either of us. I hurt her when I broke things off and told her she'd be better off with someone else. She said she'd never felt so betrayed, and I felt like the biggest asshole in the world. But...she lied to me too."

"Do you know what happened to her?" Taylor asked.

"She met someone else and got married recently, just like she wanted. My sister saw the announcement in the paper. I'm truly happy for Amanda. I never wanted to hurt her."

"That's noble of you," Taylor said. "I never wanted all that stuff either. I'm too fucked-up to be anyone's mother, and I'm not even sure I could be someone's girlfriend. It's easier to keep things casual."

Layne held Taylor's face and moved closer to her. "It's only easy if both people agree. You and me, Taylor, we could be good together if you'd give me a chance—a chance to be more than just your fake boyfriend when you want guys at the gym to leave you alone."

Taylor stood up and grabbed her keys off the counter, clearly avoiding Layne's proposition. "Come on," she said. "We need to go get your car from the gym."

Layne worried he'd said too much because Taylor didn't turn around once as he followed her downstairs to the parking lot. He caught up with her and grabbed her hand. "I'm sorry. Just think about what I said, okay?"

"Please, just not now," she pleaded. "I need more time."

Layne nodded and let go of Taylor's hand, fighting the urge to pull her back into his arms and never let go.

chapter 16

Taylor hadn't spoken to Layne during the drive to the gym. Now alone in her car on the way back to her apartment, she couldn't stop thinking about what he'd said about giving him a chance. She wanted to do that so badly, but it wasn't the right time—not yet.

When she got back to her apartment, Taylor gathered Layne's things and had them waiting for him when he walked into the hallway.

"Thank you for taking care of me," he said as he took his things.

"I'll see you Tuesday on set," Taylor said.

"What about tomorrow?"

"Don't you have Memorial Day plans with your family?"

"I do, but you could come with me."

"I have plans with Willow, but thanks anyway."

"Okay." Layne looked down at the floor, unable to hide his disappointment. "Can I give you a ride to the set on Tuesday?"

"No," Taylor said. "I have something to take care of after work."

"Well, I guess I'll see you on set Tuesday."

As soon as Layne closed his door, Taylor went to Willow's apartment and knocked.

Willow seemed surprised to see her. "I figured you'd still be busy with Layne," she said.

"I've spent the whole weekend with him," Taylor said. "Is Kayla home?"

"No. She had to work tonight."

Taylor sighed and looked at the floor. "I need to talk. Is that okay? I'm sorry I've been a bitch to you lately."

"Come in. I just made some tea like a proper old lady," Willow said with a laugh.

Taylor followed Willow to her dining table and sat down. After a couple of minutes in the kitchen, Willow returned and placed a cup of tea in front of Taylor.

"So, what's up?" Willow asked, tapping her fingers on the table as she sat across from Taylor.

"I think I have feelings for Layne."

Willow raised her eyebrows. "And? Tell me something I don't know."

"*And* it's only been a week, not counting when we met briefly ten years ago."

"That doesn't matter. I knew I wanted to be with Kayla for the rest of my life after our first date."

"How though?" Taylor was always amazed and skeptical of anyone who claimed to fall in love so fast, and love at first sight sounded even more foreign to her.

"There was just something about her...the way her eyes sparkled when she told me she wanted to be a doctor to save people's lives someday. I realized I wanted to know every single thing about her—good or bad—and wanted to tell her everything about myself too. She was easy to talk to, and I felt like she wasn't judging me for not wanting a career as prestigious as hers. She brought out the best in me and was responsible for supporting me and giving me the courage to come out to my family."

"And you've been together ever since then? No breakups?"

"That's right. It's been twelve years. I'm not saying it wasn't hard while she was in college and med school. Some of my insecurities resurfaced during that time because I was worried she'd meet someone else who was more exciting than me, but Kayla told me she could see the passion I had for fitness and said I shouldn't give up on that to try to impress anyone."

"That's how I felt about Michael at first," Taylor said.

"Michael?"

"My high school boyfriend. He said all the right things, and we talked about our futures. Investment banking for him like his father. I told him I wanted to sing more than anything, and he said it was something great to get back to after school. He didn't seem to care about the fame I'd had before and seemed so genuine. I fell for him—hard. I made him wait a year before I had sex with him, but he never pressured me. It was how I always dreamed my first time would be—with someone I loved who loved me. I had this romantic notion sex and love should be connected."

Willow bit her lip. "For some people it does," she said. "But I find that odd considering what I've seen from you in the past."

"I know," Taylor said as she looked down at her hands. "After he finally got me in bed, Michael cheated on me, and it broke my heart. He was probably cheating on me the whole time."

"I'm so sorry," Willow said as she laid her hand on Taylor's arm. "I know how hard that is."

"He cheated with Jordan. I caught them together."

"Oh," Willow said. "No wonder you never want to talk about her."

"She went after every guy I ever liked and got him. Michael was the only one up until that point who hadn't blown me off to go out with her. He said sleeping with her was a mistake because he was drinking and begged me to forgive him, but I couldn't."

"That's a damn shitty betrayal. I don't blame you for not forgiving him, Taylor, but you can't shut off your heart from everyone else because of one asshole."

Tears formed in Taylor's eyes. "You were right when you said I was using sex as a drug," she said, feeling ashamed of herself. "It felt good and distracted me while it was happening, so I kept doing it to not feel so empty. I tried to be an evolved woman who could just have sex and not worry about another relationship to hurt me, and it worked until that jerk hit me. But now…I don't think I can ever have random hookups again." Taylor covered her face with her hands, her whole head aching from the weight of her thoughts.

"And what's made you realize that?"

"Layne, I guess."

"And why is that a problem? I'm pretty sure he's smitten with you."

"I'm not sure I'm ready for a relationship. I just don't know if I can, and what if he hurts me? Plus, he's only here for the job. In another three weeks, he'll be gone."

Willow shook her head. "Why did you have sex with him in the first place? Did you just want another hookup?"

"It started out that way, I guess, because I was annoyed about Jordan's TV interview, but when Layne kissed me, it felt different from anyone else I've ever kissed. The next day, I told him we made a mistake, that I didn't want anything serious. He said he wanted us to be friends, and we talked all day, and he was wonderful. Then, the day after that, it just happened again. He took me out on the most amazing date, and that same night we sang together at the bar. After my mom died, I just wanted to stop the pain, and Layne was there."

"Girl, you're not making any sense. You don't want him for just a hookup, and you don't want a relationship, so do you want to end it with him?"

Taylor leaned back in the chair and pulled her knees to her chest, embracing her legs. "I have to figure this out. I need to take a step back, but I still have to see him on set. I just need to make sure we're not alone together so I don't end up sleeping with him again."

"You can't control yourself?"

"Neither one of us can. It happened again yesterday after we got home from the gym and took a shower…and then again last night."

Willow shook her head. "Chemistry—another part of a successful relationship."

"The chemistry is there," Taylor said, "It's great with him…the best. I didn't know it could feel that good."

"You're attracted to him, he's attracted to you, you have great sex, and he's nice to you."

"I know…what should I do?"

"Marry him," Willow said with a chuckle.

"You're no help at all!"

"I can't tell you what to do, but if it were me, I would talk to him and tell him everything you just told me and see what he has to say. Plus, he signed a six-month lease, so the time factor is moot."

"I can't until I know for sure how I feel about him. But I think he might have feelings for me, too, or he just wants to keep me around for sex. He says little things like I should give him a chance."

Willow slapped her forehead. "Do you even listen to yourself? He's telling you he wants to be with you! You could open your heart to him and see what happens. He told me flat out he cares about you. He also said he could tell you were hurting."

"He said that? When?"

"Yeah. The day your mom died. When he asked me to stay with you, I jumped his ass and accused him of getting you drunk or stoned."

"Willow, you didn't…" Taylor was shocked Layne hadn't mentioned it.

"I apologized," Willow said as she took the cups back to her kitchen. "I can't fix this, Taylor. I can't fix you. Honey, you have to work this out for yourself. Love—or the potential of it—is worth it, but it does come with the risk of getting your heart broken again and again. It makes you stronger. Sometimes it takes the right person to heal your heart. That's what Kayla did with mine. I wanted to die after my previous relationship ended, and there was no one to talk to about it because we'd kept it secret. I didn't feel whole again until I was with Kayla."

"What if I can't be fixed?"

"Who says you're not fixed already? Have you ever considered that sex with Layne is so good because you have a connection with him? That it's more than just sex because he's making love to you?"

That was the difference. Layne was making love to Taylor. "What if I hurt him?" she asked.

"That's the risk Layne takes if he falls or has already fallen in love with you."

"I don't want anyone to get hurt."

"Then don't hurt him," Willow said. "Growing up with three older brothers, I can read guys fairly well. I've told you already, Layne has feelings for you. It's not all bullshit to get you into bed. I'm as sure of that as I am my feelings for Kayla. What do you want to do?"

Taylor closed her eyes. "What I want is to not be so fucked-up that I can't figure this out. I want the stupid fairy tales I believed in when I was a kid before everything with my family went to shit. I want to fall in love with Layne and for him to fall in love with me and for us not to hurt each other. And I want my sister to not screw this up for me when she gets here." She wiped tears from the corners of her eyes. It was all too much.

Willow moved to the chair beside Taylor and patted her arm. "That's a big wish list," she said. "Go home and sleep—alone—and think about it. Write a song about it. You'll figure it out. I know you can open up to him some more since you just did that with me. You've never talked to me so much."

Taylor nodded and stood up. "Thank you. Are we still on for tomorrow?"

"Yep. Pick you up at noon. Everyone's looking forward to meeting you. I hope my brothers won't annoy you too much."

"I'm sure it'll be fine. They can't be as bad as my family."

As Taylor walked back to her apartment, pain pulsated across her abdomen. She sighed with relief and thanked her body for providing a reason to avoid sleeping with Layne for the next week to sort out her feelings. In her bedroom, she pulled out her notebook and started jotting down her thoughts for the opening lines of the song that had been churning in her head since the night she'd first slept with Layne. After some scribbling, scratching out and rearranging, it was perfect.

If you could love me more, I think I'd run away. I never thought that I could feel this way—again.

chapter 17

Memorial Day, 2016

Taylor had never been to Willow's childhood home near the beach but figured there would be plenty of people to talk to with Willow's brothers and their families. Willow's parents were a respectable-looking couple in their late sixties who welcomed Willow, Kayla, and Mr. Cosney with warm hugs. They shook Taylor's hand and told her how much they enjoyed watching her on the sitcom when she was a little girl. Taylor humbly thanked them and tried to keep Willow's brothers, their wives, and children clear in her mind. Taylor sat beside Kayla on a lounge chair in the shade and watched the chaos around her. She lost count at eight children running around the pool.

"How do you keep up with all of them?" she asked, pointing to the kids.

"You get used to it," Kayla said, looking at Willow, who was jumping in the pool with the kids. "Look at that. They're all drawn to her. She's going to be such a good mom."

Taylor smiled. "She's a good friend," she said. "I'm glad she invited me, but I feel like an outsider."

"Girl, are you kidding? We were having dinner with them last week, and they pretty much insisted you come after Willow mentioned you lived in our building. Be warned though, they may ask you to sing later."

"Really?"

"Well, we don't have any cute kids to bring yet, so you're our honorary cute kid for the day," Kayla said with a laugh. "I love Willow's family. It's been just Dad and me since my mom died eight years ago. Missing her doesn't hurt as much when I'm here. I think Dad's happier spending holidays here too. When we have kids in a couple of years, I think it'll be even better." Mr. Cosney's roaring laughter interrupted them. Apparently, one of Willow's brothers had shared a joke that set him off.

Taylor still couldn't imagine taking on motherhood, but watching the children play by the pool was therapeutic. She wondered if Layne was enjoying his time with his family.

When Layne first arrived, his mother and sister fussed over his black eye even though he assured them he was fine. "Before you say anything, it's no big deal," he said.

"Good grief, Brandon Layne! What the heck happened to your eye?" Christina asked.

"Kickboxing accident," he said.

"Sounds dangerous," his mother said. "I didn't know you did kickboxing."

"I don't," Layne said. "It was an accident. I wasn't paying attention while I was holding the punching bag for my friend, Taylor." He looked down at his nephew, Cohen. "That's why your mom and dad always tell you to keep your head up when you're playing t-ball, so you won't get hit in the face."

"Well, your friend should be more careful," his mother said. "He could have really hurt you."

"She," Christina corrected. "Taylor is a woman."

Cohen giggled. "Uncle Brandon got kicked by a girl."

Layne's father patted him on the back and chuckled as he left the room.

Later, Layne was so tired from having played for an hour with his nephew and his niece, Cecelia, he was thrilled when their dad, Wade, told them it was time to take a nap. Layne plopped down on the couch beside his sister. "I'm exhausted," he said. "How do you keep up with them?"

"Lots of wine. After they go to bed, of course," Christina said. "I hoped you'd bring your new girlfriend."

"New girlfriend? What new girlfriend?" Wade asked as he came back into the living room.

"Yeah, Brandon—sorry, *Layne* is in love," Christina said. "With Taylor Hoffman. Remember her? She played Sierra on *The Spectacular Smiths*."

"The 'sweet puppies' girl?" Wade asked, laughing. Christina nodded, grinning widely. "Is she even of age yet?"

Layne pictured Taylor's naked body in the shower. *Oh, she is,* he thought. "She's twenty-three and strong enough to kick me in the face," he said.

Wade chuckled. "I'd be interested to know how that happened." Christina elbowed her husband. "Ow."

"At the gym," Layne said, shaking his head. "I moved the wrong way while holding the punching bag, and Taylor knocked me on my ass. It really was an accident. She felt so bad about it."

"I can't believe your girlfriend is a kickboxer," Christina said.

Layne pulled out his phone and showed them the photo he'd taken with Taylor before their date.

"Oh my gosh!" Christina said. "She looks different...but still so beautiful. I can't wait to meet her."

"We've only gone out a couple of times. Give it a rest, Chris. You'll get to meet her if things get more serious."

"If?" Christina asked. "Don't you plan to keep seeing her, Layne?"

"What are we talking about?" their mother asked as she came into the room followed by their father.

"Nothing," Layne said. "Hey, Mom, weren't you going to show us the pictures of the play your students did? I know

Christina was just telling me how much she's looking forward to seeing them."

"Of course!" Mrs. Stallings exclaimed. "Let me get them queued up. Wade, you may have to help me with this TV thing."

Christina glared at her brother while her husband set up the slideshow. Layne grinned at her. His sister hated watching the slideshows only slightly more than he did, but Layne could zone out while the hundreds of photographs flashed on the screen. He didn't want to talk about Taylor with his parents yet, but he couldn't stop thinking about her. He missed her. He discreetly pulled his phone out of his pocket and sent her a message.

> Layne: **Watching my mom's slideshow. Bored as hell.**
>
> Taylor: **LOL**
>
> Layne: **You wouldn't be laughing if you were here.**
>
> Taylor: **I bet I would be.**
>
> Layne: **I wish you were here. I miss you.**
>
> Taylor: **Go have fun with your family.**
>
> Layne: **Tell Willow I said hello.**
>
> Taylor: **I will.**
>
> Layne: **Can I see you tonight?**
>
> Taylor: **It'll be late when I get home. I might not feel like hanging out.**
>
> Layne: **Bummed. See you tomorrow at work then.**

When Willow got out the pool, she sat down beside Taylor as she dried her dripping hair with a towel. "Texting with Layne?" she asked.

Taylor put her phone down beside her. "Not anymore," she said. "Looks like your nieces and nephews are having a blast. How many are there? They're running around too fast for me to count."

"Nine," Willow said, pointing out the family members. "My oldest brother has four, next has two, and the youngest brother has three. There's one set of twins, right over there."

"They seem great. And they all seem to love Kayla."

"I think they're thrilled to have a doctor in the family. And they love Marcus. He's like an extra grandfather to the kids. They were such a comfort to him after Kayla's mom died."

"What happened to her?"

"Aneurysm. It was sudden and devastating. They didn't have time to prepare themselves."

"That's so sad," Taylor said. At least she'd had plenty of time to prepare for her own mother's death.

"Death is never convenient." Willow turned back to the children playing. "Not when you leave someone behind."

"Kayla says you'll be a great mother."

"In a couple of years," Willow said. "With her schedule, it makes more sense for me to carry the baby, but I'm not ready yet. And we need to move. I don't want to subject anyone to a screaming baby in our apartment building."

Screaming, Taylor thought, *I feel like screaming.* The idea of Willow leaving the apartment hadn't occurred to her before. She felt selfish wanting to keep her around forever, like the big sister she'd always wanted. Willow was nothing like Jordan. Willow was chosen family, but Jordan was chance. Were they not related, Taylor would never have known Jordan and figured she would have been better off.

"Have you talked to your family?" Willow asked.

"What's there to say? Dad never visited Mom at the rehab center, and Jordan only went about once a month, if that much.

I'm the only one who went weekly. She was just a burden to them."

Willow reached out and squeezed Taylor's arm. "She was a burden you bore all by yourself," she said. "Let yourself grieve however you need to."

After the slideshow, Layne's parents and Wade went to the kitchen for coffee, leaving him alone with Christina. She left the oversized armchair she and her husband had shared and plopped down on the couch beside Layne. She looked at him and grinned.

"I saw you texting your girlfriend, little brother," she teased.

"She's not my girlfriend. Not yet, anyway."

"How's she doing? You said she was having a bad day when I called."

"It was more than a bad day," Layne said. "Her mom died."

"Oh no! Is she okay? Why aren't you with her today?" Christina pinched Layne's arm and then slapped it.

"Ouch!" he said, rubbing his bicep. "Cut it out, or I'm telling Mom!" Saying that always made her stop when they were kids, not that she'd ever really hurt him.

"Big baby! You know Mom and Dad would've understood. Is Taylor with her family?"

Layne sighed. He saw no reason to keep the truth from Christina because she would pry it out of him eventually anyway. "Just between you and me," he said. "Promise?"

"Of course."

"She's not close to her sister or her dad. Her family isn't like ours. Her mom was in a rehab center after a stroke and had another one that killed her. Taylor had to deal with the whole thing by herself. I drove her to the rehab center and stayed with her all day to make sure she was okay. I invited her to come with me today, but she already had plans with a friend."

"And you did all that for a woman you claim is not your girlfriend?"

"Chris, seriously, I've only known her a little over a week…"

"Three dates with Wade was all it took before I knew I was in love with him."

"And did you tell him right away?"

"No! That's crazy-talk! I waited until he told me two weeks later."

"Then stop bugging me about it. I don't want to scare the hell out of her by—"

"Telling her you're falling in love with her?" Christina interjected with a laugh. "It wouldn't be the craziest thing you've ever done."

Layne pulled his hair over his face. "Just stop…" How was it that his sister could always read his mind?

"I just want you to be happy," she said. "Like Wade and me. Like Mom and Dad."

"I am happy," he said. "But I'll never be happy in the same way as you because I don't want the same things you did. You know that, and you know it's why Amanda and I broke up. She wanted all those things I couldn't give her. Just because I wasn't married at twenty-two like you and our parents doesn't mean I'm not happy."

"So, what, you're never getting married?"

"It's definitely too soon to propose to Taylor."

"Ha ha, little brother," Christina said. "You know what I mean."

"I don't know…maybe someday, with the right person who wants what I want. I'm not worried about it. That's your specialty."

"I'm sorry." Christina crossed her arms and looked away.

"I know you just want what's best for me," Layne said. "And right now, what's best for me is for you to butt out."

Taylor woke startled when Willow's car dipped into a pothole as they pulled into the parking lot of their building later that evening. The bump jolted her out of a dream and frightened her into calling out for someone, but not just anyone—Layne, his name still on the tip of her tongue.

"Hey, are you okay?" Willow asked.

"Yes," Taylor said, trying to slow her breathing.

"You just called for Layne."

"I was dreaming."

"Speak of the devil," Kayla said, pointing at the SUV pulling into the parking lot behind them.

Layne got out of his SUV and waved at them. Taylor stayed in the car for a moment, unsure of what to do. She wanted to jump out and run into his arms but couldn't deny how foolish that seemed. Willow and Kayla got out, leaving Taylor behind.

Layne opened the door for Taylor. "I was wondering when you'd be back," he said. "Did you have a good time?"

"It was nice," Taylor said. She walked ahead of him to the building door. "Did you?"

"It was alright, except for the slideshow and my sister bugging the hell out of me." Layne punched in the code and held the door open. He followed Taylor upstairs and waited while she unlocked her door. "I missed you today."

Taylor turned to him and bit the inside of her jaw. She had missed him, too, but couldn't get the words out to say anything.

Layne stayed close to her and didn't say anything for a moment either. Finally, he cleared his throat. "I'm sorry about last night; I didn't mean to upset you. I know you need some time. I'm trying to respect that, but it's hard to be so close and not touch you."

Taylor held her breath. *What does he mean,* she thought, *close physically or close emotionally? Maybe both.* Looking at his eyes was excruciating. She wanted to tell him everything—all the irrational reasons she was afraid—but her mouth was dry, and her voice fell silent. Taylor leaned her head against Layne's chest and wrapped her arms around his waist, allowing time to stand still for a moment, wanting him to kiss her more than anything else.

Layne wrapped his arms around Taylor, desperately wanting to kiss her. Time was something he could give her as long as he felt they were still moving forward, slowly or not. Taylor had reached out to touch him first, a sign of movement. "Did you talk to your family today?" he asked.

"No," Taylor said, finding her voice again.

Layne hugged her tighter. "I'm sorry."

Taylor relaxed in Layne's arms as he kissed her forehead. "Not all families are like yours," she said.

"I know. Do you want to come inside with me?" It would have taken little effort for Layne carry her into his apartment.

"I not feeling up for that tonight." She still had her arms draped around his waist.

"No, that's not what I meant," Layne said. "You're always taking it back to sex…dirty-minded." He tapped her temple. "I want to take you out again soon. Another real date. One wasn't enough."

"Maybe later this week."

"There's hope. It wasn't a no."

"Goodnight." She started to pull away, but Layne didn't let go.

"Can I kiss you?"

Taylor looked up and nodded.

"Goodnight," Layne said before his lips touched hers. He'd starved for Taylor all day. It took all his willpower to pull away from her to speak. "I'll see you tomorrow."

With a sigh, Taylor watched Layne go into his apartment. She went to her bathroom to wash her face and crawled into bed fully clothed, pulling the covers around her like she used to when she was a kid. The exhaustion she felt wasn't enough for sleep to come easily. It would be a restless night. Several times she contemplated getting up and knocking on Layne's door, but she couldn't bring herself to get out of bed. She missed him. Part of her soul ached for him—a part she didn't know was still intact after all the heartache she'd endured.

chapter 18

Tuesday, May 31, 2016

Layne worried he'd screwed up everything by pushing Taylor too much. She was strictly professional with him at work, not cold, but not overly friendly either. They rehearsed and recorded one of the songs together, and then the music producer split them up to record the vocals and guitar separately in case different mixing was needed. It was a long, grueling day, and Taylor was moody and distant during their brief lunch break.

He tried to talk to her several times afterward, but she was always on her way to do something else or make a phone call. As the set closed, he ran to catch up with her before she could leave. He caught her car door before she could close it.

"Hey," he said. "I feel like you're avoiding me."

"Layne, I've got somewhere to be, and I don't feel like hanging out tonight."

He kept his hand on the car door. "Are you mad at me?" he asked. "Did I do something to upset you?"

"No, I just have to go pick up my mother's things from the rehab center. It's a long drive, so I need to get going."

"You could have told me. I would have gone with you."

"I just want to be alone. I'm not feeling well today. Cramps. Please, I have to go now."

Rejected, Layne let go of the door so Taylor could close it and watched her drive away. He could be sensitive. He had grown up with a sister. Christina always wanted ice cream during her period, so he figured getting some for Taylor couldn't hurt.

He drove back to the supermarket where he had bought her cupcakes. The same woman was working the checkout.

"I remember you," she said when she saw Layne. "The cupcake guy. Wow, did you get punched in the face, hon?"

"Kickboxing accident," Layne said as he placed two pints of ice cream on the conveyer belt. He read the woman's nametag: Florence.

"First cupcakes and now ice cream," Florence said. "Chocolate and vanilla."

"Yeah. Don't know her favorite yet, so I'm getting both."

"You're so sweet. I wish my daughter could find a guy as considerate as you, but she only dates losers."

Layne laughed. "Have a good evening, ma'am," he said.

Taylor drove to the rehab center with her radio blaring. She sang along with all the songs and tried not to think too much. When she arrived at the center, Emanuel was waiting with a box of her mother's things. He was always kind to Taylor when she'd arrive to visit her mother just as his shift was ending.

"Hello, Miss Hoffman," he said. "I packed up everything for you. I wasn't sure if it would be you or Jordan who would come, but I found a bracelet near your mother's bed when we were cleaning up. I think it's something Jordan left behind."

"Thank you. I'll make sure she gets it." Taylor rolled Jordan's bracelet in her hand. The clasp was broken. She would recognize it anywhere; it was a gift Chase had given Jordan years ago. "Is there anything else I need to sign?"

"No. Everything's taken care of. Again, I am so sorry for your loss. It came as a surprise; your mother seemed stable before your sister's visit, a bit agitated in the afternoon, but stable."

Had Jordan been involved in their mother's death? Taylor broke out in a cold sweat. No. She pushed those thoughts out of her mind. Jordan had her flaws but killing their mother crossed a line she didn't think her sister could do even on a drug binge.

Taylor took the box of her mother's things out to her car and sat in the parking lot with her head resting on the steering wheel. She'd just made the last drive she'd ever take to the rehab center, and she felt guilty about the relief that flooded her mind after her realization. She cried through a few songs on the radio before she felt like driving home.

Someone knocked as soon as Taylor closed her apartment door. She looked through the peephole at Layne standing there and pursed her lips as she opened the door.

"I get it," Layne said, holding out a grocery store bag in one hand. "You've got your period and hate all men right now. I brought you some ice cream as a peace offering to show you we're not all jackasses. You like chocolate, right?"

"Chocolate cake, vanilla ice cream."

Layne pulled a pint of vanilla out of the bag. "Good thing I got both," he said as he handed the carton to Taylor. "Enjoy and feel better soon. Goodnight."

Taylor closed her eyes as Layne kissed her on the forehead. It wasn't a lustful kiss; it was a tender, caring gesture with no expectation of return. She watched Layne walk back to his apartment and had almost called out for him to stay before she was interrupted by her phone. It was her sister calling.

"Hey, Jordan."

"You never called me back or responded to my texts."

"Yeah, I was busy. How are you?"

"Great, considering everything. The fans have been really supportive."

"Have they?"

"You haven't been online?"

"Short of Netflix, no."

Jordan scoffed. "How do you expect to be famous again if you're not on social media?"

"Who says I care if I'm famous again?"

"Well, you should care. Singing in that dinky bar isn't going to get you anywhere. And now with Mom gone, you don't have any excuses left. You should change your hair back and release an album through Dad's company. With my movie releasing in the fall, you could ride on the publicity to boost the sales. It might even help with hype for the movie."

The thought of doing that infuriated Taylor. "Jordan, I don't want to rely on your fame; I just want to write my music. I'll release it in my own way when I'm ready. And nobody but you gives a shit about the color of my hair."

"Well, I'm *so* sorry for trying to help you."

"But are you really trying to help me or just trying to get more attention for yourself?"

"You ungrateful little bitch!" Jordan exclaimed.

"Me ungrateful?" Taylor laughed, falling back on her couch. "Jordan, why did you slash my tire?"

"Why the hell would I do something like that?"

"You've done crazy shit before."

"I haven't messed with your stupid car. I have much more important things to do."

"Fine. I have important things too. Bye."

Taylor hung up on Jordan, who was still yelling something at her. Usually, she tried to avoid pissing off Jordan, but it seemed to happen no matter what she said lately. When Jordan had first started abusing drugs, it happened a lot. Taylor was almost certain Jordan was using, and the thought of trying to help her get clean again was overwhelming.

Her mother was really gone now, and her dad still wasn't around the way she needed him to be. There was no hope of having a good relationship with Jordan. And how was it that Jordan had left her favorite bracelet behind at the rehab center? Taylor felt completely alone. She looked at the ice cream sitting on her counter. She didn't want to be alone at all.

Taylor wanted comfort that ice cream couldn't bring; she wanted to be with someone who cared about her. She wanted Layne to hold her. She couldn't explain how someone so soothing could also be so terrifying to her. Going to him was still not as frightening as sitting in her apartment alone with her thoughts and a box of her mother's things.

When Layne heard a light knocking on his door, he knew it was Taylor. He opened the door and found her standing there with the ice cream.

"I don't like to eat ice cream alone," she said.

"Come in," Layne said, unable to hide his smile. "You don't need an excuse to come see me. You can just come over, anytime."

"Says the guy who just brought me ice cream." Taylor walked in and looked around the apartment. "You finished unpacking." She sat on the couch.

Layne grabbed spoons from his kitchen and joined her. "I had some free time this evening before you got back."

"I guess you've spent all of your free time with me lately."

"I'm not complaining." Layne tried to hand Taylor a spoon, but she was looking at her hands. "You don't really want to eat ice cream, do you?"

Taylor shook her head. "I'm not hungry. I want to talk to you."

Layne took the ice cream from Taylor and put it in his freezer. He watched her as she leaned against the back of the couch and put her arms over her face. This wasn't the way he wanted things to end; he didn't want things to end at all. "I know things are confusing right now, and I shouldn't have pressured you..." He sat down beside her.

Taylor took Layne's hand which stopped him from finishing his thought. "Not that kind of talk," she said. "We're okay, Layne. Aren't we?"

He stopped holding his breath and kissed Taylor's hand. "What's going on?"

"I had a fight with Jordan on the phone after I picked up our mother's things," she said. "She called me an ungrateful bitch, but I did provoke her a bit. She's mad I don't want to ride on her fame parade."

"What do you want to do?"

Acting like it was the most difficult question in the world to answer, Taylor stared at the floor and began wringing her hands.

"I don't mean what do you want to do forever," Layne said. "You don't have to figure out forever right now. I mean what do you want right now at this moment, on Tuesday night?"

"I'm kind of embarrassed to tell you," she said softly.

Even though Taylor wouldn't say what she wanted, Layne figured she was in his apartment for some reason. He put his arm around her and pulled her close, surprised she hugged him back so tightly. "Well," he said. "Why don't we just hang out like this until you figure it out? Unless me holding you is breaking the rules."

"It's okay." Taylor discretely tried to wipe away her tears, but Layne had already noticed.

"Baby, please, just tell me what's wrong," he said. *Shit*, he thought, *calling her that just slipped out.* But Taylor didn't seem to mind as she buried her face in his chest and cried. He held her and smoothed her hair, wishing he could replace all her dark, painful thoughts with beautiful music and light.

It wasn't just one thing wrong—it was everything. Taylor struggled to put it into words. "I realized when I got in my car tonight I'll never make the drive again to see my mom. I think I'm okay with it, or I will be. I guess part of me always hoped she'd wake up and get better, but she couldn't. It just hit me all of a sudden. I'm just so tired of dealing with all my mom's stuff and now Jordan. It's exhausting." Taylor hated feeling vulnerable. Her jaw ached as she tried to stop herself from crying again in front of Layne. She looked at him and thought he might cry with her, his eyes dancing as they met hers.

"I'm so sorry," Layne said. He got up and grabbed a box of tissues from his countertop and handed them to Taylor.

Taylor took a tissue and wiped her face. "The funeral home told me her ashes will be ready Saturday morning. I want to spread them at my dad's private beach."

"Your dad has a private beach?"

"Yeah. He bought the beach house when he and Mom were still married, and she loved going there. Dad lived there after he left Mom until he found another place. It's where Jordan and I lived with him after Mom's stroke. He lets Jordan and me use it whenever we want, but I haven't been there in months."

"I don't go to the beach much. I'm not much of a swimmer."

"Me neither, but I love being there to watch the sunset."

"You should go, then, when you're ready to spread the ashes," Layne said. "I'll go with you."

"I need to talk to Jordan again and see what she wants to do. You don't have to go. I can handle it on my own."

"I have no doubt you can handle anything, Taylor." Layne reached out and cupped her chin. "I realize your relationship with Jordan isn't like mine is with my sister. She's not there for you the way she should be. You just shouldn't have to handle some things alone. Not when you have people in your life who care about you, like me."

"Layne, you barely know me. You shouldn't have to deal with my family drama."

"I know enough to know I care about you," he said. "And one of the rules is we get to keep learning more about each other, including the family drama."

"We did agree to that, didn't we?"

"We did," Layne said. "I don't ever want to not know you."

Taylor looked into Layne's eyes. He never broke eye contact. He wasn't lying. She realized she wanted to always know him too.

"So, can I drive you to the set tomorrow?" he asked.

"Yes, but I'll drive the day after that," Taylor said as she stood up. "I should probably go home since we have to be there so early. I'm sorry I cried on you again." She walked to his door and put her hand on the doorknob but didn't turn it. Walking through the door seemed impossible, but staying all night was a haunting melody in her head.

Layne walked over to Taylor. "Come here," he said as he hugged her. His arms were strong and warm. "You can come lay down with me until you're tired enough to go home and sleep…or you could just stay and sleep here with me."

Taylor hugged him back. "Okay," she said. "Just for a little while…"

After she had changed and brushed her teeth, Taylor went back to Layne's apartment and curled up with him in his bed. She rested her head on his chest, listening to the steady beat of his heart, and felt safer than she ever had.

"You're not just using me for my awesome snuggling abilities, are you?" Layne joked. "You fit really well in my arms."

Taylor consciously tried to match her breathing pattern to Layne's to make herself feel calmer. *Just trust him*, she thought. "I found her…"

"Found who?"

"My mom, after the stroke. I'm the one who found her."

Layne held Taylor's hand. "That must have awful for you. I can't imagine."

"I'd found her in a pool of her own vomit so many times before, I didn't think anything different when I cleaned her up that night. I didn't realize anything serious was wrong when I dragged her to bed, but then I couldn't wake her up the next morning, and one side of her body was stiff and contorted. I always wondered if she might have been okay if I would have called for help right away. I think Jordan's always blamed me for that."

"Oh God, Taylor, it wasn't your fault," Layne said.

"I guess not, but still…"

"You had to clean up after your mom a lot, didn't you?"

"All the time. At first, it was just alcohol, but then Jordan came back from filming her last horror movie and introduced Mom to cocaine. She continued with it after Mom's stroke, and it took a while before I convinced my dad that Jordan needed help. We managed to keep Jordan's rehab stay out of the press. I think Dad paid off some people to keep it from hurting his record business."

"I had no idea."

"I told you. My family is fucked-up."

Layne held Taylor tighter, kissing the top of her head. "I'm the one who found Chase after he OD'd. I found him like you found your mom, covered in puke and shit, only he wasn't breathing, and there was a needle still stuck in between his toes. A lot of the night is fuzzy because I was drunk, but I know Kyle called for help and Noah and I tried CPR. There were paramedics nearby because we had just finished our concert and the crowds were still hanging out. They gave him a shot of something and got him breathing again. I think our publicist paid off some people, too, to keep it out of the headlines. And somehow, no one got arrested for our underage drinking."

"Was it an accident or was he trying to kill himself?"

"I really don't know. I blamed myself because I upset him when I told the guys before the concert that it would be my last— that I was leaving to go to college and planned to go solo later."

"Chase's overdose wasn't your fault, either, Layne," Taylor whispered.

Layne still remembered the hurt look in Chase's eyes that evening. According to Chase, Backdraft was the only good thing in his life, and he asked Layne how he could want to throw it all away. Noah and Kyle had come to Layne's defense and said they also wanted to take a break and pursue other things. Afterward, Chase accused them of conspiring against him. Despite it all, Chase gave the best performance of his career that night—his last performance with the guys he considered his brothers. The guys who were leaving him behind. Layne had always wondered if Chase's near-death was accidental or on purpose but wouldn't have dared to ask.

"We're both fucked-up by drugs we didn't take ourselves," Taylor said, breaking the silence. "How is he now? I haven't heard anything about him since he and Jordan broke up."

"I've only kept in touch with Kyle since he's renting my house and Noah since we've stayed best friends. I haven't seen Chase since the end of his rehab. Last I heard, he'd moved to the middle of nowhere in, like, Montana or something."

"Do you think he's still clean?"

"I hope so. Do you think Jordan is still clean?"

"I don't think so. She was so angry when I worked with her on the first *Awake* movie. She and Chase had just broken up. During the second one, my classes were more time-consuming, so I didn't spend a lot of time with her. She never seemed like she was on anything then. She's different now, more up and down than usual on the phone, but I don't know if it's just grief over our mother or something else. I'm pretty sure she's responsible for my tire. She did it to a guy's car when we were in high school. I couldn't prove it, just a gut feeling."

"What are you going to do?" Why would Jordan be so destructive to her sister's car?

"I'm really sleepy, so I should probably go home now." Taylor turned away.

"You don't have to go," Layne said as he pulled her close again.

"Against the rules," Taylor said. She got up, but Layne wouldn't let go of her hand, silently begging her to stay

"Screw the damn rules. Please stay." Layne would have held her all night if she'd let him.

Taylor gave him a quick peck on the lips. "You know I can't," she said. "But I'll see you tomorrow."

Disappointed, Layne's heart ached to follow Taylor, but he understood she wasn't ready yet. They were already closer since Taylor had admitted she didn't want to be alone. He took her face in his hands and kissed her goodnight. "Sure," he said. "I'll pick you up tomorrow morning, okay?"

As soon as Taylor got back to her apartment, she crawled into her bed and cried again. She couldn't go to sleep for another couple of hours as she tried to figure out why she couldn't relax enough to stay the night with Layne. It had taken him staying overnight after the accident for her to realize she might have feelings for him. Now that she had talked with Layne while lying on his chest and listening to his heart, Taylor was certain of her feelings. The terrifying sensation was growing stronger, and if she could fall in love again, it would be with him.

chapter 19

With a glass of wine in her hand, Jordan sat on her patio to cool off after her fight with Taylor. It was the best place for quiet reflection after an emotionally exhausting day of acting. With their mother gone and their father distant as always, there wasn't much left connecting Jordan to her sister except fame—something Taylor had made clear she didn't want. Jordan couldn't understand her sister not wanting adoring fans and publicity. In fact, she lived for those things.

For someone who didn't want fame, Taylor sure hadn't minded all the attention from singing on the sitcom during its last two seasons. Jordan had been extremely frustrated when her storylines were cut to make room for Taylor's songs.

The only good thing about the last two seasons of the show was when Backdraft visited, and she had hooked up with Chase. For the next few years, they would meet up when he was in town. It was fate they had ended up in the same rehab facility. While there, they started an exclusive relationship that lasted almost a year.

After Chase kicked his heroin habit and Jordan convinced the doctors that cocaine was in her past, she had flown out to visit him at his ranch in Montana.

2012

Chase met Jordan at the door. "Hey, beautiful," he said.

"Good to see you," she said, kissing him.

They didn't make it all the way to his bedroom; they made love in the middle of his living room floor near the fireplace. Afterward, they wrapped up in a blanket together.

"I've missed you," Jordan said. "I wanted to see you again before I go to an audition next week. This new project is a trilogy, so it could really be the boost I need after the break."

"Babe, it was more than a break. You tried to kill yourself."

"I didn't know what I was doing," Jordan said. "It was the drugs. I won't do it again."

"But you're going back to the lifestyle where you'll be around it again."

"It'll be fine. I can go do movies and then come back here to see you during the breaks."

"I can't do that."

"What do you mean?"

"I don't think I can be with you if you can't leave all that behind."

"How can you ask me to do that when you know it's all I've ever wanted? You should understand that."

"I do understand, but I can't sing again. I almost died, and it took that for me to realize I'll always be an addict. I can't be around the temptation or even associated with that lifestyle. That's why I bought this ranch. I'm staying here and giving up fame to save myself."

"And you're giving me up too?"

"Not you—us. I think I have to."

"Sounds like you've got this all thought out. Why did you even let me come here?"

"I hoped you would stay with me, and we wouldn't have to say goodbye."

"I thought we had a good thing going here," Jordan said as tears spilled over her cheeks.

Chase kissed her. "Jordan, I love you, but I see now you'd never be happy here with me, and I can't go back to LA with you because I'll die out there."

Jordan dried her face and got dressed. "This could have worked if you weren't so damn selfish," she said as she gathered her bags to leave. "You'll regret this."

"Every day for the rest of my life," he called to her as she slammed his door.

About a month after their last encounter, and right after she'd landed the trilogy, Jordan discovered she was pregnant. Three tests she'd taken alone in her bathroom confirmed it. She'd planned to tell Chase with hopes to get him back but never got the chance because the pregnancy ended on its own a few days later—before she could wrap her mind around what having a baby might have done to her career.

She'd suffered through the miscarriage alone, having told no one. With the pain at its worst, Jordan had picked up her phone to call Taylor but passed out before she could dial. Later, she woke in a pool of blood, no longer in physical pain, and knew her pregnancy was over. She sobbed while she cleaned up and decided to never tell anyone. She still thought about it often, reminded every time she took her birth control pills. She'd never forgotten them again.

Some nights, more than others, Jordan missed Chase. There had been other guys since him, but they weren't the same. Jordan always thought Chase was the only guy who hadn't considered her replaceable. She picked up her phone and sent him a text. It had been months since she'd sent a message to him, and she desperately hoped he'd answer right away.

Jordan: **Chase, I wanted to check on you to make sure you're okay. Please respond.**

Chase: **I'm okay. Staying busy with the ranch.**

Jordan: **Are you happy?**

Chase: **Yes. Are you happy?**

Jordan: **Sometimes. Sometimes I miss you.**

Chase: **I saw your last movie. You were incredible.**

Jordan: **I was hoping to hear from you after what happened on Friday.**

Chase: **What happened?**

Jordan: **My mom died.**

Jordan saw that her message was read, but Chase wasn't typing back. The phone rang in her hand.

"Hey, Chase," she answered.

"Jordan, I am so sorry," he said. "I didn't know, or I would have called sooner. I don't get online much."

"Thank you," she said. "It's been hard, but it was for the best. You know how she was. She never improved much after the first stroke."

"That doesn't make it any less hard," Chase said. "Are you okay? Is Taylor okay?"

"I'll be fine. I have outdoor shoots starting next week, so that will keep me busy. I'll be working with Taylor again. And also, Brandon from Backdraft. He's going to play guitar for the last movie."

"Ah, Brandon," Chase said. "He saved my life, you know. Please give him my best."

Jordan heard a female voice in the background. "Who's that?" she asked, but she already knew. Her eyes filled with tears.

"I'll be right there, babe," Chase said, his voice muffled.

Jordan felt like she'd been stabbed in the heart.

"That was my fiancée," Chase said. "It was good to talk to you again, Jordan. My deepest sympathies for the loss of your mom."

"Thanks," Jordan said. "Take care of yourself."

"You too."

Jordan started sobbing and threw her phone on the patio, cracking the screen. She reached for the bracelet Chase had given her and discovered it was no longer on her wrist. Lost, like everything else. Chase had moved on, but she couldn't because everything always went back to him.

chapter 20

Friday, June 3, 2016

L ying in bed with Taylor felt more intimate than sex, and by the end of the week, Layne felt closer to her than he'd ever felt to anyone else. They had carpooled, worked together, and eaten dinner together every night. They'd repeated their ritual of lying together in Layne's bed until Taylor was ready to go home to sleep. The nights ended with a tender goodnight kiss initiated by Layne, and then Taylor would leave even though Layne had wanted her to stay wrapped up in his arms. He was getting a taste of what it would be like to have her for a girlfriend, and it was exactly what he wanted.

On Thursday night, they had returned to the Mocking Bird to sing another duet, "When the Stars Go Blue," with more applause than their first duet at the bar. After that, Layne began thinking about the possibility of them officially recording a duet to help launch both of their solo careers but hadn't mentioned his idea to Taylor yet.

By Friday, Taylor was tired of all the take-out options in the immediate area, so Layne drove them to the grocery store where he'd bought the cupcakes and ice cream to pick up the ingredients to make pasta and salad for the two of them. Taylor went back to get salad dressing while Layne stood in line to pay. The same cashier, Florence, was working the checkout when Layne placed his basket on the counter.

"It's you again," Florence said. "You're becoming a regular."

"What can I say? The service here is excellent," Layne said with a smile.

"Your eye looks better."

"Finally."

"We get celebrities in here sometimes," Florence said, barely speaking above a whisper. "Did you know that the child star, Taylor Hoffman, lives nearby? I haven't seen her this week, but she's been in here before. I think she's trying to keep a low profile, so I don't let on I know who she is. She looks different than she did on the show, but still so beautiful. I wish she'd take that stud out of her nose. I hate those darn things."

Layne laughed. "Oh really? I'll have to be on the lookout for her."

"I know who you are too," Florence said, matter-of-factly. She picked up a tabloid off the rack beside her and pointed to the cover. "Right here, a full exclusive interview with an insider who says Brandon Stallings from Backdraft will be working on the *Awake* set soon."

Layne glanced at the magazine with his photo on the front and shook his head. It was recent, taken as he'd walked into the gym with Taylor steps ahead of him.

"Don't worry, hon," Florence said. "Your secret's safe with me. Will this be all for you?"

Layne looked behind him and saw Taylor coming. "Add in the magazine," he said. "And wait...she's bringing something else."

Florence grinned at Taylor as she put the salad dressing on the counter.

"I got two kinds since I didn't know what kind you wanted," Taylor said to Layne.

"Thank you," Layne said. "Anything's fine. I'm not too picky."

Taylor pulled out her wallet. "Let me pay for half," she said.

"No," Layne said, covering her hands with his. "I've got this one; you paid for dinner last night."

165

Florence gave Layne the total and winked at him afterward. Taylor raised her eyebrows at Layne.

"Florence knows who we are," Layne said in a loud whisper. "But our secrets are safe with her." He pulled the tabloid out of his bag and showed it to Taylor.

"That's a terrible picture of you," Taylor said with a laugh. "A great photo of my butt, though." She turned to the cashier. "Hi, Florence, I didn't realize you knew who I was. I appreciate your discretion."

"Of course, hon," Florence said. "You kids go have a nice dinner."

Taylor went back to Layne's apartment where he impressed her with his ability to cook. She watched him as he pulled his hair back, washed his hands, and got started on their meal. Layne cooking for her made him even sexier.

"Think you can handle chopping things for the salad?" he asked.

"Probably," Taylor said. "If you don't care how it turns out."

"I don't."

Taylor helped him, and before long, they were sitting on the bar stools eating the best pasta she'd ever tasted. "This is incredible," she said. "Who taught you how to cook?"

"My mom," Layne said.

"The only things my mother ever taught me were how to mix drinks and not get pregnant." Taylor reached for her mouth, realizing what tomorrow would bring. "I have to pick up her ashes tomorrow morning." She had almost forgotten.

"My offer still stands to go with you."

"I know, but I need to call Jordan again to find out if she's changed her mind about going with me." Taylor doubted Jordan would go, but she still needed to give her the option.

"Okay, but I'll still go with you whether she goes or not."

Taylor stood up and took her plate to the sink. "Thank you for dinner," she said. "I can't remember the last time anyone's cooked for me."

"I'll do it more often, then. Are you staying awhile tonight?"

"Not tonight. I'm already sleepy enough to go to bed. It's been a long week."

"Noah said he'd be passing through tonight, but he hasn't called me yet. If you change your mind about being sleepy after you talk to Jordan, you should come hang out with us. I was hoping you'd meet him. He wants to see the bar."

"He's not worried about someone recognizing him?"

"Nah," Layne said. "He's determined to out-sing me tonight, but he can't. He's got these dark glasses he wears when he wants to go low-profile."

Taylor laughed. "That's original," she said. "I'm going home now." She kissed Layne beside his lips and immediately felt strange because she had done so without thinking—like an involuntary reflex. Being with him felt completely natural now.

Layne embraced Taylor so tightly she felt breathless. "We've had a great week together," he said before kissing her lightly on the lips. "Go dream about me."

"You wish."

"I know."

When Taylor got back to her apartment, she sent Jordan a text, which was always preferable to talking to her.

Taylor: **I have to pick up Mom's ashes tomorrow. Are you going with me to Dad's beach house or not?**

Jordan: **No. I've already said my goodbye to her. There's no need to drag it out.**

Taylor: **Fine. Are you still coming to my apartment Monday morning so we can ride to the set together?**

Jordan: **Probably.**

Taylor: **Great. Have a good night.**

Jordan: **I will.**

Taylor sent Layne a message next.

Taylor: **Road trip with me tomorrow?**

Layne: **To spread the ashes?**

Taylor: **Dad won't be there, and Jordan doesn't give a shit.**

Layne: **Just come get me when you're ready to go. Are we spending the night there?**

Taylor: **Probably. I'm going to try to get some sleep now. Goodnight.**

Layne: **Ok. Goodnight.**

Noah arrived just before nine o'clock in the evening. Layne buzzed him in and waited in his doorway. As soon as Noah got to the hallway, Layne met him and gave him a hug. Noah's blond hair was shorter, and he had a neatly trimmed beard, but his clothing was the same preppy style he had worn when Backdraft was together.

"Man, it's been too long," Layne said.

"It has," Noah said as he looked around Layne's apartment. "Nice place you've got here. A bit small, isn't it?"

"It's fine," Layne said as he closed his door. "I don't need much space, and it's close to the set."

"How's it going? I saw the TV interview with Jordan Hoffman. It's got to be crazy working with her. I think everybody knows who she is now."

"She's not on set until next week," Layne said. "I'm just recording some of the guitar music for now and singing some harmonies with Taylor."

"Taylor? Jordan's sister?"

"Yeah, but she's using the last name Lee in the credits. She's done all the singing for Jordan during the whole trilogy. Her voice is amazing."

"Yeah, and she used to be hot," Noah said. "I didn't realize she was still working."

"Went low-profile at college. She's writing songs right now."

"She still hot?"

"Yeah," Layne said with a grin.

"You think she'd go out with me?"

"No." There was no way Layne would let that happen.

"Why not?"

"Because you're a whore, and she's seeing someone."

"Ouch." Noah stroked his beard. "That's too bad."

"Come on, I hear the karaoke. It's what you came for, right?"

Noah pulled his fake glasses out of his shirt pocket. "It's on," he said. "Think you can out-sing me?"

"Oh, there's no competition, I'm way better than you."

Noah laughed as they walked downstairs.

169

Taylor had just changed into sweatpants and stretched out on her bed when the music started downstairs. She pulled up her Netflix account and started browsing her selections, hoping to find something to distract her until she could fall asleep. Tomorrow would be a long drive and an emotionally exhausting day. She was ready for the whole thing to be over and for her mother to finally be at rest.

Jordan's impending arrival made Taylor's stomach ache. Things were going well with Layne, and she didn't want Jordan to screw it up. He was already the perfect boyfriend even without that definition in their relationship.

The movie Taylor picked didn't hold her attention long. She woke up later to the sound of her phone buzzing on her nightstand. It was Willow calling.

"Girl, you've got to get down here," Willow said, barely audible over the loud music in the background. "Layne and his friend are killing it on stage. The regulars are backing off, and everyone keeps requesting more songs from them."

"I'm all trashed out," Taylor said. "You just woke me up."

"Un-trash and get your ass down here to support your boyfriend," Willow said.

Taylor sighed. "Fine," she said. "And he's not my boyfriend."

"Yeah, yeah, keep telling yourself that. Come on."

"Be there in a sec."

Taylor went to her bathroom, quickly brushed her hair and put on the jeans she had worn earlier. She put on eyeliner, mascara and a small amount of blush and lipstick before she moved her hair around to hide the pillow crease on her forehead. She was presentable enough for a dimly-lit karaoke bar.

After sneaking in through the employee entrance, Taylor sat beside Willow at the counter in the only available seat in the whole place. People were standing at the back, and everyone's eyes were glued to the stage where Layne and Noah were singing "Beautiful Soul."

As they finished, the crowd cheered, and everyone stood up. Cries of "More" and "Sing another one" filled the space after the applause had tapered off.

"Thank you all so much for the support," Layne said. "Who's next? You guys are turning this into a private concert up here."

No one volunteered to sing next. Layne noticed Taylor sitting at the counter and motioned for her to come up on stage. Taylor shook her head, and Willow started laughing.

"Go on," Willow said.

"I didn't come here to sing," Taylor said.

"Hey guys," Layne said into the microphone. "Let's get a returning performer up here. You all know Taylor Lee? She's right there at the counter. Come on, let's give her some encouragement."

The crowd applauded even louder and left Taylor with no choice but to join Layne and Noah on stage. Noah shook her hand and introduced himself while Layne looked through the other song selections. Noah left the stage to get a drink.

"You can punish me later," Layne said.

"Definitely," Taylor said. "What are we singing?"

The opening notes to "Heart to Face" started playing. Taylor laughed as Layne grabbed her hands and began dancing like the boys had in the old music video. He whispered into her ear, "It's guilty pleasures night. I know you know the words. We've got this. You sing lead, and I'll back you up."

Taylor took a calming breath and sang, conveniently substituting the word "boy" for "girl" for her lines. Layne sang with her during the chorus.

You're the one that I want, girl
You're everything I can see
In this great big world
Baby, please don't ever leave me

With my heart to face, I can't escape this place.
When I see you, I know we're winning the race.
With my heart to face, I can't escape this place.
Your time's well-spent, memories I can't erase.

You have my heart, baby
I see it in your face,
Don't break my heart, girl
Let me give you the world.

With my heart to face, I can't escape this place.
When I see you, I know we're winning the race.
With my heart to face, I can't escape this place
Love like yours, I will never replace.

You're my whole world, girl.
Everything's so clear
Nothing is ever wrong, baby,
Whenever you're near.

With my heart to face, I can't escape this place.
When I see you, I know we're winning the race.
With my heart to face, I can't escape this place.
Your time's well-spent, memories I can't erase.
With my heart to face, I can't escape this place
Love like yours, I will never replace.

With my heart to face, I can't escape this place.
With my heart to face, I can't escape this place.

When the song ended, the crowd cheered so loudly, Layne could feel the noise in his chest. He couldn't help but laugh when Noah stood on a stool and cheered for them.

Layne put his arm around Taylor and kissed her on the temple—taking a risk to do so in front of the crowd. "You were incredible," he said. He wanted to kiss her again.

"Thank you all," Taylor said into the microphone. "Now, let's hear it again for Layne!" She turned to him and clapped, looking stunning in the luminescence of the stage lights.

The crowd cheered again as Taylor left the stage and returned to the counter where Willow sat. Layne followed Taylor and put his arm around her again, thrilled she didn't pull away.

"Thanks for calling me," Taylor said to Willow. "I needed that."

"You want to come back to my place to hang out with Noah and me?" Layne asked. "You can hang out, too, Willow, if you want."

"No," Willow said as she got up to leave. "I've got an early class tomorrow. I'm out."

Noah came over and shook Taylor's hand again. "Wow, Taylor, your voice is amazing. I never thought his cheesy old song could sound that good."

"Thank you," Taylor said. She turned back to Layne. "I'm still exhausted. Willow woke me up and said you guys were killing it in here, so I came to see for myself. I'm going back to bed. You guys have fun."

"We're done here anyway. Can we follow you back through the employee exit?" Layne asked.

"Sure," she said.

They went back upstairs, and Layne let Noah back into his apartment before he walked over to Taylor, who was still unlocking her door. "Thanks for singing with me," he said, leaning against the wall beside her.

Taylor laughed. "It's not like I had a choice," she said as she opened her door. "But it was fun. And Noah seems nice. You two were great up there."

"We were always the two most awesome in the group," Layne said.

"Yeah, I guess you were," she said with a smirk as she tried to go into her apartment.

"Hey, wait." Layne grabbed Taylor's hand and pulled her back into the hallway for the longest goodnight kiss of the week. Her body relaxed in his arms, and she didn't open her eyes right away. "I'll see you tomorrow."

Taylor snuggled against Layne's chest. "Goodnight," she said. She pulled away and closed her door.

When Layne turned around, Noah stood in his doorway with his eyes wide. "I was wondering if you got lost," he said as Layne closed the door. "Now it's clear what's going on."

"And what's that?"

"You and Taylor are hooking up," Noah said. "She's hot, man. I'd tap that if I could."

Layne glared at him. "Dude, don't be a dick. It's not like that."

Noah laughed. "You're definitely sleeping with her. Nice."

"Yeah, and so what if I am? Stop being an ass." Layne shoved Noah's shoulder.

Noah playfully shoved him back. "Sorry. Just screwing around with you. She seems great. How long's that been going on?"

"Long enough," Layne said. "What's up with you? Have you talked to the other guys?"

"I'm going to be a judge on one of those reality shows coming up. They're going to have these kids audition to make a boy band and a girl band. Sound familiar?"

"Vaguely," Layne said as he started laughing.

"Kyle's probably judging with me, at least that's what he said last week. Now that he's engaged and renovating his house, I don't know from one week to the next what he's doing."

"Yeah, he's renting my house until construction on his is finished. I still can't believe he's engaged. I thought he'd be the last one of us—if ever."

"No kidding. We had our bets on you being first since you've always been a sappy romantic. Chase is doing well. His ranch is nice. I saw it when he first bought it, and then I went out there again last year. He's still clean, going to meetings. He thanked me for helping save his life."

"I guess I should call him. I haven't talked to him since right after he got out of rehab. He thanked me, and that was it. I didn't have anything else to say to him."

"I've kept in touch and let him know how you were. The first time I went out there, he had just ended things with Jordan for good, and he was really messed up about it. He said he couldn't be with her because the temptation for drugs was too much."

"I guess I didn't realize they were that serious," Layne said. "I thought he was just hooking up with her."

"None of us did," Noah said. "He shocked the shit out of me when he broke down crying about her. I always thought she was a little too wild, but he loved her. Taylor's not anything like Jordan, is she?"

"I don't really know Jordan," Layne said. "But she and Taylor aren't close, and Taylor…well, she's amazing." And she was, deep down where it mattered most.

"What's this song you were texting about?"

Layne handed his notebook to Noah and waited for him to finish reading it.

"You've upped the cheese, man," Noah said, stroking his beard again. "The chicks will love this song." He handed the notebook back to Layne.

"You think?"

"Yep. Desperate love song. Moderately good-looking guy with a decent voice. You got this."

"I'm still working on the melody, but I think I want it to be soft, acoustic guitar only, no bass."

"I thought all of your stuff was going to be that way, just you and your guitar. Are you planning to get a band together?"

"Maybe. I want something different than what we did with Backdraft. No singing and dancing to pre-recorded tracks."

"So, you went straight back to writing love songs?" Noah asked. "Not saying it's a bad thing. It'll be a hit with the Backdraft crowd for sure, but I think other people will like it too."

"I didn't set out to write a love song, but..." Layne couldn't finish his thought. He had written a love song, but it was more than that. It was the first song he'd ever written with a specific person in mind rather than generalized ideas of what love should be.

"Man, you're in deep," Noah said, pulling Layne from his thoughts.

"What? Deep shit? I thought you said the song wasn't that bad."

"It's fine, but sweet puppies! You're in love with Taylor!"

Layne pulled his hair into a ponytail and looked at Noah. "Shit," he muttered. His feelings were definitely moving in that direction. If it was already obvious to Christina and Noah, it was only a matter of time before it was obvious to Taylor as well.

Noah crashed on Layne's couch for the night, and Layne barely slept at all. He stared at the ceiling half the night. Spending the night with Taylor the next evening was all he could think about. It would be a sad situation for her, but he also hoped it would bring them closer.

The next morning, Layne got up before Noah and woke him by making coffee in the kitchen.

"Dude, how do you get up so early when you didn't go to bed until after I did?" Noah asked, rubbing his eyes as he sat on a bar stool.

"It's a gift."

"Hey, Kyle's having a party at his place—well, your place tonight. You should come."

"Not interested," Layne said. "I've got plans with Taylor. And you guys better not trash my place."

"Bring your girlfriend with you. It'll be fun."

"We're going to her dad's beach house," Layne said.

"Her dad's that record exec, right, Miles Hoffman?" Noah asked. Layne nodded. "You going to try to hit him up for a deal? Is that what this is about?"

"No. He's not even going to be there."

"Ah, a booty weekend." Noah chuckled.

"Jordan and Taylor's mom died last week. I'm going with Taylor so she won't have to spread the ashes alone. Jordan won't go with her."

"Man," Noah said with a sigh as he looked at Layne. "I really feel like an asshole now. I'm sorry. I was just teasing you last night, but you really are in love with Taylor, aren't you?"

"It's way too soon," Layne said. "But I can't stop thinking about her."

"Well, judging by the kiss last night, she's into you too."

"Yeah, I hope so. She's been hurt before, so I'm trying hard not to be a jerk." Layne handed Noah a cup of coffee.

"Nah," Noah said as he took the cup. "You're not a jerk. Not even when you were hooking up with those women when we were on tour. You always chose women who wouldn't get attached."

Layne sat down on the stool beside Noah. "I'm done with all that," he said. "Taylor's special. I don't want to be with anyone else. I just love hanging out with her doing nothing."

"Then tell her," Noah said. "Chicks dig that shit."

Not Taylor, Layne thought. *Telling her will scare the hell out of her.*

chapter 21

Saturday, June 4, 2016

Layne was speechless from the moment Taylor opened her apartment door. His eyes met hers, and he was absolutely mesmerized by her beauty.

"Are you ready?" Taylor asked, a slight blush forming on her cheeks. "We have a long road ahead of us." Layne hoped Taylor's words were truer than she realized.

She wore a white dress with little yellow flowers printed on it. Instead of her usual heavy eye makeup, she wore just a hint of mascara and lip-gloss. She had removed her nose stud and all but one set of earrings, accented by the fact that her hair was pulled back off her face. Layne pulled Taylor into his arms and waited while her lips met his halfway.

After their lips broke apart, Taylor grabbed Layne's arms to steady herself. "You've got to stop doing that," she said. "You're making me dizzy."

Glad it's not just me, Layne thought as he followed Taylor out of the building.

He waited in the car at Taylor's request while she went inside the funeral home to retrieve her mother's ashes. His main goal, besides being supportive of Taylor, was to convince her to remove the casual label from their relationship and agree to be his girlfriend. Crazy or not, two weeks in or not, he hoped she had feelings for him too.

Layne's phone rang. "Christina," he answered. "I'm going out of town today, so I probably won't be responsive to texts."

"Mom said she didn't hear from you this morning like she normally does, so she called me."

"Why didn't she just call me?"

"Because I may have told her you're dating your friend, Taylor, and seemed pretty serious about her, so Mom didn't want to bother you."

"Chris!" Layne exclaimed, slapping his forehead. "Why the hell would you tell her that? I told you it's too soon!"

"I'm sorry; it just slipped out. She was worried you were lonely and was wanting to set you up with someone."

Taylor came back to the car carrying a small silver box. She opened the back door and placed it on the floor.

"I have to go," Layne said as he watched Taylor get into the driver's seat. "I'll call Mom later. Just tell her I'm busy, okay?"

"Fine. Have a good weekend," Christina said.

Layne hung up and placed his hand on Taylor's knee. "Are you ready to go?" he asked. "I can drive if you want."

"I'm fine to drive," she said softly. "Was that your sister?" Even when Taylor smiled, her eyes were still mournful.

"Yeah, my mom worries, but she won't call me; she calls my sister. Christina never minds calling me. I don't think they'll bother me again. I told them I'd be out of town."

"At least they care. I'm practically an orphan. My dad can't even remember my birthday."

"What about Jordan? Did she remember?"

"She sent me a text with the word 'shitty' in it."

"What happened with you two?"

"I don't want to talk about it."

"What do you want to talk about?"

"Can we just listen to some music and not talk?"

"I thought of another song I think you'll like," Layne said. "Have you heard 'Honey and the Moon' by Joseph Arthur?"

"I don't think so."

Layne found the song on his phone and played it through Taylor's speakers as she drove out of the parking lot. He watched her smile as she listened to the lyrics that had spoken him when he first heard the song several years ago. "Well," he said when the song was finished. "What did you think?"

"It's really pretty. Is it older?"

"Yeah. It was released for the first time over ten years ago. I heard it in the background of a movie and had to look it up. I know it dates itself a bit with the mention of an answering machine, but I still think it's relevant."

"Lots of things are dated, but it doesn't mean people won't figure out what things are," Taylor said. "I mean, I've never used a typewriter, but I still know what one is. I think teenagers today who hear his song will figure out what an answering machine was."

"True. I just love that it seems like he wrote it about a specific person."

"You really like those love songs," she teased.

"Don't you? What's your favorite love song?"

"This is hard," Taylor said. "Does it have to be about someone specific like 'All of Me,' or can it be hoping for love without a specific person in mind?"

"It doesn't matter to me. 'All of Me' is an awesome song, though."

"Yeah, it is. I guess I'd have to say it's a toss-up between 'I'm With You' by Avril Lavigne and 'London Rain' by Heather Nova."

"I get the Avril one since it's a lot like my favorite, 'I'll Be,' but I've never heard of Heather Nova."

"Look it up and play it," Taylor suggested.

As he closed his eyes and listened to the lyrics, Layne wondered if Taylor was trying to tell him something with the song she couldn't say to him directly. He hoped he was doing his part to help Taylor heal. Sharing the music they loved with each other was the best conversation he could imagine.

They arrived at the beach house just before sunset, having stopped for burgers along the way. After parking, Taylor pulled a blanket out of the trunk of her car and handed it to Layne. "I want to wait until sunset," she said. "It used to be her favorite time of day when we'd visit here when I was a kid."

"Okay." Layne followed Taylor to the back of the house to access the beach. He spread the blanket out on the sand.

Taylor sat down with Layne and placed the silver box beside her. "How is your song coming, the one you sang for me? Was that a first line?" she asked.

Layne worried he might scare her if he sang the whole thing. "Yeah, I just have a couple more lines so far. I could sing it for you."

"Sure."

Layne took a deep breath and sang his first few lines.

There's more beauty in you,
Than could ever be true.
I've spent all of my life
Waiting for you.
You push me away
While I beg you to stay.
I'm new to this place
And I won't be the same.
I'll take all your pain
And lock it away.
If I don't kiss your lips
I might go insane.

No one had ever written anything for Taylor before, and she was fairly certain Layne was pouring his heart out. "It's beautiful," she said, hoping her intrigue and distress weren't flashing like strobe lights on her face.

"Thank you. Do you really like it?"

She nodded. "The lyrics are good, and I like the melody you have going. It has a kind of a haunting feeling to it. Not really desperate but determined."

"You nailed it," Layne said. "That's what I was going for. I figured some light guitar music with it, and another verse or two and I'll be done. It's not meant to be a long song."

"Do you want to hear one I've been messing with? It's a different one than the one I sang for you."

"You know I do."

"All I have is the possible main chorus right now. I'm not sure where I'm going with it or how to start it, and I may end up changing some of the words."

"It's okay, just sing what you have."

Taylor sang for him the song she'd started while dwelling about Jordan.

I could take all the blame
And hide from the pain
But the scars will remain
'Cause you don't know my name.

Layne cleared his throat. "Your voice…it's such a sad song."

"Is it too sad?" Taylor didn't want to depress everyone with her music despite how she felt sometimes.

"No. Some of the best songs out there are sad. Like 'Jar of Hearts.' It's sad and angry, too, but it's also beautiful just like your song will be when it's done. I know it."

"That's funny. 'Jar of Hearts' is probably my favorite song right now."

"Now I know something else about you," Layne said. "What's your favorite book? It's not the *Awake* trilogy, is it?"

Taylor laughed. "No. It's probably crazy, but *The Bell Jar* comes to mind."

"It's not crazy. My favorite's *The Catcher in the Rye*."

"I think we're both crazy," she said.

"Favorite color?"

"What is this, twenty questions?"

"Yes."

"Fine, green," Taylor said.

"What kind of green?"

"Emerald—like your eyes."

"Okay, you'll think I stole your answer, but my favorite is sky blue like your eyes." Layne brushed a strand of hair out of Taylor's face.

"You copied me." Taylor stood up and walked to the water's edge just as the last sliver of the sun disappeared behind the ocean. As she knelt on the shore, Taylor imagined shrinking away to nothingness and letting the grief overpower her, but she had to get up and keep moving. She opened the silver box, letting the ashes blow in the breeze and fall into the waves at her feet. The burden of her mother was gone, but the memories remained etched in her heart. Taylor went back to the blanket and sat in front of Layne. No words could convey how she felt.

Layne reached for Taylor's hand. "There's a lot going on behind those eyes of yours," he said. "Please, talk to me."

"Layne, do you believe in God?"

Taken aback by her question, Layne let his mouth drop before he could respond. "Wow, that got deep fast."

"I'm sorry, you don't have to answer." Taylor pulled her hand away and looked out at the ocean.

Layne watched as Taylor nervously twisted her dress in her hands. "Do you?" he asked.

Taylor hesitated for a moment. "Sometimes," she said. "I want to believe there's someone in control, someone who knows the 'why' of everything. Even if I don't understand it."

Belief was beyond understanding; it was all about faith. "I do believe in God," Layne said. "I have to believe every time I see a sunset. Just look at it. It's all too perfect to just be chance." He took Taylor's face in his hands and looked at her under the soft glow of the sky. Her beauty was enough proof for him that God existed. "And every time I look at you...my God, Taylor, you're so beautiful."

Taylor closed her eyes. "Beauty fades."

"That's not all I'm talking about when I say that. I mean, you are physically beautiful, but..." He took Taylor's hands and placed them on her chest, over her heart. He had to make her understand what he saw. "Right here is where you're most beautiful, where it doesn't fade—your heart, your soul. The best parts of you. I think we're all drawn to certain people for different reasons at different times. All in a quest to find a true match—a soulmate. That's what I believe, anyway."

Taylor looked out at the ocean again before turning back to Layne, her lip quivering. "Maybe you can believe enough for both of us," she said as tears spilled over her cheeks.

Layne wiped away her tears. "Baby, I already do," he whispered just before Taylor kissed him. With that kiss, Layne knew he was no longer in danger of falling in love with Taylor; he was already in love with her. There was no doubt in his mind. If he could have picked any moment to be trapped in for the rest of his life, it would have been that moment right before they made love on the beach.

chapter 22

Jordan pulled up to her father's house just in time for sunset, her favorite time of day. Bright sunlight was unforgiving, and besides, nothing worthwhile ever happened before dark. Now, the memories of summers spent running around the beach with her sister seemed like almost-forgotten movie roles. Taylor's car was in the driveway, but none of the lights were on inside the house. Jordan left her bags in the car and walked around to the beach.

She looked toward the water just in time to see Taylor kissing someone. Based on the silhouette, Jordan suspected it was the same guy she had seen with Taylor in her apartment. They kissed like a couple in a movie—people who were in love. The sight of them made her skin crawl.

When Jordan noticed they were progressing to more than kissing, she went back to her car and decided to leave. Taylor hadn't really wanted her there since she brought her boyfriend with her. Being around happy couples triggered Jordan's gag-reflex now that she knew there was no chance of rekindling her relationship with Chase. She had hoped to convince him they could be together without him having to move back to California.

It wasn't fair that Taylor seemed so happy with her life out of the spotlight. Everything had always come so much easier for her. Acting, singing, dancing. Taylor never had to practice much because she was naturally good at all three. And people seemed to genuinely like Taylor more no matter what Jordan did.

She remembered overhearing the producer and director discuss Taylor right before everything had changed on the sitcom.

2005

"Taylor can sing," the director said to the producer. "We need to talk to the writers about working in another talent show or something to showcase Taylor's talent. I think it will be a much bigger hit than the Sierra and Laken tap-dancing act we had planned."

"I'm not sure if we need to completely rework everything for some kid singing along to her music player. Jordan and Taylor have rehearsed for hours to get that dance act down. I don't want to have wasted all that time."

"It would be a disservice not to feature Taylor's singing on the show this season. Could we talk to the writers and bring in Taylor for a soundcheck? She's a natural and won't even need voice lessons from what I heard. She wasn't pitch-matching to any music; she was just singing on her own, and she's incredible."

"Fine," the producer said. "Let's do it."

Jordan would never forget the tightness she'd felt in her chest while watching Taylor audition for the key people. The entire soundstage had gone silent as everyone stopped what they were doing to listen to Taylor sing her own rendition of "Somewhere Over the Rainbow." Jordan had known then things would be changing. She hated Taylor for stealing her spotlight since the show was supposed to be centered around Jordan's character, Laken, as it had been for the first eight seasons. Afterward, the screen time per episode featured Taylor's character, Sierra, an average of two minutes longer than Jordan.

During the talent show episode where Sierra wins, the writers included a touching moment with Laken expressing her jealousy to her on-screen parents. That was the only time Jordan hadn't been acting as she'd cried to them. It was also the first time she'd won an award for her performance. For the next two years, Taylor had won in the same category for best young actress in a sitcom, even though Jordan was also nominated.

As Jordan drove away from her father's beach house, she cried for her past. The past before things got too hard. The past when things were simpler. She scratched at the faint scars on her wrists, the skin tight and unforgiving. A new feeling choked her—a sickening feeling she refused to acknowledge.

chapter 23

Sunday, June 5, 2016

The sun had just begun to rise when Taylor woke to the sound of waves crashing on the shore. Having slept on the beach all night wrapped in the blanket with Layne, she took a deep breath as she stretched, inhaling the scent of the salt water. No one had ever said anything to her as profound as what Layne did the night before, and with such sincerity. He was almost too kind, exactly the type of guy Jordan loved to chew up and spit out. Taylor dreaded the two of them meeting. She smoothed Layne's hair and touched the stubble on his chin to wake him.

He smiled and opened his eyes. "I wish we could wake up like this every day." His eyes were beautiful in the morning light.

"We fell asleep out here," Taylor said. "I guess we were worn out."

Layne sat up and wrapped the blanket around Taylor's shoulders. "You can wear me out like that anytime." He moved her hair and kissed the back of her neck.

Taylor looked out at the ocean and wondered if she should feel different now that her mother's ashes were gone, but she felt the same. There was still a slight numbness in her chest that had been there for as long as she could remember. Even with the burden of her mother's impending death gone, she still felt something nagging at her—something she couldn't quite put into words. She wanted to run away from it all. The only difference now was that she couldn't imagine Layne not coming with her.

Layne caressed her cheek. "Hey, are you okay?"

"I will be," she said as she stood up. "Come on, let's go inside and get cleaned up. I have sand in some very uncomfortable places."

"Hey, you started it," Layne said, laughing as he stood up.

"Thank you for coming with me," Taylor said. "You were right; I didn't want to do this alone."

"There are only a few people I'd do anything for," Layne said as he took Taylor's hand. "And you're one of them." He held her hand as they walked from the beach through the patio door of the house.

After they had showered and eaten breakfast, they left the beach house. Still physically and emotionally exhausted, Taylor asked Layne to drive back so she could sleep.

They stopped to eat a late lunch, then continued their drive and arrived back late in the afternoon. Just as they pulled into the parking lot, Layne's phone rang and connected through Taylor's speakers.

"Hey, Christina," he said.

"We're driving through town on our way home," she said. "Can we stop by and visit for a few minutes? I know the kids just saw you, but they miss you."

"Yeah, that's fine," Layne said. "We just got home. When will you be here?"

"Now," Christina said with a laugh. "I just pulled into the parking lot behind you I think."

Layne ended the call. "You want to meet my sister and her family?" he asked.

"Okay," Taylor said as she followed Layne out of her car.

Two blond-haired kids, about four and five years old ran over to Layne and jumped into his arms.

"Uncle Brandon!" they screamed.

"Hey guys," Layne said. "Come here and meet Taylor. Taylor, this is my niece, Cecelia, and my nephew, Cohen."

"Hello," the kids said in unison.

Taylor crouched to greet them. "Very pleased to meet you," she said. As she rose, she saw Layne's sister and her husband standing behind the kids.

Christina resembled Layne, with wavy light brown hair and green eyes. Her husband was tall and blond like their children.

"Taylor," Christina said as she extended her hand. "I feel like I know you already. It's so good to meet you, I'm Christina, and this is Wade."

Taylor shook their hands. "It's nice to meet you both," she said. She grabbed her bag out of the car and handed Layne's bag to him. "I hope you all have a nice visit."

"Hey," Layne said as he grabbed Taylor's hand. "Let's talk later."

"Okay," Taylor said before she walked away. She turned around before going inside and watched Layne hug his sister and brother-in-law. She couldn't imagine having a family like theirs.

Layne chatted with his family in the parking lot for a few minutes before taking them to see his apartment.

"This place is smaller than I expected. A lot smaller than your house," Christina said as Layne showed her around.

"I like it," Layne said. "It's easier to keep clean."

"The perfect bachelor pad," Wade said. He turned to Christina "Remember? It looks like my old place."

"That it does," she said. "So, you and Taylor went out of town? Sounds pretty serious."

"We went to her dad's beach house," Layne said.

"Is Taylor your girlfriend?" Cohen asked.

Layne hadn't realized the kids were paying attention. He picked up Cohen and tossed him on the couch. "I want to hear about all your girlfriends in kindergarten, little man," he said, tickling him.

"Girls are gross," Cohen said, unable to stifle his giggles.

"That's not nice," Cecelia said, putting her hands on her hips, modeling her mother's stance.

"That's enough, kids," Wade said.

"So, is Taylor your girlfriend?" Christina asked as she tugged on her brother's hair. "She's adorable."

It wasn't a question Layne could answer until he had a conversation with Taylor.

"Babe, we can't stay long," Wade said. "The kids are already tired, and we still have a couple of hours left to drive."

Christina sighed. "Thanks for letting us drop by," she said. "We'll have to come again sometime when we can stay longer, and maybe Taylor can join us next time."

The kids groaned and let Layne hug them goodbye. He looked at his sister's probing eyes, silently begging her to give up asking about Taylor.

After his family left, Layne looked for his phone to send Taylor a message but couldn't find it. He pulled out his laptop to track it and located it nearby, most likely still in Taylor's car.

Taylor was sprawled out on her couch reading a book when a knock on the door startled her. Having grown accustomed to Layne's knocking over the past two weeks, she knew it was him.

"Hey," he said as she opened the door.

"I figured you'd still be with your family," she said. "Did they leave already?"

"Yeah, the kids were tired."

"They seemed nice."

"They're great. Hey, I need your keys. I left my phone in your car."

"Sure," Taylor said, handing him the keys from the hook by her door. "But no joy rides, okay?"

Layne laughed. "I prefer different rides."

Taylor pushed him out the door. "Your mind always has to go there, doesn't it? Right into the gutter."

"I didn't mean it that way," he said as he walked backward down the hall. "You're way more dirty-minded than I am."

Taylor's phone alerted her to a text message from Jordan as she watched Layne walk down the stairs.

Jordan: **How was the memorial? You didn't look too broken up.**

Taylor: **What are you talking about?**

Jordan: **I saw you on the beach.**

Taylor: **I thought you weren't coming.**

Jordan: **I can't believe you took a random guy to spread our mother's ashes. Stop being such a skank.**

Taylor: **You're one to talk. You don't have any idea what's going on with me or how I'm feeling.**

Jordan: **I saw exactly what you were feeling.**

Taylor: **Who I'm sleeping with is none of your business. He wasn't just a random guy.**

Jordan: **I won't care once I get to work. I'll be hooking up with the guitar player.**

Taylor: **He won't be interested.**

Jordan: **There's never been a guy who wasn't interested in hooking up with me.**

Taylor: **There's a first time for everything.**

Jordan: **Brandon Stallings won't be able to resist me. I wonder if he's as good in bed as Chase? I'll be sure to let you know.**
Taylor: **He's seeing someone.**
Jordan: **That's never been a problem before.**
Taylor: **Leave him alone.**

Taylor felt sick that Jordan had seen her with Layne on the beach. She would never hear the end of it. Jordan was typing another message, but Taylor turned off her phone to avoid it. Had she been skanky having sex on the beach right after spreading her mother's ashes? *It wasn't Layne who started it,* Taylor thought, *I did. Was it just because I was hurting or because I care about him? Oh God, I care about him, and Jordan's going to try to take him away.*

She remembered the aftermath of catching Jordan and Michael together.

2010

Taylor arrived home after dark, having wandered around her neighborhood for hours, not knowing where to go or what she would do when she got there. She heard someone in the kitchen as soon as she walked in the house. Expecting her mother or the housekeeper, Taylor walked through the dining room into the kitchen, finally allowing her shock to dissolve into tears.

Jordan looked up as Taylor walked in. "There you are," she said. "I didn't know if you'd gone to Dad's house."

"What the hell, Jordan?" Taylor asked. "How could you do that to me? You're my sister. You're supposed to care about me!"

"I'm sorry, Tay. Boys and their hormones. Michael's been coming on to me for weeks. We were both drinking, and then it just happened. He probably got tired of waiting around for you to sleep with him."

"Are you fucking kidding me?" Taylor asked through her tears, swallowing the bile burning the back of her throat. "He told me he loved me. He said he wasn't interested in you. I had sex with him last night, so that

blows your whole theory. What did you do? Why do you do this with every guy I've liked? Every single guy I wanted to date at school you've ended up sleeping with! Why, Jordan? What did I ever do to you? How can you not have any loyalty to me?"

"Taylor." Jordan sat on a bar stool and placed her hands on Taylor's shoulders. *"I can't help if guys like me more. And I can't help it if they use you to get to me. You'll have to learn to be smarter and not give your heart away to these losers. Just use them for sex like I do. It's so much easier. Michael was the perfect guy for you to use. He was outstanding—a natural in bed. Maybe you were the problem."*

Something snapped inside Taylor. She threw Jordan's hands off her shoulders and slapped her hard across the face. Jordan grabbed Taylor's hands, but Taylor wrestled free and grabbed Jordan's hair. With all of Taylor's anger surfacing, Jordan took several punches before the housekeeper came in and broke up the girls by turning the retractable faucet on them.

"That's enough, girls!" the housekeeper yelled. *"Sisters should take care of each other!"*

"You're not my sister!" Taylor screamed. *"You're dead to me, Jordan! I hate you!"*

"You had no right to hit me!" Jordan yelled as she ran upstairs. *"You better not have broken my nose. Filming starts in three weeks!"*

Taylor watched her sister leave and sat down on the kitchen floor, still crying.

It felt like high school all over again. *Hell, I can't deal with this tonight,* Taylor thought, *Jordan's coming tomorrow and will screw up everything.* But if Taylor didn't act like she cared, Jordan wouldn't either.

Layne retrieved his phone and took Taylor's keys back to her. He watched her toss the keys onto the couch instead of hanging them up. Her whole demeanor was different than before. "What's wrong?" he asked.

"Just family drama. I'm fine." Taylor crossed her arms.

"So," Layne said. "Can I come in?"

"Aren't you sick of me?" she asked, devoid of emotion.

"No…I actually wanted to talk to you. It's important."

Taylor moved so he could get by and then closed the door. She shoved Layne against the wall and kissed him.

Knocked off-balance, Layne grabbed the doorframe to steady himself. "That's quite a welcome back."

"I don't want to talk right now," Taylor said before kissing him again.

"We can talk later," Layne said, his heart pounding. He picked up Taylor and carried her to the bed without saying another word.

chapter 24

As they lay in bed exhausted, Layne thought the timing was perfect to tell Taylor he loved her. He snuggled against her, ready to say what was in his heart. Taylor had to feel it too—the intense connection they had and the energy their bodies released when they connected.

Taylor's voice broke the silence. "You should go home now," she said.

The perfect moment he'd envisioned was slipping away. Something told Layne if he didn't express his feelings soon, the world would implode, and he would lose her forever. "Please let me stay," he said. "We'll get something to eat and stay in bed...maybe take a bath."

"No," Taylor said, pushing him away. "That's not what we agreed to." She got out of bed and picked up her clothes off the floor.

Layne got up and hastily dressed. The conversation was not going how he'd planned. "What the hell is wrong with you?" he snapped as he put on his jeans. "You're so damn frustrating! I can't figure you out. You're hot and cold all the time."

Taylor didn't look at him as she dressed, and Layne felt like an asshole, regretting what he'd said. "I'm sorry," he continued, slamming his palm against his forehead. "But, damn it, Taylor, I can't do this anymore. I can't be casual with all these stupid rules that seem to change every day. It's not what I want. It was never what I wanted with you."

"We agreed to keep things casual," she said, her tone distant and icy. "What did you expect? A relationship?"

"Yes! Isn't that what we have? I thought you were just...scared. We've been so close this past week. You're telling me it hasn't meant anything to you? And last night on the beach, you didn't feel that?" All he wanted was to pull Taylor into his arms, but he could do nothing but stare at her and fight the threat of tears.

Taylor turned away from him, avoiding his eyes. "Layne, she's coming tomorrow. It'll take all of my time and energy just to deal with her. I can't deal with anything else right now. She takes everything I have."

Layne's heart was breaking for her, but he had to push a little more. "So that's what this is about? Jordan? You can't keep hiding behind your sister's fame. Take back some of your own if that's what you want. Or don't. Just do something and stop screwing around!"

"You didn't mind the screwing around a minute ago!" Taylor yelled as she turned to face Layne. "You have no idea what it's like to live in her shadow!"

"Then explain it to me. Explain everything to me! Like how you can kiss me the way you do and look at me the way you do but not let me stay."

"No one really cares about me or what I do once Jordan's around." Taylor sat on her bed and covered her face with her hands.

Layne twisted his shirt and threw it against the wall. "I care," he said as he sat down beside Taylor. He clenched his teeth to keep from crying. "Believe it or not, I do know what it's like to live in the shadow of fame. I may not make it solo or write anything more than cheesy pop songs, but I have to try. You can try with me."

"I can't…"

"Taylor, just talk to me. Enlighten me about life with the great Jordan Hoffman. Tell me why you never talk about her. What did she do to you? How did she hurt you?"

Taylor's body stiffened as she lay back on the bed and answered Layne's questions. Jordan expected everyone to kiss her ass after filming the first horror flick. She was sugar sweet to everyone, especially Taylor's boyfriend, Michael, but was horrible to Taylor. She broke Taylor's phone and bleached all her clothes. Even their mother noticed Jordan's erratic behavior but didn't do anything to help because of her own addiction. The saga ended with Taylor catching Michael and Jordan having sex in the middle of their living room.

"Man, that's cold," Layne said, still trying to process everything Taylor had shared. He watched tears drip from Taylor's eye and pool near her ear.

"Yeah." She wiped her face. "He claimed he was drunk and didn't remember what happened, but Jordan wasn't drunk. She had a pretty high tolerance for alcohol by then. She knew exactly what she was doing, and she knew I loved him."

"Did she?"

"Yeah. I told my mom, and Jordan must have heard me. I lost my virginity to Michael the night before he had sex with Jordan. I loved him, and he said he loved me. My mom still had brief moments when she was sober. I talked to her that same morning, the morning after Michael and I had sex, because I was scared. I had just read *The Bell Jar*. There was this part in it…"

"Ah, I know which part you're talking about—the part where she was bleeding. I can see how that would have upset you."

Taylor raised up on her elbows and looked at Layne differently, like she was seeing him for the first time "You've actually read it?"

"I'm smarter than I look," he said. "So, seeing them together, that's what broke you?"

"I just stood there, still bleeding from the night before. I couldn't move or speak. Everything hurt. It was so out of character for him. I never thought he would do that to me. Jordan told me she was sorry I saw them and said Michael had been coming on to her for a long time. I always thought she was just jealous that Michael had asked me out instead of her. It started with a double date about a year before. Michael asked us to go out with him and his cousin.

"Jordan thought Michael was asking her out. We all went to the movies, and Jordan was fuming when she realized her mistake. Michael's cousin was extremely obnoxious, which didn't help, but the real problem was when Michael put his arm around me during the movie. Jordan was livid by the time we got home and especially so when Michael kissed me goodnight. It was my first real off-screen kiss right in front of her. She thought it was just a momentary thing that wouldn't last, but he and I were still together when she came back from filming. It was before I knew he was a cheater."

"What did you do after you caught them together?"

"I stopped caring, I guess. I went to live with my dad when my mom got sick a few months later. I never could get away from Jordan, though. I needed the money for college when she recommended me for the trilogy, so I took the job. I couldn't touch the money from the show until I turned twenty-one. The one smart thing my mother did was put our earnings into a trust for each of us. I work with Jordan when I have to, but I still don't trust her. I feel like she's always got some scheme going. If I can't trust my own sister…"

And there it was. Taylor couldn't trust anyone because of Jordan's betrayal. "You can't trust me?" Layne asked. "I haven't given you any reason not to."

"Neither did he."

"Taylor…" Layne moved to close the gap between them.

Taylor got up from the bed and walked toward her bedroom door. "You have to go home," she said, almost whining. She seemed afraid of what Layne might say next. "Jordan will be here tomorrow morning."

"Damn it, don't walk away! I'm…" Layne's throat constricted as he choked out his next words. "I have feelings for you."

Taylor stopped and leaned against the wall, struggling to catch her breath.

Layne went to her and held her face in his hands, worried she might faint. "Breathe. You don't have to say anything," he said. "I just wanted you to know…"

Taylor slid down the wall and pulled her knees up to her chest.

Layne sat beside her in silence for what seemed like hours. "Taylor, how many guys have you let into your bed more than once?"

She looked at the floor and sighed as she spoke. "Just you."

"Then you already trust me more than you have anyone else." Layne kissed Taylor on the temple before she pulled away. He moved closer and pressed his head to hers. "This hasn't been just sex to me. I care about you."

"You should go now."

"Please, Taylor, don't push me away," Layne begged. "I…" He couldn't get the words out; he might lose her.

Taylor's eyes filled with tears as she looked at Layne. She stood up and went into her bathroom. "Go home," she said as she closed the door. "Please!"

Layne stomped through the living room and threw open the main door, slamming it behind him. He stood in the hallway for a moment unsure of what to do. Hot tears stung in his eyes as he cursed and pounded his door with the side of his fist.

Willow's apartment door flew open. "Hey!" she yelled. "The landlord can be a real stickler about someone mistreating his property. Knock it off."

Layne hastily wiped his eyes and turned to face her. "I'm sorry. Bad night."

"No shit." Willow walked over and grabbed his arm, her eyes full of compassion. "I'm sorry for what I'm about to do, which is interfere."

"Look, I'm not in the mood."

"Don't care," she said, her eyes drilling a hole in Layne. "I heard you yelling, but not a lot of what was said, but I get the gist."

Layne relented. He might as well listen to Willow. Maybe she knew more about Taylor than he did and could help him understand what the hell was really going on with her. "That she's afraid of me? That she doesn't care about me the way I care about her?"

"Bullshit."

"Bullshit what?" Layne asked as Kayla stepped into the hallway and glared at him, her arms crossed defensively.

"Everything okay, babe?" Kayla asked Willow.

Willow turned around. "Everything's fine. I'll be back inside in a minute. Love you." She turned to Layne as Kayla closed their door. "Taylor's afraid of Jordan swooping in here tomorrow and seducing you."

"That's crazy. I would n—"

"I didn't say it was a rational fear." Willow leaned against the wall with him. "I've broken her trust to tell you what's going on. Now, get your ass back in there and tell her you love her. Because you do, don't you?"

Layne ran his fingers through his hair and tilted his head back. "Yes," he said through gritted teeth. "But it doesn't matter if she doesn't feel the same."

Willow walked to her door. "It matters," she said, turning back to Layne. "She told me she has feelings for you, too, which was a big deal for her—trusting me with that. Everyone she's ever loved has hurt her. She needs you to fight for her. Be the knight in shining armor little girls dream about."

Frustrated that Taylor could open up to Willow but not him, Layne shook his head and scoffed. "Are all you women crazy with this knight in shining armor crap?"

Willow chuckled. "Well, in my case, it was a dream about a maiden, but yeah, we're all crazy. But don't act like you don't want to be that for her. Be her hero, Layne. Don't give up. She loves you. She just isn't ready to tell you yet, and she's scared to death of getting hurt again."

Layne sighed. Women were too complicated sometimes, but Willow made sense.

"And Layne..."

"Yeah?"

"If you hurt her, I swear I'll break all your fingers."

"I won't," he said before going back to Taylor's apartment. He crept into her bedroom and stood outside the bathroom with his hand resting on the door as he listened to Taylor sob. He wanted nothing more than to go in and hold her, but instead, he waited on Taylor's bed for her come out on her own.

Taylor sat on the bathroom floor and cried for her sixteen-year-old self and everything that had happened to her since then. Her face was a streaked mess of running mascara and eyeliner when she looked in the mirror. She wondered why her love life was such a disaster as she washed her face and closed her eyes to calm down. After a long, hot shower, her face looked better when she glanced in the mirror again, but her eyes were still puffy. Jordan's impending visit was nerve-wracking. Whenever Taylor saw her sister, she remembered the ice-cold look of satisfaction on Jordan's face when she had caught her on top of Michael all those years ago.

But Layne and Michael weren't the same, were they? Layne would resist Jordan's advances, right? *Damn it,* she thought, *why did I just push him away? Is it too late?* Taylor had to talk to Layne and apologize for being crazy.

She ran out of her bathroom and found Layne curled up on her bed asleep. He was lying on his side with his arms crossed over his chest, his hair hanging over his shoulder. He had meant it when he said he didn't want to leave. Watching Layne sleeping so peacefully made Taylor want so much more, despite the unwieldy voice in her head screaming at her to stop. She crawled beside him and woke him by caressing his cheek.

"You're still here," she said.

"I had to know you were okay." He brushed Taylor's hair out of her face. There was an uncomfortably long silence before Layne spoke again. "Taylor, if you don't have feelings for me, I promise I'll leave, and I won't bother you again."

Taylor looked at his pleading eyes and feared she would lose him if she didn't say something. It was her last chance with him. "Don't go," she whispered. "I was coming to find you."

"You were?"

"I'm sorry."

"Don't be sorry; be honest." Tears formed in his eyes.

"I'm scared, Layne."

"Of me?"

"I don't want to get hurt again," she said as tears filled her eyes. She quickly wiped them away. "I don't think my heart can take it. And I don't want to hurt you."

"Baby, you're already hurting, or you wouldn't be crying right now." Layne pulled Taylor back into his arms, but this time she didn't pull away. "I'm not some stupid high school boy trying to screw you over so I can screw your sister. I know how I feel, and I know what I want. I want to be with you—only you. And you never have to cry alone, not when you have me. You have me, Taylor. I won't hurt you, I promise."

"How can you promise me that?"

Layne laughed and wiped his eyes. "Do you really not know?" He raised Taylor's chin until their eyes met. "Taylor, I'm in love with you."

Taylor had only a moment to decide which fear was greater— losing Layne or having him.

Layne kissed Taylor's forehead. "Just tell me. Do you have feelings for me?"

She looked into his glassy eyes and trusted his sincerity. "Yes," she said before falling into his arms.

Layne embraced Taylor and exhaled. "We don't have to label anything tonight. I just want to hold you."

"I need you," Taylor said through her tears, clinging to Layne as tightly as she could. Everything would be okay as long as she had his love.

Layne kissed Taylor so softly and timidly, it reminded her of her first off-screen kiss at fifteen. She cried with him as they passionately made love, Layne whispering "I love you" whenever their lips parted. Jordan would complicate everything when she arrived the next day, but that night, there was nowhere Taylor would have rather been than in Layne's arms.

chapter 25

Monday, June 6, 2016

A slamming door startled Layne, and immediately, Taylor shook his shoulder. The light from the windows stung his eyes as he struggled to get untangled from the sheets. He pulled a pillow over his face for a few more seconds of darkness. "It's too early." His head ached from their emotional night.

"Someone's in my apartment," Taylor whispered. "We left the door unlocked."

Layne sprang up in bed. "Stay here," he said, pushing Taylor behind him. He looked around Taylor's bedroom, searching for anything that could be used as a weapon if needed, and realized they were both still naked. He also remembered that the whole building was locked.

Just then, Jordan appeared in the doorway, her long blond hair pulled back in a messy bun with sunglasses resting on top of her head. She crossed her arms and glared at them. "Oh, looks like I got here a bit too early," she said.

"How did you get in here without ringing the buzzer?" Taylor asked, pulling a shirt over her head.

"I got here when your neighbor was leaving, some tiny woman with blah hair," Jordan said, glaring at Layne. "Who the hell are you?"

Layne looked at Taylor before answering. She appeared fragile as she sat there, wringing the blanket in her hands. "I'm Layne."

"Who?" Jordan asked, smirking at Taylor. "The guy from the beach? Or wait, was it someone else on the beach with you Saturday night, Taylor? Sorry, this is awkward."

Everything about Jordan infuriated Layne, especially the way she talked to Taylor. And how the hell did she know about the beach? "I'm Layne Stallings," he said. "Taylor's boyfriend."

"Stallings? Any relation to Brandon Stallings? I can't wait to see him again on set today."

"You just did. I went by Brandon when I was in Backdraft."

"God, what happened to you?" Jordan asked with a gasp as she studied Layne. "You look so different than I remember you."

"And you must be Jordan," Layne said as Taylor rested her head on his back. "I vaguely recall meeting you once. I don't remember much about it."

Jordan laughed. "Everyone knows who I am," she said. "People always remember meeting me."

"You look different in person. Those makeup artists can work wonders, huh?"

Jordan's mouth dropped open. "Taylor," she said. "Your boyfriend's rude. Are you going to let him talk to me that way?"

Layne whispered into Taylor's ear. "Don't let her get to you." He kissed Taylor on the cheek before he looked at Jordan. "Would you mind leaving the room so I can get dressed?"

Jordan sneered. "It's not like you have anything I haven't seen before." Layne had no doubt it was true.

"Jordan," Taylor said. "Please, just give us a minute."

Jordan rolled her eyes and closed the bedroom door behind her. Layne got up and put on his clothes while Taylor put on a pair of pajama pants. After they got dressed, Taylor walked Layne to the door, where he hugged and kissed her while Jordan scowled at them.

Jordan turned to Taylor after Layne had left. "I don't like him at all," she said. "What an asshole."

I don't like him either, Taylor thought, brushing her fingers across her lips. *I'm in love with him.*

"You should've told me he was your boyfriend when I texted you," Jordan continued. "I think you purposely try to make me embarrass myself."

Taylor sighed. "I told you he was seeing someone," she said. "I don't want to fight with you. I'm exhausted. I'm going to take a shower, then we'll go. I won't be long."

Jordan plopped down on the couch. "Do you expect me to sleep on this piece of shit?"

"You can have my bed."

"After you change the sheets."

"Of course. I have a brand-new set just for you."

"You should really get some new furniture, Taylor," she said, shifting around on the couch. "You live like you don't have any money at all."

There was no point responding because it wouldn't make a difference. Jordan would always find something to complain about.

Later, Taylor found Layne near the food table on set while Jordan was getting prepped for her scenes. He was dressed in black jeans and a concert t-shirt—so sexy that Taylor stopped breathing when she saw him. Layne winked at her and motioned for her to come over.

Taylor chuckled as she reached Layne. "You really pissed off Jordan. I don't think I'll ever forget the look on her face. She bitched about what an asshole you were the whole way here."

Layne took a deep breath. "Glad I made an impression," he said, resting his hand on Taylor's shoulder. "I'm sorry, but it pissed me off the way she talked to you. I probably shouldn't have insulted her or told her I was your boyfriend when we hadn't finished our talk about that."

"I'm sorry I was such a spaz about everything. Something happened with Jordan yesterday, and it freaked me out."

"It's alright. What happened?"

"She texted me about her plans to hook up with Brandon Stallings, and it upset me. The thought of losing you, especially to her, felt like déjà vu."

Layne hugged Taylor. "Baby, that would never happen, even if you weren't my...wait, you are my girlfriend, right?" He grinned, pulling her close enough to kiss.

"I'm good with that label." Taylor wrapped her arms around Layne's neck and kissed him. Having him for a boyfriend was how it always should have been.

The production crew clapped and whistled before someone yelled, "Guys, get a room!"

Taylor pulled away. "Sorry!" she said, blushing profusely.

Layne didn't seem upset at all. He was still smiling when they started rehearsal.

From her makeup chair, Jordan watched the exchange between her sister and Brandon Stallings. As Jordan snapped a photo of them with her phone, the makeup artist gave her a funny look.

She turned on her best smile. "Isn't it sweet that my baby sister is in love?" Jordan asked. It seemed to be enough of an explanation.

"Wait till you hear them," the artist said. "Everything around here stops when they're singing. I've never heard two people sing so well together. I didn't realize they were a couple since they were discreet until today."

"Please hurry," Jordan said curtly. "I don't want the director yelling at you for making me late."

The artist went back to work, covering the mild acne on Jordan's chin.

Brandon was nothing like Jordan remembered. Ten years ago, he'd looked a lot like Chase with blond hair and green eyes. Now, she knew Brandon, *Layne*, had never been a true blond since he didn't seem like the type of guy who would color his hair now, considering his new grungy look. The drab brown was his natural hair color.

The crew and all the other actors nearby watched in silent awe as Layne and Taylor sang together. Jordan's stare could have burned a hole through the camera lens had she looked at it directly. Taylor and Layne had more natural chemistry than Jordan did with the lead actor, Blake. Jordan and Blake had attempted to date to help with the publicity after the first installment in the trilogy, but Blake wasn't feeling it and wanted to be just friends. Jordan wasn't used to that kind of rejection. Not since Michael had she been so openly rejected.

At the urging of the producers, Jordan and Blake had agreed to pretend to be in a relationship to help with the publicity for the premiere of the final installment in the fall and all the coverage leading up to it. A public breakup afterward would keep the attention on the actors long enough to help with download and DVD sales.

Even though the guy she'd envisioned starting a fling with didn't exist, Jordan decided then her next conquest would be Layne. It might be enough to get Chase back, and since the relationship seemed new, Taylor would bounce back like she had before—straight into someone else's bed.

chapter 26

The guitar music coming from Layne's apartment was the same melody of the song he'd sung on the beach. Taylor closed her eyes, letting the music envelop her and waited until it stopped before she knocked on the door.

Layne smiled as he opened the door. "I thought you'd be too freaked out to be around me tonight." He grabbed Taylor and pulled her into his apartment, giving her a quick kiss. "You weren't home earlier."

"I was out with Jordan helping her get prepped for another photo shoot for a magazine. I just now got home. She and Blake are going to a press event, and I've had my limit of her today, and him. He hit on me."

"What?" Layne clenched his teeth as he spoke.

Taylor sat on the couch. "It was this afternoon when I was looking for Jordan. I saw Blake first, and he told me he wished I had the lead role instead of Jordan. He said the kissing scenes would be a lot easier with me and tried to touch my face. He hasn't ever talked to me like that before. It was weird. I think he was the only person who didn't know about you and me by then."

"Do I need to have a chat with him?"

Taylor leaned over and kissed Layne. "I told him to back off because I have a boyfriend."

Layne pursed his lips. "So, you haven't been online today, have you?"

"No," she said. "What's going on?"

Layne got out his laptop and pulled up an article for Taylor. The headline read: "Exclusive: Backdraft's Brandon Stallings and former child star Taylor Hoffman—Total PDA on the *Awake* set." Below it was a photo of Layne and Taylor kissing near the food table.

"Shit!" Taylor said as she took the laptop from Layne, suddenly feeling sick to her stomach. "So much for privacy."

"Embarrassed to be seen with me?" Layne joked.

"No, it's not that. I just hoped to leave my old name behind. I thought you wanted that too."

"Yeah, but now this is out there. It goes on to say stuff about Jordan."

"Jordan! She did this. She took the photo."

"Why would she do that?"

"More publicity. She's counting on all the buzz about you in the tabloids lately, and now she's throwing in stuff about me since no one knew I'd changed my last name for the credits in the first two movies."

"I guess everyone knows now."

Taylor sighed. "There's already a lot of stuff about me online. I looked a few days ago. A lot of speculation and 'whatever happened to Jordan's sister?' I know I shouldn't have, but I read some of the comments. A lot of people think I got strung out on drugs and others guessed correctly that I took a break. Several people wrote they hoped I would sing again. I didn't think so many people cared what happened to me."

"Of course, they do," Layne said. "You're amazing."

Taylor skimmed the article, which revealed her voice-over work for the previous two *Awake* movies and also that she had changed her appearance since her role on *The Spectacular Smiths*. Thanks to the "insider source," the article also revealed secrets about Layne's changes and alluded to his relationship with Taylor. "Insider? It had to be Jordan. I doubt anyone else on the crew cared. My God! They have links to videos of Jordan and me dancing together on the show."

"A lot of people care," Layne said. "There are tons of comments saying us being together is the best thing ever. I think we could use this to our advantage. We could release a duet online and include it on both solo albums. This could be just the push we need. Let's turn Jordan's own game against her. I know you wanted your music to speak for itself, but this momentum will allow a lot more people to discover how incredible you are."

"We don't have a song to sing together," Taylor said. "And I don't know when I'll be ready to release an album. I don't feel like any of my songs are done yet, or good enough."

"We'll write one or release a cover," Layne said. "I've read your lyrics. They're good enough, I promise."

"You really think I can do it?"

"I know you can," Layne said. "We can. Don't let fear stop you anymore."

Taylor hugged Layne. "I have to work on one fear at a time," she said. "I don't think I can let go of another one today."

Layne wrapped his arms around Taylor. "Baby steps," he said. "I want to show you something, but you have to try not to freak out about it." He took the laptop from Taylor and started a video for her.

Taylor heard the opening notes for "Leather and Lace" exactly how the karaoke machine had played it the night of their first date. She watched the video of them singing that someone had taken with their phone. "We do sound good together," she said. "Who took this?"

"Someone in the crowd recorded us and uploaded it today. I think it's great. We could probably get the rights to release a studio version."

Taylor stared at the number of views in disbelief. "Is this right? In the last five hours, the video has been viewed more than half a million times. Are you kidding me?"

"Baby, we couldn't ask for better publicity."

"I guess not." Taylor watched the rest of the video, mainly focusing on Layne. Even when he wasn't singing, he had looked at her with awe and love. It was before Taylor knew Layne loved her. Had he already known then, after their first date?

"Will you stay here with me tonight?" Layne asked. "We can work on our songs and get them ready for the next songwriter's night."

Taylor and Layne had worked on basic melodies for each of their songs and were ready for bed when someone stumbling and cursing in the hallway interrupted them.

Layne got up and opened his door. "Taylor," he said. "It's Jordan. I think she's drunk."

Taylor joined him at the door and looked out at her sister sprawled out on the floor in the hallway. For a moment, she imagined her mother lying there. "Shit," she muttered.

Mr. Cosney came up the stairs. "I thought this mess might belong to you, Taylor," he said. "She's your sister, right?"

"Yes," Taylor said. "Though I'm not sure I want to claim her right now."

"She said she was staying with you for a couple of weeks. I just wanted to make sure she got up here in one piece. I had to cut her off when she got belligerent with another customer."

"Thanks," Taylor said. Mr. Cosney went back downstairs, and she turned to Layne. "Will you help me get her inside?"

Layne dragged Jordan to Taylor's bed.

"You're my shining armor guy—my knight," Jordan stammered as Layne straightened her legs on the bed. Taylor removed her shoes. "Where's my goodnight kiss?"

"Not happening," Layne said. "Sleep it off."

Taylor looked at Jordan with disgust, then turned to Layne. "I shouldn't leave her alone. I'll see you tomorrow."

Layne glanced at Jordan. "Call me if you need anything," he said. "Do you have stuff to give her to fight the hangover?"

"Yeah," Taylor said. "I'll give it to her after she gets done puking. Should be soon by the looks of her."

Jordan got sick within an hour of Layne leaving. Taylor sat on the bathroom floor holding her sister's hair back. "God, Jordan, why do you do this to yourself?"

"Yeah, my slutty sister is judging me."

"Slutty? How the hell would you even know? I haven't seen you in months. Have you been spying on me?"

"Spying? I just came by to see you at the bar a few times when I was passing through. You were always leaving with a different guy."

Taylor flushed the toilet and handed Jordan a wet washcloth. "You're one to talk, and I'm not the one puking my guts up," she said. "You have everything." She couldn't tell if her sister was laughing or crying when she spoke again.

"Everything? Ha! I didn't get it. I have nothing left after this."

"Didn't get what? What are you talking about?"

"The audition. They don't want me."

"You'll get the next one," Taylor said. "You can't be in every movie. You could always try television again." She took the hair tie off her wrist and used it to pull back Jordan's hair in preparation for the next round.

"That was the next one. Three—three times they didn't want me. Chase..." she sobbed. "And Dad doesn't want me."

All Taylor could do was sit and wait for it to end. She was dumbfounded as she watched her sister. These weren't the tears of the actress Jordan or the lying, manipulative Jordan, they were real tears—the first Taylor had seen.

Taylor helped Jordan back to bed where she made her take some pain relievers and drink a glass of water.

"I'm empty…everything comes so easy to you," Jordan said.

"No, it doesn't." Taylor sat down beside her sister and removed the hair tie, combing her fingers through Jordan's hair.

"I miss Chase…"

For the first time in their lives, Taylor pitied Jordan. She'd never seen her sister so vulnerable and out of control before. "Jordan, I'm sorry. Maybe you can get him back."

"The baby…gone."

Baby? What baby? "Jordan, what are you talking about? Are you pregnant?"

"No!" Jordan cried. "I'm all alone. You think you're better than me. You sing…beautiful…you have Chase—no, Layne. I screwed up with Chase…love…my fault you're a slut. Michael didn't want me. He said your name."

Taylor clenched her teeth. "Shut up," she said as she stood up. "I'm done listening to you tonight."

Jordan turned over and squeezed the pillow. "I killed Mom," she murmured before closing her eyes.

Taylor violently shook her sister, all her pity gone. "Wake up, Jordan!"

"Leave me alone…so tired."

"What the fuck is wrong with you? You didn't kill Mom; she killed herself by snorting poison into her body. The same thing will happen to you if you don't stop all this bullshit! You have everything, and you're pissing it all away!"

"Go away, Taylor!" Jordan yelled, pulling a pillow over her face. "Go be perfect somewhere else! I hate you!"

"I'm not perfect," Taylor growled as she left her room and slammed the door. She'd had enough of taking care of drunk people. Her mother had never appreciated it either.

217

Layne seemed surprised by Taylor's reappearance at his door. "I thought you'd still be babysitting," he said as he let her inside.

"I don't think she has anything left inside her. She's passed out in my bed."

"You think she'll be okay by herself?"

"She'll have to be," Taylor said. "I don't want to be around her. She said she hated me and told me to go away, so I did. Can I still sleep here?"

"Anytime you want," Layne said, pulling Taylor onto the couch with him.

"She talked about Chase, saying she missed him and screwed up everything with him. Do you know anything about that?"

"I knew they were seeing each other and that he loved her. That's what Noah said the other night. I wasn't really around them during our downtime. I always went back home to visit my family."

"She said something else...about a baby. She said the baby was gone when she was talking about Chase. She wasn't making much sense."

"Maybe she was," Layne said. "People don't usually lie when they're that drunk. Could Jordan have been pregnant with Chase's baby?"

"There was a long time when she and I didn't speak, but I don't think she could have kept a whole pregnancy secret since she was always in the public eye."

"She could've had a miscarriage or a private abortion. The doctors who treated her wouldn't have been able to talk about it."

"I guess it's possible."

"You can ask her when she's sober. What would you do?"

The question seemed to hang in the air above Taylor's head. What would she do? "I'm so tired, can we just go to bed now?" she asked.

Later, wrapped in Layne's arms, Taylor thought about his question again. Through all the guys she'd been with, she'd never considered what she would do if she got pregnant. The idea of having a baby on her own terrified her. The idea of being responsible for another life at all sent chills down her spine. She loved Layne, but he didn't want children either, so how would he feel about an unplanned baby? Taylor turned to Layne and woke him.

"What's wrong, babe?" he asked.

"I can't sleep. I keep thinking about what you asked me earlier, about what I'd do if I got pregnant."

"I thought you didn't want kids?" Layne sat up in bed and rubbed Taylor's arms.

"I don't, but it's all hypothetical. You said you don't want any either."

"I don't see myself with kids with the kind of lifestyle I want. We've always been careful, every single time, and you're on the pill. I don't think we have anything to worry about."

"Yeah, but what if? What if I got pregnant anyway despite all our precautions?"

Layne smoothed Taylor's hair and kissed her. "I would be a man and support you and be a father to our baby. If you didn't want to, I would support you through that too."

"Sorry I woke you; I just couldn't sleep thinking about it."

Layne kissed Taylor on the tip of her nose. "Stop apologizing to me so much. Wake me up whenever you need to talk. I love having you here with me. I know we haven't known each other very long, but we've gotten a lot of mileage out of these late-night conversations in my bed. I missed you when you weren't here on Friday."

"I missed you too."

"I know you're still scared, and I am too." Layne pressed his fingers against Taylor's lips to keep her from speaking. "It's okay; I get it. I pushed you to admit feelings you weren't ready for and asked for a relationship—a serious one." He moved his fingers and kissed her. "There's nothing your sister or anyone else can do to take my mind off us. I will never cheat on you."

Taylor rolled over and pulled Layne's arms around her. "I'm less afraid with you, Layne." He held her tightly while he drifted off to sleep again. Still unable to sleep, Taylor got up and went back to her apartment to check on Jordan. She looked down at the mess of her sister and wondered how the two of them got where they were. What had changed in Jordan to make her so hateful? But Taylor had uttered "I hate you" first. She still felt the sharpness of the words on her tongue mostly because she had meant every word at the time. What would their mother have thought? Would she have ever beaten her addiction and helped Jordan? Taylor would never know.

2001

At Jordan's tenth birthday party, Taylor watched with awe as her big sister sat surrounded by more than a dozen other kids who were all child actors involved with their show.

Jordan scanned the room and smiled when her eyes met Taylor's. "Sis!" she called. "Come up here and sit by me."

Taylor eagerly ran to the front of the room. "Happy Birthday, Jordan!"

"Help me blow out my candles, Taylor," Jordan said. "I can't do it without you."

After blowing out the candles, Taylor looked at her sister with admiration. "You're my best friend, Jordan," she said. "Forever."

"You're my best friend too," Jordan said as she hugged Taylor.

Their mother watched her girls closely because as she had told them, her beautiful roses were admired by everyone. Mr. Hoffman was in the back of the room, clearly more interested in his phone call than his own daughter's party. He did the same thing during Taylor's party, which her mother had missed due to a supposed "stomach flu." Taylor knew it was really because her mother had drunk too much of her grown-up drink the night before. After that, Taylor figured the only person she could count on was her big sister.

After ensuring her sister was still breathing, Taylor pulled Jordan's broken bracelet out of the dresser drawer and placed it on the nightstand. She went back to Layne's apartment and found him in the living room.

"Is she okay?" he asked.

"She's still passed out." Taylor grabbed Layne's hand and led him back to the bedroom.

"I didn't realize what an insomniac you were," he said. "I woke up, and you weren't here."

"Only since you and me. I've had a lot on my mind." Taylor stretched out on the bed beside Layne. "I didn't mean to wake you again."

"It's fine. I sleep better when you're here with me. Until the night we spent together after you kicked me, it had been a few months since I'd gotten a full night's sleep."

"Why?"

"I switched anxiety meds recently, and this one makes it hard for me to sleep sometimes. I'm still getting used to it."

Ashamed she hadn't been a better friend to Layne, Taylor sat up and leaned against the wall. "I didn't know…"

Layne laid his head in her lap. "No one knows," he said. "You're the only person I trust enough to tell."

"Not even your family? Or your ex-girlfriend?"

"They don't know about the panic attacks either. You're the only non-medical person who knows. I thought it was just stage fright at first, but even after I'd left the band and finished college, there were still times when I felt like I was on the verge of freaking out for no apparent reason. About six months ago, I got home from a composing job that went well, but I felt like my throat was closing up. I didn't leave my house for a week trying to chill out. After that, I found out I passed the audition for the replacement guitarist for *Awake* and figured I'd better get my shit together."

Taylor smoothed Layne's hair. "You seem like you have the type of family who would understand."

"My parents are great, really, but they were raised with more of a 'suck it up' attitude about mental stuff. I was too embarrassed to tell them when I was a teenager. I can't tell Christina either because I don't think she can keep a secret from them."

"Is the medicine helping?"

"This one is," Layne said. "The first one made me jumpy and nauseous. Being with you helps too. I feel like I can talk to you, like I've known you my whole life."

"What you said last night, when did you know?"

Layne chuckled. "Like the exact moment?" he asked as sat up beside Taylor. "Why is that important?"

"Because you are."

Layne caressed Taylor's cheek and kissed her. "I knew I had feelings for you from the moment we first kissed. And then I knew for sure it was love when we were on the beach at your dad's house."

Saying "I love you" had come easily with Michael, back when Taylor was young and dreamy. On her sixteenth birthday, they had gone for a walk and stopped underneath a tree. There, Michael kissed Taylor and told her he loved her. As effortlessly as he uttered the words, Taylor had said them back. How could such serious words come so easily at sixteen, but not now at twenty-three? Still, she wanted to say something to Layne. The beach was a turning point for her too. "I think that's when I knew too," she said.

Layne smiled and began kissing Taylor all over. She hadn't told him she loved him, but it seemed to be close enough for Layne. "I know we have to be up for work soon," he said. "But I want you so bad right now."

"Sleep's highly overrated," Taylor said, returning Layne's affection.

chapter 27

Tuesday, June 7, 2016

Sprawled out on Taylor's bed, Jordan woke with her head pounding. "Taylor?" she called. Nothing. Her sister had ditched her. She grabbed a pain reliever bottle from the nightstand, knocking over a small trash can on the bed in the process. She shook out two tablets and reached for a bottle of water, quickly swallowing the pills before they could dissolve on her tongue. It was just like Taylor to buy the cheap stuff. Something shiny on the nightstand caught the light from the window. Jordan reached for it and was surprised to find her own bracelet, the clasp broken. How had it ended up in Taylor's apartment?

Parts of the previous evening began taking shape in her mind. She'd been out with Blake again. After all the smiles and drinks, she'd gone back to his hotel room with him, and once again, he rejected her in favor of the mini-bar because he said kissing her felt like kissing his sister.

Jordan didn't care that much about Blake, but once he'd finished a few drinks with a little something extra she mixed in to help him relax, he responded differently the next time she kissed him until he passed out from being too drunk in the first place. Frustrated and lonely, Jordan had returned to the Mocking Bird. She couldn't recall how she got inside Taylor's apartment but could tell by the taste in her mouth she'd vomited a lot.

The apartment door slammed, and soon Taylor was standing at the foot of the bed. "I see you're still alive," she said.

"I don't have to be on set until noon," Jordan said. "Where were you last night?"

"Well, I was up half the night checking on you and holding your hair while you puked. It wasn't how I wanted to spend my evening. I thought you would have outgrown all the partying since you're almost twenty-five."

"It's not like you stayed here with me."

"I came back to check on you!" Taylor yelled, slamming her hand against the doorway and sending ripples of pain through Jordan's head. "Don't act like this is my fault for not going to the press event with you. You're old enough you shouldn't need a babysitter."

"I had a date with Blake, remember? We hooked up in his hotel room last night."

"Yeah, before you came back and drank yourself stupid downstairs? He didn't want you to stay?"

"He and I have an understanding," Jordan said.

"Does it include him hitting on me yesterday?"

"I'm sure you just misread his signals. He's not into you."

"Blake's not that complex. The only signals he sent were sleazy." Taylor turned away from Jordan's scowl. "I don't want to talk about him anymore. Some of us have to be on set early. I just want to get dressed and get out of here."

"You should really consider getting a better place so you can have a guest suite."

Taylor glared at Jordan. "If you don't like the accommodations, you can pay for a room down at the Palisades Hotel. I'm sure they'll be happy to serve a celebrity of your status."

"You're just jealous," Jordan muttered as Taylor closed the bathroom door.

When Taylor came out of the bathroom, Jordan rolled over to face her. "You should shower," Taylor said, covering her nose. "You smell like puke and bourbon."

"I'll look my best when I get on set. I always do. Hey, how did you get my bracelet?"

"It was mixed up with Mom's stuff. I figured it broke when you were visiting her."

"Yeah, I was wearing it that night," Jordan said.

Taylor sat on the edge of the bed. "Are you on drugs again?" she asked. "Do you need help?"

Jordan started laughing. "You're crazy," she said. "I'm fine."

"Whatever."

She has no idea what it's like to be me, Jordan thought. *I was the only person with the courage to end our mother's suffering.* The doctors and Taylor would have let her live as a vegetable forever, prolonging the inevitable.

There was so much pressure to be perfect. Perfect skin, perfect body, perfect boyfriend. Taylor wasn't even trying and had all those things. She'd never had to try. And now she was rubbing her boyfriend in Jordan's face again.

Blake avoided Jordan on set until it was time for them to shoot scenes together. She finally caught up with him at the door to his trailer.

"Why are you avoiding me?" she asked. "You know we still have to convince the press we're in a relationship, don't you?"

"I'm looking forward to the public breakup after the movie's finished," he said. "What the hell kind of drink did you give me last night? I woke up naked and hungover."

"You got drunk and put the moves on me, but then couldn't rise to the occasion," Jordan said. "Don't be embarrassed. I hear it happens to all guys at some point—I've just never seen it happen."

Blake glared at her. "I guess it was a reaction to you, then," he said. "Because it's never happened to me before."

"Asshole." Jordan turned away from him and walked back to her own trailer. *He has no idea what he's missing,* she thought.

She glanced over at the set and saw Taylor and Layne walking out in the field. Layne held Taylor's hand. They sat together near the base of a tree and kissed. The whole thing made Jordan feel sick, especially when she noticed they were in costumes, and a cameraman was filming them.

For the next two weeks, Jordan stayed at Taylor's apartment, only seeing her sister on set and when she arrived in the mornings to get clothes. Taylor stayed distant but remained cordial on set. She didn't talk to Jordan at all any other time. Jordan wondered what she might have said to Taylor when she was drunk. It was the most she'd drunk at one time in months. All the preoccupation with Taylor caused her to miss her marks and forget lines more often than she had in the past. The worst part was when the director yelled at her in front of everyone. He told her she was lucky it was the last movie and the last day of filming because he never wanted to work with her again due to her lack of professionalism.

Blake seemed happier the more Jordan messed things up during their last day of filming. His performances were perfect, the best work he'd done according to the director. *Suck-up,* Jordan thought. *Neither one of them would be known for anything if it wasn't for me starring in these movies.*

Jordan caught up with Taylor at the wrap party later that evening. "Why are you being such a bitch?" she asked.

"I figured it was a language you'd understand," Taylor said as she crossed her arms, her eyes cold and apathetic.

"Why didn't you say anything when the director was being such an asshole to me? We're sisters. You're supposed to have my back."

Taylor scoffed. "Are you kidding me?" she asked. "Who do you think taught me how to be a sister? And when you came home drunk the first night you stayed at my apartment, you told me how much you hate me. I've sung for you, been your assistant when no one else would, let you stay in my apartment this whole time. What more do you want from me?"

"Appreciation."

"Appreciation?"

"I'm the one who got you this job!" Jordan exclaimed. How could her sister be so blind? Several people turned to look at them.

"Jordan, you got me the audition," Taylor said, speaking quietly. "I got the job on my own. You weren't as famous then as you are now. But just because you're famous doesn't mean you can treat people like shit. I'm not taking it anymore."

"Yeah, you're all confident now when you're sleeping in some guy's bed. It was the same way with Michael."

"Don't you dare mention him!" Taylor yelled.

All eyes were on them now. Blood rushed to Jordan's cheeks. She stepped forward and got in Taylor's face. "You'll only be able to ride on Layne's fame for so long until he dumps you, and then you'll be begging to come back and ride on mine."

"Don't count on it," Taylor said as she walked away. She crossed the room to where Layne was speaking to some of the crew members and whispered something in his ear. He looked at Jordan then back at Taylor and nodded. Taylor spoke to the crew before Layne took her hand and led her out of the room. He was always holding her hand and kissing her in front of other people. *It's disgusting*, Jordan thought.

chapter 28

Friday, June 24, 2016

Despite how close she felt to Layne, Taylor still hadn't told him she loved him. Each time she tried to get the words out, an invisible force came out of nowhere threatening to close her throat and cut off her air. It was nothing Layne had done wrong; something deep inside Taylor still made her afraid to tell him how she felt. Layne didn't seem bothered by it, but Taylor noticed he hadn't said he loved her again since the first night he'd admitted it to her. Still, though, he showed her with the way he reached for her hand when they went for walks, their late-night conversations in his bed, the way he held her after they'd made love, and the way he kissed her like it was the first time every time.

Late at night, Taylor would slip out of bed long enough to grab her notebook and pour her heart out with all the thoughts she couldn't say to Layne in any other way. She watched him work on his song and found herself humming along to the melody as Layne strummed his guitar, whispering the words.

By the next songwriter's showcase, they were ready to debut their songs and had agreed to wait until the big night to hear each other's songs in their entirety. They had arranged to have the standard house band come back for their performances by paying them for the whole evening and rehearsal the night before.

On the night of the showcase, Christina was in the crowd. She came up to the area behind the stage, greeted Taylor, and wished Layne luck.

"Don't hate me," Christina said to Layne. She pointed to a table near the door where a man and woman, who looked to be in their early sixties, were seated. The woman waved fervently at Layne.

"Mom and Dad are here," Layne said, leaning his forehead on Taylor's shoulder, letting his hair cover his face.

"It just slipped out that you were performing tonight," Christina said. "I'm sorry."

Layne took Taylor's hand. "Come on," he said. "Now's as good of a time as any."

A lump rose in Taylor's throat. She wasn't prepared to meet his parents right before performing her song, which would tell Layne things she hadn't been able to say before.

Layne's parents stood up and embraced him as he reached their table.

"We're so excited about hearing your song, Brandon," his mother said. "Sorry, *Layne*. I'm just so happy you invited us."

Layne glanced at his sister, who shrugged her shoulders and mouthed, "What?"

"Of course, Mom, I wouldn't want you to miss this. I also want you to meet my girlfriend." Layne pulled Taylor in front of him. "Taylor, this is my mom, Pamela, and my dad, David."

"Hi," Taylor said shyly as she took David's outstretched hand. "It's nice to meet you both."

"Oh, honey," Pamela said, pulling Taylor into a hug and rocking her back and forth. "I'm thrilled to meet you. Are you singing tonight too?" Her hair smelled like sunflowers.

"Yes, ma'am," Taylor said. "I'm the opener tonight."

"None of this 'ma'am' nonsense. Call me Pam."

"Thank you, Pam," Taylor said.

"Christina and I used to watch you on TV," David said. "I watched you grow up with my own kids. You've got some serious talent."

"Thank you, sir." Taylor beamed at Layne. "So does your son."

"We know," Layne's parents said in unison.

"And it's David," David said to Taylor.

"We have to get ready," Taylor said. "The show starts soon." She led their way back to where their guitars were waiting.

"I hope that wasn't too brutal," Layne said.

"Not at all," Taylor said. "Now, I'm just so nervous, I feel like I'm going to throw up. I'm sure it'll pass, or I'll make an ass of myself and puke all over the microphone."

"Hey," Layne said as he grabbed Taylor's shoulders. "You're going to be amazing out there. I'm the one who's nervous having to follow you."

"You can go first…"

"Not a chance. This is your show. You're the star. Now go kick some songwriting ass. I'm ready to hear the rest of your song."

Taylor looked out at the packed crowd. Her hands were clammy as she gripped the microphone. She took a deep breath, exhaled slowly, and looked at Layne one last time before turning the mic on. "Thank you, everyone, for coming out to support us independent songwriters," she said, silently willing herself to not throw up. "This isn't my first time singing on this stage, but it's my debut performance of a song I wrote. I hope you all like it."

As the cheers died down, Taylor focused on Willow's smiling face. "It's called 'Love me more,' and it's dedicated to my amazing and talented boyfriend who's supported me through the whole process of writing it and with countless other things since I met him." She turned to Layne, who was looking at her as if no one else were in the room. "Layne, thank you for helping me find the courage to get up here, and thank you for just being who you are."

Taylor started playing her guitar and sang her message to Layne.

If you could love me more
I think I'd run away
I never thought that I would feel this way—again
But I never want to leave this place
I think so every time I see your face—I do
I do
I do—

Baby, if you're nice
I'll let you come inside
Into this secret place where I go to hide
I'm so afraid with every breath I take
There's no one else who makes me feel this way—like you
Like you
Like you—

If you could love me more
I think I'd run away
I never thought that I would feel this way—again
There's something with us that I can't replace
I think so every time I see your face—I do
I do
I do—

Baby, please don't go
I've been so alone
You're the only one who feels like home
There is nothing left for me to say
I'd do so much if I could make you stay—I would
I would
I would—

If you could love me more
I'd never run away
I never thought that I would feel this way—again
You're the only one worth fighting for
'Cause no one else will ever know me more—than you
Than you
Than you—

There's nowhere left to hide
In this place of mine
I never knew exactly what I'd find
There is nothing left for me to say
I'll love you more with every single day—I will
I will
I will—

If you could love me more
I'd never run away
I never thought that I would feel this way—again
There's nothing in this world that I wouldn't do
If in the end, I'd still end up with you—again
There is nothing left for me to lose
It all comes down to, baby, I love you—I do
I do
Love you—

If you could love me more

After she finished her song, Taylor felt an incredible sense of empowerment. She closed her eyes and bathed in the crowd's applause before she introduced Layne as the next performer.

"Wow," Layne said to the crowd. His hands were trembling as he gripped the microphone "I'm not sure if I can follow that performance. Now, this amazing band behind me has been so good to rehearse with me, but I've decided this song is meant to be soft, just me and my guitar, so I've asked them to drop out and just let me sing it myself. I haven't named the song, so maybe you all can help me."

As Taylor tried to leave the stage with the band, Layne grabbed her hand to stop her. "Taylor, please stay because this song is for you," he said into the mic. "When you helped me work on it, I told you it was a generic love song, but that's not true. It was always about you. I started writing it while we were getting to know each other and finished it when I realized I was in love with you."

Taylor tried to conceal her own trembling hands. She scanned the crowd for Willow, who was standing behind the counter reminding her to smile. Taylor looked at Layne's family. His mother and sister were crying, and they were watching him with something she hadn't seen in a long time—pride. Layne began to sing after Taylor's knees had given out, and she was barely holding herself upright on the stool beside him.

There's more beauty in you
Than could ever be true
I've spent all of my life
Waiting for you

You push me away
While I beg you to stay
I'm new to this place
And I won't be the same

I'll take all your pain
And lock it away
If I don't kiss your lips
I might go insane

There's more beauty in you
Than could ever be true
I've spent all of my life
Waiting for you

You won't let me in
And I know you're scared
But if you'll let down your guards
I'll show you I care

I'll love you the same
With each passing day
True to your soul
My heart will remain

I'll take all your pain
And lock it away
If I don't kiss your lips
I might go insane

There's more beauty in you
Than could ever be true
I've spent all of my life
Just waiting for you

The crowd stayed silent, waiting for Taylor's reaction to Layne's public declaration of love. She had just admitted she loved him via her song, but now it all felt real to her after hearing him say it in the presence of other people.

Taylor cleared her throat and wiped the corners of her eyes as she grabbed the microphone. "I think the song's title should be 'Waiting for you,' and it's the most beautiful song I've ever heard."

The crowd cheered and jumped to their feet as Taylor wrapped her arms around Layne's neck and hugged him. Before she pulled away, Taylor said into his ear, "Layne, I love you." Immediately, she felt vulnerable and hoped he would say something to acknowledge what she'd wanted to tell him for weeks.

Layne put down his guitar and pulled Taylor back into his arms, lifting her off the floor and embracing her like she might float away if he didn't hold tightly enough. "Baby, I know," he said. "I love you too." He kissed her, their intimate moment engulfed by the deafening roar of the crowd.

chapter 29

Jordan scowled behind her dark glasses as she watched Taylor and Layne from a stool at the back of the bar. The crowd loved them, and it made Jordan angrier the longer she looked at the happiness on her sister's face and watched the camera flashes going off all around them. It wasn't fake publicity kissing; it was real. She'd watched Taylor and Layne through the peephole in Taylor's apartment while she stayed there. They'd held hands and stolen kisses in the hallway when no one else was around.

The fake public relationship with Blake was all Jordan had. Originally attracted to him, she now loathed him. He was too high-maintenance, even for Jordan. The fact he had no feelings for Jordan was his loss, she'd told herself at the time.

Finding someone to have sex with was never a problem. Actors, singers, athletes, production assistants, wannabe directors, and models—all the guys had thought their one-night stands with Jordan Hoffman were the stuff porn star dreams were made of. None of them stuck around, and she hadn't wanted them to. They all made Jordan miss Chase even more. No one else understood her like he did. He had loved her; she was sure of it.

Later that evening, after the crowd had stopped applauding long enough for other songwriters to perform, Jordan went back to her sister's apartment to wait, but Taylor never came home.

Before midnight, Jordan heard thumping in the hallway and looked out the peephole in time to see Taylor and Layne practically ripping each other's clothes off as they rolled across the walls kissing and stumbled into his apartment.

Jordan pulled out her phone and began looking at celebrity gossip sites to see if anyone had picked up the story on her sister's song. Instantly, she found a video that must have been shot from the front of the bar with clips from Taylor and Layne's songs and a long shot of the two of them kissing. The headline read: "A fairy-tale romance for two former child stars."

After going to Taylor's freezer, Jordan took out her vodka, a safer bet than the bourbon she preferred, and drank it straight from the bottle as she walked to the bathroom to run a bath.

A few weeks later, when she returned for reshoots, Jordan was still annoyed by the sickening hand-holding, kissing, and constant sex her sister was having. Jordan donned her dark glasses and hoodie while she went for a run around Taylor's apartment early one morning. As she rounded a corner several blocks away, she crashed into a man she instantly recognized.

"Holy shit," she said as she removed her glasses to look at him. "Michael?"

"Jordan, what are you doing here?" he asked.

"I could ask the same thing. What are you doing here?"

"I'm staying in the Palisades Hotel a few blocks back. Thought I'd get some exercise by walking around a bit. Now you. This neighborhood seems a little under-developed for your taste."

"Taylor lives nearby. Her taste is not as refined as mine."

He let out an audible sigh and looked at the ground. "I'm surprised she still speaks to you. How's she doing?"

"God, Michael, are you not over her yet?" Jordan asked.

He didn't answer; he just stared at Jordan with a look of contempt.

"She's fine," Jordan continued. "I am too. Thanks for asking. We've both had a rough time with the death of our mother, but it's brought us closer."

"I find it hard to believe you two are close," he said. "I'm sorry about your mom."

Jordan stretched her legs. "You're ruining my workout," she said. "Walk with me, and I'll tell you all about Taylor."

Michael agreed and walked with Jordan, who slowed her fast pace when he struggled to keep up. He had packed on a few pounds since high school.

"I've been staying with Taylor for a few weeks while we're filming the final scenes for the last *Awake* movie. Have you seen the other two?" Jordan asked, batting her eyes at him. "They've made me a household name."

"No," Michael said. "I haven't watched your movies since Taylor broke up with me."

"Well, she's not around too much. She's too busy fucking the brains out of her new boyfriend. I doubt it'll last. It seems all physical just like all her other boyfriends. There have been so many, I've lost count."

"I don't want to hear about that," Michael said.

"You're pathetic," Jordan said. "I can't believe you're still hung up on her when you could've had me."

Michael laughed. "I never wanted you," he said.

Jordan huffed and thought of a new plan. "Well, if you're not done with Taylor, now's your chance. She's working at the Mocking Bird later this afternoon. It's several blocks back. Go see her. Her hair is dark now, so you might not recognize her at first."

"Thanks. Maybe you're not such a bitch after all, now that you've aged."

Jordan smiled as she watched Michael walk toward his hotel. It would be a night Taylor's fairy tale would crash and burn.

chapter 30

Thursday, July 28, 2016

Mr. Cosney was in a huge bind when he'd asked Taylor to work for a couple of hours, having tried everyone else first. She didn't mind helping him out. He'd been amazing by giving her the job in the first place after she'd moved in and earned her license. Most of the drinks she already knew from her mother's parties and the rest she'd learned quickly.

Lost in her thoughts, Taylor looked up absentmindedly at the bar's front door as the bell dinged. At first, it didn't register who was walking toward her. Were her eyes deceiving her? The room felt colder in an instant, but Taylor was sweating. Michael didn't look much different than he had in high school. His dark brown hair was neatly cut and styled, and his eyes had a slight hint of sadness in them. He was clean-shaven and wore a blue polo shirt and jeans. Taylor continued filling the napkin dispensers on the counter as Michael sat on the stool in front of her. She avoided his eyes.

"Hey, Tay," he said.

"Don't call me that." Jordan was the only person who still used her nickname. "What are you doing here?"

"I'm staying at the Palisades Hotel for a friend's wedding. I ran into Jordan this morning, and she told me you would be here. I'm so sorry about your mom."

"You could have just called to express your condolences, or not at all. Mom died two months ago."

Michael reached for Taylor's hand, which she promptly snatched away. "I didn't think you'd answer if I called," he said.

Taylor stopped what she was doing and walked around to the other side of the counter. There were no other customers in the bar. She sat one stool away from Michael. "You're right. I probably wouldn't have. What do you want?"

Michael stared at Taylor's hair, then touched the clover tattoo on her arm. "I'll never get used to your new look," he said. "You don't look like yourself at all."

"There's no reason for you to get used to it. What the hell do you want?" She jerked her arm away.

"I don't think we ever finished our last conversation."

2010

"Taylor, please talk to me," Michael said as he ran after her. Everyone in their high school hallway turned to look at them.

"Leave me alone!" Taylor yelled. "All of you!"

Michael stayed in front of her at her locker. "Please," he begged. "I don't know what happened."

Taylor glared at him, trying to control her tears. She got in his face and spoke as quietly as she could through her gritted teeth. "You had sex with my sister. That's what happened. We're done!"

"I don't remember. Everything's so fuzzy. I was drunk."

"I don't care if you were drunk," Taylor said. "You cheated on me. I saw you!"

"Can we please talk about this?" Michael asked. "In private? I love you, Taylor."

"No! I don't want to talk to you ever again. Fuck off, Michael!" She ran away from him and hid in the bathroom, sobbing on and off until the final bell rang.

Taylor shook her head and laughed in disbelief. "Me telling you to 'fuck off' wasn't enough closure for you? We have nothing left to say to each other."

"Taylor, I'm sorry for how things ended with us."

"It's ancient history," Taylor said, looking at him again.

"Not for me," Michael said. "Everyone since you just hasn't been the same. I miss what we had. I miss you."

The words stabbed her in the heart, causing all her feelings from their breakup to bubble up to the surface. She would always love him, but she no longer trusted him. It had taken her so long to get to the point where she wasn't crying into her pillow every night over the pain he'd caused her. She had been so connected to Michael, that even at sixteen, she thought she would spend the rest of her life with him.

"A lot can change in six years, Michael. You don't know me anymore."

"A lot can stay the same too," he said. "I still love you, Taylor, and I hope you still love me. We could try again."

"Thank you for your condolences, but you need to leave," Taylor said. "I don't want to try again…not with you. I can't."

"Why not? We could have such an amazing future together, just like we talked about when we were younger."

Now, Layne was the only person Taylor envisioned in her future. "I don't want the same things I thought I wanted back then. And I could never trust you again."

"I'm sorry. I made a huge mistake drinking with Jordan that day. I didn't know how my body would react and…"

Taylor slammed her hand against the counter, causing Michael to jump. "Mistakes have consequences. Move on. I have. It's been all over the internet, something I guess Jordan failed to tell you."

He leaned on the counter and ran his hand through his hair. "She mentioned you were seeing someone."

"Then coming here was an especially shitty thing to do since you know I have a boyfriend."

"She said it wouldn't last—that it was casual."

Taylor rolled her eyes. "She's not the best judge of relationships."

"I guess I was hoping you might forgive me and give me another chance," Michael said with a sigh. "Do you love him—the guy you're seeing?"

Taylor didn't want to continue her conversation with Michael any longer, so she was relieved when one of the band members came in to start a soundcheck.

"Is it too early?" the band member asked.

"No, you're good," Taylor said. She turned to Michael to tell him to leave but decided to answer his question instead. "Yes, I love my boyfriend. It's not casual at all."

Layne took a deep breath before knocking on Taylor's apartment door. He knew only Jordan was there because Taylor had sent him a text earlier to let him know she'd be working at the bar for a couple of hours. She would be home soon, so Layne figured he could try to have a decent conversation with Jordan for Taylor's sake. He wanted Taylor in his life, and unfortunately, it meant Jordan would also be around.

"Hey, Layne," Jordan said as she opened the door. "You can wait with me; I'm sure Taylor will be back soon. She's only supposed to fill in for a couple of hours until the other bartender can make it in."

"Yeah, I know," Layne said as he stepped inside. "You done with reshoots? Shouldn't you be going home soon?"

"I just wanted to spend a little more time with my sister before leaving." She scanned Layne's body, focusing on his groin a bit too obviously.

"Uh huh." Layne knew she was up to something. It was laughable that Jordan expected every guy to stand at attention in her presence.

"Why don't you join me for a drink?" Jordan asked as she walked into the kitchen.

"No, I'm good without one, thanks. Taylor and I are going out tonight, and I'm driving."

"Oh, where are you going?"

"There's a concert at a coffeehouse with some up-and-coming indie artists we want to check out. Competition, you know?"

Jordan made him a drink and took a tiny pill out of her pocket. Layne watched her pour the capsule's powder into the glass and mix it with a spoon, thinking she had gone unnoticed. "Oh, come on, you have to try this," she said. "I'm a really great bartender. Taylor didn't get all the talent in that area."

She sat on the couch with Layne and handed him a glass. There was a slight variation in color between the drinks. Layne studied Jordan and her psychotically sweet smile. He took the glass from her but didn't drink it.

"Aren't you going to try it?" Jordan asked.

"I told you I didn't want a drink." She was trying to drug him to hurt Taylor, wanting her to walk in on them. The crazy bitch had probably done the same thing to Taylor's first boyfriend.

"Just one won't hurt you. Taylor can drive if you're that worried about it."

"Fine, I'll try it in a minute," Layne said, taking great care to not smash the glass in his hand against Jordan's head. "I was hoping to get to know you a bit. It's been a long time since I've been around anyone so famous."

Taylor arrived at her door just in time to hear Layne's statement. *Not again,* she thought as bile filled her throat. She stood outside and listened, afraid to go inside. Not Layne. He wouldn't betray her, too, would he? Willow walked out of her apartment into the hallway. Taylor held her finger up to her lips and motioned Willow over to the door. Willow cupped her hand around her ear as she listened with Taylor.

Jordan seemed surprised and flattered by Layne's attention. "What do you want to know?" she asked as she twirled her hair around her finger and leaned forward.

"Well, first, I want to know why you hate Taylor so much. What did she ever do to you?"

"That's a stupid question. Taylor's not here."

"You're jealous of her," Layne said. Everything was obvious to him now. "Taylor's more talented than you, and you know it. That's why you hate her, and it's why you're so mean and vindictive. You slashed her tire, didn't you?"

"What are you talking about? I got her the job. Why would I do that if I hated her?"

"You did it to save your own ass. They were planning to replace you when they found out you couldn't sing, but you begged them to let your sister do the voice-over work. I know because a buddy of mine worked in production."

"That's not true. I've always wanted Taylor to be successful."

"Bullshit. She told me what you did with her high school boyfriend. That was really low."

"He came on to me," Jordan said, delicately caressing her collarbone. "Taylor didn't need him."

Layne pointed at Jordan. "I think you came on to him, and he rejected you over and over again. I think, in the end, you got him drunk and forced him to have sex with you just to hurt Taylor."

"That's not true. Michael wanted me. He didn't really love Taylor; he just wanted to get in her pants." Jordan crossed her arms and turned away. "I don't have to force anyone. I can have anyone I want."

"You can't have me." Layne shuddered at Jordan's death-stare, wanting to throw the glass at her even more.

"Who says I want you?"

"It has nothing to do with me. You want what Taylor has, and she has me. You did more than just get Michael drunk; you drugged him."

Jordan laughed. "You have no proof."

"Proof? I have this drink in my hand. You're trying to drug me now with the same shit you gave him, aren't you?" Layne asked. "It's not going to happen. You and me—never going to happen. Even if I wasn't with Taylor, it would still never happen. You're nuts." He turned his back and walked to the kitchen.

Jordan followed him and backed him into the corner, jabbing him in the chest with her finger. "Taylor won't believe you. She's crazy. She can't trust any guy. I'll tell her you came on to me and tried to drug me."

"It's not her who's crazy." Layne put the glass on the counter and pushed Jordan away. She followed him back into the living room, but he wanted to get as far away from her as possible. "It's always been you. I was trying to be nice and get to know you because you're Taylor's sister, but I don't want to be around you at all. You're bat-shit crazy."

Out in the hallway, Taylor covered her mouth with her hands and started crying. It all made perfect sense. Michael had begged for forgiveness and claimed to have no memory of what happened after drinking with Jordan. Taylor's trust was gone from the moment she saw them together, so she had refused to listen to any explanation from Michael. Jordan had destroyed them.

Willow wrapped her arms around Taylor. "You need to keep that man," she whispered.

Jordan laughed maniacally. "I could ruin your career if I wanted to. You have no idea how connected I am."

"Go ahead and try!" Layne said, moving behind the couch to get away from her. "I already have more money than I'll ever need. Say whatever the hell you want about me. I don't give a shit. Taylor and I know it was you who sold our picture to the tabloids."

"Why would I do that?"

"The hell if I know!" Layne said, growing angrier every moment. He wanted to wrap his hands around Jordan's throat for all the pain she'd caused Taylor. "Why did you drug Michael? Was it just to hurt Taylor? Or, hell, can you only get a guy if he's incapacitated?"

"I gave Michael a little something to take the edge off. Is that what you want to hear? He was begging for it."

Layne couldn't believe Jordan had admitted it. "There's something broken in you," he muttered.

"He and Taylor wouldn't have lasted anyway. I did her a favor. She's not cut out for playing house and having kids—all the things Michael wanted. You just wait. She's the one who's broken. You'll get tired of her before long."

247

"I'll never get tired of her. I want her just the way she is with all the scars from all the shit she's been through. We have what you never will because you're such a cold-hearted bitch. Nothing about you is special. Taylor has so much more going for her."

Jordan huffed. "Yeah, an emotionally damaged has-been outside of Hollywood—she's not that special." She stretched out on the couch and propped her feet on the arm.

"You're the worst person I've ever met, Jordan, and I've met a hell of a lot of people."

Jordan growled at him. "You don't know me, and you don't know Taylor as well as you think."

Layne knew the parts Taylor was scared to share with anyone else. "I know her heart, and I already know I want to spend the rest of my life with her if she'll have me. There's nothing you can do to change that. I'm completely in love with her."

"Of course, you are. It's all over the internet—your pathetic declaration to poor, helpless, broken Taylor. And you think I'm crazy? She doesn't really love you. She's not capable. She was just caught up in the moment after your cheesy song. I've watched my sister. She's a whore, and you're a loser with a hero-complex."

"You're sick and twisted for spying on her! Taylor doesn't have to answer to you, and she doesn't have to answer to me either. The only thing wrong with her is that she has you as a sister. You need to get out of her life. Pack your shit and get out!" Layne yanked Jordan off the couch by her arm.

"We'll see if Taylor really wants me to leave," she said, jerking her arm away and rubbing it. "She wouldn't dare. I could destroy her reputation if I wanted to."

"No, she could annihilate yours, but she's too good of a person," Layne said, getting in Jordan's face. "She's the most beautiful person I've ever met, and only a fraction of her beauty is on the outside. That's the difference between you and Taylor. I have no idea why, but deep down, she still loves you and doesn't wish you any harm. I don't share those sentiments. You can rot in hell. Get the fuck out of her apartment. Now!"

"You know, Michael's planning to see Taylor at the bar today," Jordan said, sitting on the couch. "He thinks he's still in love with her, so it might be you who's leaving by the end of the day."

"I trust her. Get out." Layne grabbed Jordan's purse from the floor and chucked it at her. He opened the door, startling Willow and Taylor in the process.

"You can't make—" Jordan stopped abruptly as Taylor stepped into the apartment, her jaw tight and her fists clenched at her side.

Layne's heart broke as he looked at his girlfriend's tear-streaked face. "Are you okay?" He pulled Taylor into his arms.

Taylor wiped her face. She grabbed her car keys and looked at Jordan, who sat there with her mouth gaped open. "Jordan, do what he said. Get the hell out of my apartment!"

"If you're not gone in ten minutes," Willow added. "The landlord will be notifying the police."

With Layne and Willow right on her heels, Taylor slammed the door and ran out of the building. In the parking lot, she dropped to her knees and threw up in the storm drain. She caught her breath and leaned against the driver's side door of her car. Knowing Taylor was in no condition to drive, Layne wrestled away her keys, holding them out of her reach when she tried to get them back. "I have to go," she argued.

"I'll take you anywhere you want to go," Layne said. "But you're not driving when you're this upset."

Taylor looked at Willow, who nodded at her. "Take me to see Michael. He should know what Jordan did to him."

"Done," Layne said. "Let's go."

chapter 31

Layne held Taylor's hand while he drove her to the Palisades Hotel, unsure of what to say. Taylor had loved Michael once, and learning what Jordan had done to him had to be tearing her apart inside. Selfishly, Layne worried how the revelation would impact their relationship.

As soon as they arrived at the hotel, Taylor went straight to the front desk. "Will you please ring Michael Bulloch's room, and tell him Taylor wants to speak with him?" she asked the desk worker.

The worker called Michael and relayed Taylor's message. "He's in room 307."

Layne followed Taylor to the room and endured the awkward introduction. Michael seemed disappointed she wasn't alone. Layne sat on one of the beds beside Taylor and continued to hold her hand while she recounted the past event.

Michael acted like he'd had the wind knocked out of him. "My memory of that day is fuzzy, and I was hungover and hazy for a couple of days. I didn't drink that much." He rubbed his eyes.

"I'm sorry Jordan did that to you," Taylor said. "I'm sorry I didn't believe you back then."

Michael sighed and ran his fingers through the back of his hair. "How did you find out?"

"She tried to pull the same shit on me today," Layne said as he squeezed Taylor's hand. "I caught her and confronted her. She admitted she drugged you."

"My friend and I were in the hallway, so we heard Jordan say it too," Taylor said.

"Does this change anything about our conversation earlier?" Michael asked Taylor. He looked at Layne nervously when Taylor didn't answer right away.

"No. Goodbye, Michael. I'm so sorry." Taylor left the room and headed toward the elevator.

Layne turned to Michael. "What did you say to her earlier?"

"I'm sorry, man," Michael said. "I told Taylor I'm still in love with her and wanted her back."

"That's a shitty thing to do." Layne stepped closer to Michael and clenched his fists. "You need to leave her alone. Being around you hurts her."

"I know." Michael took a step back and put his hands out. "She told me she's in love with you. If I'd known, man, I wouldn't have said anything. Jordan told me she didn't think you two were serious. I'm sorry. I won't bother her again."

"You shouldn't trust Jordan," Layne said as he stepped into the hallway. "Especially after what you learned tonight."

Michael stood in his doorframe and looked down the hall at Taylor. "Do you love her?" he asked. "Because if you don't…"

Layne looked at Taylor, who was waiting for him at the end of the hall. "I do," he said to Michael. "More than anyone else."

"Then don't fuck it up. Stay away from Jordan."

"You should consider pressing charges against her."

"Why?"

Layne shook his head in disbelief. "Dude, she drugged you and raped you."

"Over six years ago. What good would it do now?" Michael pulled the chain lock beside the door and twisted it around his fingers as he looked down at the floor.

"Closure? Justice? She shouldn't get away with it. Who knows how many guys she's drugged?"

"I would rather just put it behind me," Michael said. "There's no evidence, and Taylor was the only witness. Pressing charges would cause publicity. I think I've hurt Taylor enough." He had a good point, and Layne couldn't deny that reliving the situation would hurt Taylor, although he was still furious there would be no justice.

Layne extended his hand to Michael. "Take care of yourself, man," he said as Michael shook his hand.

"Take care of her."

Layne nodded and walked away from Michael. When he arrived at Taylor's side, she pushed the elevator button.

"Thanks for not hitting him," she said as they stepped into the elevator.

"I've never hit anyone," Layne said. "I never wanted to until tonight, but not him. Jordan. I feel like an ass for wanting to hit a woman. I can't blame Michael for still being in love with you." He kissed Taylor on the forehead and held her until they reached the lobby.

Taylor remained quiet as Layne drove. "Do you still want to go to the coffeehouse?" he asked.

"I need the distraction. I don't want to think about all this tonight."

"You know you can talk to me." Layne hoped Taylor knew she could tell him anything without changing his love for her. "I can't imagine how you must be feeling right now. I understand if you want to talk to Michael again alone."

"That's not fair to you."

Her words were a punch to his gut. "Baby, this isn't about me. You do what you need to do to get through this."

"I think it's better for both Michael and me if we don't talk."

chapter 32

Friday, November 4, 2016

With continued magazine and online interest in Taylor and Layne's romance and music careers, they were getting more coverage than Jordan and Blake by the time *Awake* premiered in Hollywood. Taylor hadn't returned any of her sister's calls or texts since learning the truth about what had happened with Michael; she didn't know what to say to Jordan.

Cutting off communication with Michael was easier since he'd only sent one text, but Taylor still felt lingering guilt about the whole situation even though she knew it wasn't her fault what Jordan had done. Focusing on her relationship with Layne and her music career were the only things keeping Taylor's mind clear throughout the summer into the fall.

The *Awake* director compelled the hottest new couple to walk the carpet along with the lead actors. Reluctantly, Taylor had convinced Layne to agree, but now she doubted her original idea because she didn't want to see Jordan. Maybe she wasn't cut out for fame again.

Layne was more nervous than Taylor had seen him since he was a teenager hiding in her dressing room. He was handsome in his tux with a royal blue tie to match Taylor's dress. "You okay?" she asked him from the back of their limo, moments before they were due to get out.

"I'm good." Layne took a deep breath and exhaled slowly. "I've gotten used to the cameras in my face over the last couple of months. Haven't you?"

Taylor laughed. "It's just like riding a bike, right?" Through the window, she watched the camera flashes surrounding her sister and Blake. Blake stood as far away as possible without letting go

Jordan's hand. Jordan wore a black dress, different from her usual red. As Jordan and Blake cleared the carpet, the door beside Taylor opened. "Here goes nothing," she said to Layne.

Blinding light from camera flashes disoriented Taylor as she stepped out, walking carefully to avoid falling in her heels. Hearing her name shouted all around her was as bewildering as the flashes of light. Keeping her smile plastered on, she reached for Layne, who hesitated before he stepped out of the limo. Their eyes met, and Taylor tried to transfer some of her calmness to him. Layne nodded at Taylor and placed his hand on the small of her back as he led her down the carpet.

Reporters shouted questions about the status of their albums as they stopped to pose for photos. Layne had a death grip on Taylor's hand by the time they reached the theater entrance.

"That wasn't so bad, was it?" she whispered to him.

"I'm good," he whispered back before releasing her hand to kiss her. Dozens of cameras flashed in rapid succession. "Oops, that'll be out soon."

"It's okay," Taylor said, wrapping her arms around his waist. Being in a relationship, especially with Layne, was something she no longer feared.

The audience watched the movie in silence. The music was better than it had been in the previous two installments, and the storyline flowed well. All the actors had given the best performances of their lives—all except Jordan. Her performance was mediocre at best. Her timing and line delivery were off in ways that had been helped by editing and reshoots but not completely fixed. Only those who'd scrutinized Jordan's previous performances would notice.

Taylor glanced at her sister's seat in the middle of the theater. Jordan sat beside Blake, expressionless, watching the movie. One of the final shots included far-away footage of Taylor and Layne kissing under a large tree at the edge of the set. The scene cut to Jordan's character, Helena, looking wistfully at them from across the field stating, "As long as there's love, we still have hope."

Unaware their brief fill-in as extras would make the final cut, Taylor rested her head on Layne's shoulder, enjoying the comfort of his arm wrapped around her while she watched the credits roll. Layne kissed Taylor on the temple. When the movie was over, Jordan got up and walked to the VIP room entrance without speaking to anyone.

Layne removed his arm from Taylor's shoulder and helped her to her feet. "Your songs were the best parts of the whole movie," he said, grazing his lips on her forehead.

"It wouldn't have been as good without the duets with you," she said. "I can't believe they included the shot of us."

"Does it make you want to start acting again?"

"Definitely not. Do you want to go to the VIP room?"

"Nope. I want to take you somewhere else."

Later, after the driver had taken them back to Taylor's car, Layne drove them to a gated neighborhood in the hills outside of Hollywood.

"Where are we going?" Taylor asked. She looked out the window at the small houses illuminated by the streetlights. If not for the modern cars, she'd think she was transported back to the 1920s. "I love all these old houses."

"I want to show you my house."

"You own one of these?"

"That one." He pointed to the last house on the street, which was dark except for a soft light in the front window. "Not what you expected?"

"Wow," Taylor said. "I love it." She sat in her car in awe of the house while Layne came around to open the door.

"Come on," he said.

"Is Kyle still here?"

"I sent him a text earlier. You won't believe it; he and Heidi eloped last week and managed to keep it out of the press. He moved into their new house since the renovations were done early. He left timers on the lights until I can figure out what to do with this place."

The house was bigger than it looked from the outside and was cozy and masculine with its dark woodwork, features that had appealed to Layne when he bought it. He took Taylor downstairs to the basement to show her his favorite space in the whole house—his recording studio.

"This is incredible," Taylor said, her eyes wide as she looked around. "I wouldn't have dreamed this little house was hiding so much."

Layne took her hand and led her into the soundproof booth. "It's the main reason I bought it. I always planned to record my album here. I think I'm about finished with all the songs I want to use." He sat on the stool and pulled Taylor into his lap. "The acoustics in here are incredible."

"Sounds like you've decided not to sell."

"What I was thinking? I can't sell this place. I love it here."

"Are you wanting to move back in?"

"My apartment lease is up at the end of the month. Mr. Cosney said I could go month-to-month if I want to, but I think I do want to move back here. I told you about that cartoon composing job opportunity. I got it. The studio is only a short drive from here."

Taylor sighed. "It makes sense for you to move back for a job." She left the room and went upstairs.

Layne sat for a minute, staring at the floor before he went after Taylor. He would never intentionally upset her. He could imagine spending the rest of his life living in the house, but only if Taylor would come with him. Would she? He found her at the kitchen window looking out at the backyard. He stood behind her and pulled her close. "So, what do you think?" he asked, kissing her neck.

"About what?" She leaned into him.

"The house, me moving back here…"

"The house is beautiful, and you moving makes sense for you and the job."

Layne turned Taylor around to face him. "Taylor," he said, lifting up her chin to reveal her red eyes holding back tears. "When is your lease up? Are you planning to fill in at the Mocking Bird awhile longer?"

"I am already on month-to-month, and Mr. Cosney found a permanent replacement for me who'll start in two weeks."

"Come with me."

"Move in with you?" A grin spread across Taylor's lips as her tears retreated. "Are you serious?"

"Yeah. It's not such a stretch. We're practically living together already. Do you realize we haven't spent a single night apart in over five months?"

"Has it been that long?" Taylor asked. She loosened Layne's tie and pulled it off his neck. "It's gone by so fast."

"It has," Layne said. "The greatest five months of my life so far." He couldn't stand the thought of her not coming with him, especially with the special-order awaiting his approval at the jewelry store, a gift planned for New Year's Day.

"You really want me to move in here with you?"

"If you want to. I'll miss you like crazy if you don't and would have to drive all the way back to your apartment every single day—twice a day—to kiss you every morning and every night." He kissed her cheeks, her forehead, and the tip of her nose before finding her lips. "Please say you will."

"I will. I'll move in with you."

Layne let go of Taylor and jumped with his fist in the air. "Yes!" he exclaimed before he picked her up and spun her around twice. "We can stay here tonight to see how you like our place."

Taylor laughed and pulled at the sides of her long formal dress. "What will I sleep in?"

Layne laughed with her. "Nothing...or you could sleep in one of my t-shirts."

"Alright."

"But first, I have to show you the claw-foot bathtub."

Relaxing with Layne in the bathtub, Taylor closed her eyes and listened to the song playing on the satellite radio, a cover of "The Sound of Silence" by Disturbed. Some people loved it, while others hated it based on the reviews she'd read. Taylor adored it and wanted to know Layne's opinion, but discovered he was asleep. She was also having trouble keeping her eyes open as she traced Layne's tattoos with her fingertips.

Layne jumped a little, splashing the water. "I'm sorry. I'm so exhausted from the drive and having to talk to all those people. I'm glad we're staying here. I don't think I could have driven us back home tonight."

"Have you forgotten already? We are home." Taylor pulled out the stopper to allow the water to drain and managed to drag Layne from the tub. After Layne had provided her with a t-shirt to sleep in, Taylor followed him to the master bedroom on the second floor. The skylight above the bed allowed the stars to shine through. "This view is so perfect."

"It never was before," Layne said as he wrapped his arms tightly around Taylor. "You weren't here. But it is perfect now."

Everything was as it should be. Layne fell asleep long before Taylor, and she lay awake watching for shooting stars and listening to his slow, steady breathing. Later, as she kissed his brow, Taylor couldn't imagine ever loving anyone else as much as she loved Layne.

Chapter 33

Sunday, November 27, 2016

Packing up her apartment was bittersweet for Taylor because it had been her first place out on her own. The place where she'd written her song for Layne, which was still getting thousands of downloads a week since she'd placed it on her new music website.

Layne had packed up his apartment the day after Thanksgiving and moved his things back to his house. They'd spent Thanksgiving with Layne's family, and Taylor felt like she belonged with them. There was no pressure and no backlash after Layne told his parents Taylor would be moving in with him, which relieved Taylor since she hadn't heard from her dad or responded to Jordan's messages in months. For the first time ever, Taylor hadn't acknowledged her sister's birthday in October.

The last things left to pack were Taylor's clothes. She'd already arranged to have Salvation Army pick up her bed and the old couch she'd taken from her father's storage unit, to which she had no sentimental attachment.

Taylor had said her goodbyes to Willow and Kayla, knowing she'd still see them, just not as often. She'd have to end her gym membership since a long drive was out of the question when there was workout equipment at Layne's house.

Mr. Cosney gave Taylor back her full deposit since she had taken care of her place. He told her he was never worried about it. He was a good judge of character and had always known Taylor was a good person. He hugged her goodbye, like a father would hug his daughter, and told her how proud he was of the success of her song. He was quick to remind Taylor to tell everyone she had launched her new music career at the Mocking Bird. Taylor promised she would.

Taylor sealed the last two boxes and waited for Layne to come back upstairs after loading the previous two into his SUV. She looked around her apartment, remembering how she'd fallen in love with the place earlier in the year.

Scary things had happened to her inside its walls, and wonderful things too. Layne had told her he loved her for the first time there. It was there she'd realized she loved him too. Now she was moving on to start a new adventure with the man she loved.

It was in this apartment she'd accepted that Jordan was the unhealthiest relationship in her life. Taking a step back from it had relieved most of the impending doom Taylor felt about her sister. She knew she might eventually forgive her, but it wouldn't be easy, and it wouldn't be soon. Holding on to the hatred would only cause more pain for Taylor. She'd had enough.

"You ready, babe?" Layne asked from the doorway.

Taylor pointed to the boxes on the couch. "That's the last of it," she said.

Layne walked behind Taylor and wrapped his arms around her. "You sad to leave this place?" he asked. "A lot's happened here."

She turned around to face him. "I was just thinking about that. It's fine. I'm surprised your mom wasn't upset about us moving in together. She seems conservative about other things, so I thought she might have a problem with it."

Layne laughed. "I think she gave up her illusion I was still a virgin a long time ago," he said. "It's not up to her; it's my house. I'll be twenty-five next week; what's she going to do?"

"Do you want a birthday party at your place?" Taylor asked.

"Our place," he corrected. "And yes, but you're the only person invited, and clothing is strongly discouraged. We'll do a bigger party for New Year's Eve."

Taylor smiled. "I'm ready to go home now. Home with you."

In the SUV, Taylor tuned to a radio station airing a discussion on music in films. One DJ brought up the amazing music from *Awake.* Everyone who called in agreed the music was the best part of the film. One of the movie songs played next, the main duet, titled "Awake" which Taylor and Layne had recorded their second day on set. The DJ talked about the emotion conveyed in the song and how it could stand alone without the listener needing knowledge of the book series or the films.

Layne took Taylor's hand as they listened to a second DJ talk about the exceptional performance of Blake and some of the other actors. After a while, Jordan's name came up. The first DJ said what Taylor thought, that Jordan's performance was fine, but unexceptional compared to the other actors' performances and Jordan's previous ones. The DJs discussed the very public breakup of Jordan and Blake. One claimed the relationship had already seemed strained at the movie premiere and noted the distance between Jordan and Blake as compared to Taylor and Layne on the red carpet.

Tabloids had covered the breakup more than anything else, featuring photos of Blake with an exotic lingerie model on his arm at a press event for his next movie. "Blake's moved on," the headlines read. "Leading man, Blake, with new love."

The photos of Jordan were less flattering. She was shown wearing baggy sweats, holding a Starbucks cup. Another photo captured Jordan at the market wearing no makeup, and she looked like she hadn't washed her hair in several days. The headlines were brutal and unforgiving. "Jordan Hoffman taking the breakup hard." "Jordan Hoffman on a downward spiral." "Is Jordan's Career Over? No upcoming roles."

Coverage continued when anonymous insiders revealed information about Jordan's terrible work ethic during the filming of the last *Awake* movie. The main crew had all signed non-disclosure agreements, so Taylor figured the insiders were likely caterers or technicians who only worked a few days and never signed such agreements. Any of them could have witnessed one of Jordan's frequent temper tantrums, many of which Taylor had squashed by reminding Jordan she was the star and needed to keep things moving along. Reporters now approached Taylor and Layne wanting comments. They always replied with the same monotone "no comment."

"They're getting pretty harsh about Jordan," Layne said, flipping to a different station and breaking Taylor's train of thought. "You okay?"

"I'm apathetic about it at this point," Taylor said. "I mean, she brought it on herself. You saw her behavior at work. There were days when she was just downright nasty to people. I'm surprised nothing came out sooner." Jordan was so much worse than she was during the previous two movies. She had her diva moments, but she usually only yelled at Blake or Taylor behind closed doors. Blake was an asshole anyway, so Taylor didn't feel sorry for him because he usually egged it on by grabbing Jordan's ass or doing something else stupid.

"She was pretty bad."

"And with what she tried to do to you, and what she did to Michael," Taylor said, shaking her head. "I can't believe he didn't press charges against her. The headlines would never end."

Layne gave Taylor's hand a squeeze. "He told me he didn't want to hurt you since you'd have to testify as a witness. He said he still couldn't remember exactly what happened, so it was best to let it go."

The knowledge of her sister being a non-convicted rapist sat like lead in Taylor's stomach. "I don't think I could let it go."

"Me neither."

The song "Chandelier" came on the radio. Layne turned up the volume, much to Taylor's surprise. "I didn't care for this song at first, but now that I've studied the lyrics, I think there's a lot of pain expressed in this song. It has more merit than I originally thought. I'm glad you made me think of Sia's music differently by sharing 'Breathe Me.'"

"This song makes me think of Jordan now."

"Hmm," Layne said. "I get what you mean."

Something bad was going to happen. Jordan was on a downward spiral like the tabloids claimed, living each day like the next would never come. She would do something drastic soon to gain attention, and there was nothing Taylor could do to help or stop it. She was an observer, powerless like everyone else.

chapter 34

Friday, December 30, 2016

After another month, the ruthless headlines had finally ceased about Jordan. Taylor had predicted things would blow over eventually. She figured her sister would find a new boyfriend and a new movie by the end of the year, but so far, there were reports of neither. There was nothing at all, which added to Taylor's apprehension that Jordan would do something desperate soon to get back in the headlines.

Layne and Taylor arrived early for the songwriter's showcase at the Mocking Bird hoping to see Willow. As they walked through the door, Taylor stopped so suddenly Layne ran into her. There was an exclusive interview airing on TV, but this time Jordan wasn't decked out in red. She was dressed in a muted beige shirt with gold sequins along the neckline with her hair piled on top of her head. Taylor walked to the TV and stood underneath it.

"We appreciate you being so candid with us, Jordan," the interviewer said.

"Well," Jordan said as her eyes filled with tears. "It was so many years ago, but I still remember all the confusion and the aftermath of it all." She continued to cry silently as the interviewer handed her a tissue.

Layne walked behind Taylor and put his hand on her shoulder as Jordan began to speak again.

"It happened when I was nineteen. So many things were up in the air for my family. My mother was a drug addict and had just suffered a stroke after an overdose. I was away filming a movie, so I wasn't paying attention to what was going on in my own family. All the warning signs were there..."

Taylor leaned against Layne, her increasing heart rate pulsing in her ears, debating whether the knot in her stomach would result in crying or vomiting. *Warning signs?* Jordan wasn't talking about herself. Who the hell was she talking about?

"I should have been a better sister to Taylor and then maybe I would have known she was considering ending her life," Jordan said.

Taylor gasped and covered her mouth, a cold sweat breaking out all over her body. "What the fuck?" she whispered. She looked at Layne, who couldn't hide his own shock and disbelief at what Jordan was saying.

"I came home from a publicity event and found Taylor in our bathroom," Jordan continued. "She had taken a bunch of pills and was unconscious, so I called for help. It was the scariest situation of my life. My sister had always been my best friend, but she shut me out after my career took off and hers stalled. Then she had a breakup with a boyfriend and felt like she had nothing to live for. I want all the young people out there who are watching to know there's always hope. My dad and I got Taylor the help she needed."

"It must have been so hard on you," the interviewer said, taking Jordan's hand.

"It was…" Jordan said, wiping more tears from her eyes. "My sister is my best friend, you know. I would do anything for her."

Taylor stormed out of the bar with Layne right behind her. "You've got to be fucking kidding me!" she yelled as soon as she got to the parking lot.

Other people in the lot stared as Layne pushed Taylor into his SUV and closed the door. He ran around to the driver's side and got in.

Taylor couldn't control the shaking in her hands. "What the hell? How could she do this to me? She's trying to destroy everything I've been working for!"

"Taylor," Layne said, grabbing her hands to steady them. "I had no idea it was so bad."

Taylor felt sick to her stomach again. "Wait, you believed her? Everything was total bullshit except for the part about our mom."

"No, I didn't believe her."

"I can't deal with this right now. I don't want to stay here. Please, take me home."

Back at home, Taylor sat on the couch with Layne and told him everything about what had happened with Jordan. After ending her relationship with Michael, Taylor hadn't talked to Jordan much, even though they lived with their dad after their mom's stroke. Taylor told their dad Jordan was high all the time, hoping he would punish her and get her help. Of course, the main reason Taylor tattled about her sister's drug use was for revenge over Michael, something she hated to admit. Jordan managed to act her way out of trouble and fool their dad with her sob story, swearing Taylor had lied due to jealousy.

After Jordan's last horror movie got terrible reviews and crowned her the weakest link (who should go back to TV acting), Taylor picked up a printed copy of the movie review magazine to bring home. After getting into a petty fight with Jordan, Taylor brought up the review, which Jordan hadn't seen. Taylor regretted telling her the article was right, that Jordan was a washed-up child star who needed to give it up. Jordan told her to go to hell. It was the same night Taylor met up with some kids from school at a party and had gotten drunk for the first and last time.

Layne moved closer as Taylor spoke, taking her hands, and Taylor worried he might think less of her for being so horrible to her sister.

"Late that evening, I came home from the party and found Jordan in the bathroom," Taylor continued, watching Layne for his reaction, which showed no judgment. "White powder was all over the side of the tub that the police later identified as cocaine. Dad's straight razor was on the floor. Jordan had cut both of her wrists. I immediately threw up from the sight of all the blood. I thought she was dead. When I realized she was still breathing, I called for help. No one even noticed I was drunk because I was crying so hard. I should have known. She was my sister, and I should have known how fragile she was."

"You can't blame yourself," Layne said.

But Taylor did blame herself, even after her father had apologized for not believing her about the drugs. He put Jordan in a private rehab facility for several months after she got out of the hospital for detox treatments and intensive therapy. Somehow, Mr. Hoffman's lawyers made all drug charges against Jordan go away. She stayed sober for several months, got her own place, and tried to make amends, but Taylor didn't want anything to do with her. After Jordan landed the *Awake* trilogy and needed help with the singing, she'd begged Taylor and swore she was sorry for everything in the past.

"Jordan's drug use and her suicide attempt were not your fault," Layne said.

Taylor rested her head on Layne's shoulder. "She really was my best friend, you know, before the show started taking more of a focus on me and before I started dating Michael. It hurt that she went from having my back to wanting to stab me in it. Even after all the shit she's put me through, she's still my sister." Taylor knew what she had to do. Jordan was her blood, like it or not. "I have to help her."

Layne pushed Taylor away by her shoulders and looked her in the eyes. "Oh God, Taylor, she's toxic. I don't know if you can help her by yourself."

"I'll reach out to my dad. They're my family, Layne. I understand if it's too much for you and you want out." Taylor coughed as her throat tightened.

"Don't say that," Layne said. "You act like you're a burden to me, but you're not. I love you. I don't want out. What I'm saying is I'm in this with you; I'll help you get help for Jordan."

"I'm sorry." Taylor held out her hand for Layne to take. "I can't think about this anymore."

Layne stood up and cradled her head against his chest. "You don't have to."

Relaxed in Layne's arms, Taylor pressed her ear against his chest as they swayed to the rhythm of his heartbeat while he sang the song he'd written for her. She closed her eyes and absorbed the vibration and melody coming from within him, focusing on nothing else.

chapter 35

Saturday, New Year's Eve, 2016

Jordan paced back and forth in her living room. She figured her sister would eventually forgive her after what she'd tried to do to Layne since nothing had actually happened, but so far, not a word. All her calls and texts to Taylor had gone unanswered.

I didn't really hurt Layne. I was just trying to protect you because I thought he was a cheater like Michael.

No reply

You have no idea how much pressure I'm under.

No reply

This could help your career. Everyone will be talking about you.

No reply

Taylor, you can't avoid me forever. You're my sister.

Again, no reply

She'd done terrible things before, but this time, she had lied to the world about Taylor. The fallout would be catastrophic, and Taylor might never speak to her again. She intended to be truthful with the interviewer but panicked at the last minute. Before she could stop herself, the lies had come pouring out. Any potential retaliation from Taylor would be viewed as a desperate cry for attention, but the publicity might be worth it for both of their careers. Jordan sat on the floor beside her couch and rested her head on her knees while she cried.

Deep down, Jordan knew it wasn't her sister's fault things came so easily to her, but it still infuriated Jordan. *Why am I feeling sorry for myself when I have way more fame than Taylor now,* she wondered, *who cares if she can sing? A lot of people can sing. Layne can sing. Chase can sing. Chase…it's too late to get him back.*

She went to her favorite spot—her patio—with a glass, a bottle of wine, and a small container of pills she'd picked up earlier in the day. *It's just something to take the edge off,* she told herself, *perfectly safe.* Jordan took two and waited half an hour but felt nothing, not even the wine. She poured herself another glass, took three more pills, and pulled out her phone to look at the trending posts.

As Jordan scrolled through the hundreds of posts, she found most were supportive of Taylor, wishing her good health and healing from her struggle with depression. Jordan couldn't find a single post addressed to herself.

Then she found it, a new account active in her feed, "The Jordan Hoffman Insider," with only one post:

You know what you did, Jordan. You're a liar. Come clean. Tell the truth or I will.

Who was it, and which lie was the person threatening to expose? How would she recover from it?

"My career is over!" Jordan screamed into the darkness as she smashed the wine glass at her feet. After the devastating reviews on the last *Awake* movie, Jordan's agent, whom she'd promptly fired, told her she'd be lucky if she could get an infomercial for her next acting job. Taking a break, as her former agent had suggested, was not something Jordan could afford to do. She'd blown through her movie salary and had used almost all her trust fund to purchase her house. Earnings were still pending from the proposed syndication of *The Spectacular Smiths.* The next property taxes would leave her broke.

Jordan picked up her phone and sent a quick message to Chase and Taylor. One of them would respond. They were the only two people she was certain had loved her once.

Just know that I loved you. I'm sorry.

Drinking from the wine bottle, Jordan took four more pills to numb the pain before drowsiness blurred her vision. She checked her phone several times for a text from Chase or Taylor, but none came through before she drifted off to sleep.

chapter 36

Monday, January 1, 2017

Layne thought their first party hosted as a couple had gone perfectly. Taylor was the bartender for their friends while they welcomed in the new year. Having cut off the booze right after midnight, the guests were gone by three o'clock that morning. Layne made a final round through the living room with a bag to collect the remaining red cups. Nothing was too messy; the party had been small.

After he had taken the trash to the kitchen, Layne plopped down on the couch. "Come here," he said, reaching out to Taylor. "I don't think you've sat down at all. Our friends loved the drinks."

"It's been a long day," Taylor said, only offering her hand. "Let's go to bed."

Layne looked up at Taylor as he took her hand. "But what if I'm not tired?"

"Come on. I'll make you tired."

Layne jumped up and followed her to the bedroom.

It was just past sunrise when Layne woke to the sound of his phone vibrating on his nightstand. He had only slept for a couple of hours. He reached over Taylor to pick it up, surprised by the name on the screen.

"Chase, what's wrong?" he answered. "It's early, man."

"Brandon, I need your help. Jordan sent me a strange message last night, and now I can't get her on the phone, and she's not responding to my texts."

"How am I supposed to help with that?"

"I saw the interview where she lied about Taylor. I'm worried about Jordan. You're still with Taylor, right? When I talked to

Noah, he said you two were serious. Will you get ahold of her and tell her what's going on and have her call me?"

"What did Jordan say to you?"

"She wanted me to know she loved me and said she was sorry. I didn't get the message right away."

"Shit. Just a minute." He shook Taylor's shoulder. "Babe, wake up. Taylor!"

She groaned as she rolled over. "What is it?"

"Where's your phone? Did Jordan text you? Chase can't get ahold of her."

Taylor looked around. "I think I left it downstairs," she said as she got up. "I've been ignoring her texts."

In the living room, Taylor found her phone on the couch, the ringer on silent. She read the cryptic message from Jordan as goosebumps crawled up her arms and legs. She tried to call her sister, but Jordan's phone just rang several times and connected to voicemail. "Jordan, we need to talk. Call me back." She went back to the bedroom.

"Did you reach her?" Layne asked as he held out his phone.

"No," Taylor said. "I think something's wrong. I can just feel it. We need to go."

"Shit." Layne put the phone back to his ear. "We're going to go check on her; I'll call you back." He got up and walked over to Taylor, who was still standing in the middle of the bedroom feeling bewildered. She needed direction and let Layne lead her to the closet and hand her clothes to wear.

After they were dressed, Taylor followed Layne to his SUV, and they started their drive to Jordan's house. She couldn't stop thinking about what Jordan had written. *Just know that I loved you.*

I'm sorry. What did Jordan mean? Why wouldn't she pick up her phone? Taylor tried several more times to reach her and left messages.

"She's probably just asleep or left her phone somewhere," Layne said. "I bet she went to a New Year's party somewhere and is sleeping off the hangover."

Taylor shook her head. "There's something going on," she said. "That text isn't like anything she's sent before. With what happened and the way I yelled at her..." Taylor made another call and hung up, frustrated at not knowing. "Damn it!"

"She's not there, Taylor," Layne said.

"I was trying to call my dad to see if he's in town. No answer, of course," she said. She made another call. "Hey, it's Taylor. I'm sorry for calling so early; I need to reach my dad, is he around?" She paused to listen to her dad's girlfriend's explanation of their breakup, not caring enough to absorb the details. "Oh, I didn't know. Take care of yourself."

"What's going on?" Layne asked.

"Dad's girlfriend. Well, his ex-girlfriend. They broke up a couple of months ago."

"I'll get us to Jordan's house as fast as I can."

"Do you think I'm right that she's on drugs again? I mean, from what you saw when we were last around her? She's more than just crazy, right?" Taylor already knew the answer, but she needed someone else to believe her.

"Considering she tried to roofie me, I'm going to vote 'yes' on that."

Taylor ran her fingers through her hair and held her head, which had begun to throb. "Why me?" she asked. "Why do I have to deal with this?"

"You don't. I'll turn around right now, and we can call the police to have them check on her."

"They'll never believe I am who I say I am. And even if they do, she's not missing that we know of. It hasn't even been a whole day since she contacted me. Don't they make you wait two days for an adult?"

"I really don't know how it works. We'll be there soon."

"I'm just worried since it's happened before…" It couldn't be like it was before, not when Jordan's career would bounce back at any moment. Yet Taylor still felt sick to her stomach as Layne drove them closer to Jordan's neighborhood. "I never talked to Jordan about her suicide attempt after she got out of the hospital or out of rehab. She apologized for hurting me, but neither of us brought it up again."

"I can't believe you were able to keep it out of the press."

"My dad has a lot of money and a lot of influence." Taylor covered her eyes, silently praying everything would be fine.

Layne drove up to Jordan's gated house and entered the code Taylor gave him. He didn't want to deal with more of Jordan's bullshit, but he needed to be supportive of Taylor. As they pulled up in the driveway, they found Jordan's garage open with her car inside. Taylor jumped out and ran inside the house through the garage.

"Jordan?" she called. "Where are you? Are you alright?"

Layne followed her and started looking in all the downstairs rooms while Taylor bolted up the stairs, taking them two at a time. As Layne scanned the living room, he caught a glimpse through the patio doors of Jordan's hair blowing in the wind. "Hey, babe, I found her! She's on the patio!" He opened the door and approached the lounge chair where Jordan was conked out. "Hey, Jordan, you scared the hell out of your sister and Chase. What are you doing out here?"

She didn't move. "Jordan?" Layne walked closer and stepped over a broken wine glass on the concrete. A spilled bottle of pills and a puddle of vomit lay beside Jordan's head. Layne moved Jordan's hair out of her face and jumped back, knocking over a mostly-empty wine bottle and spilling its contents onto the chair. It was already too late for Jordan. Layne covered his mouth and concentrated on breathing slowly, his quickening pulse drowning out all other sounds. Taylor would blame herself. The whole situation was as bad as it could get, and there was nothing Layne could do to make it better for Taylor.

"Jordan, what the hell!" Taylor yelled as she stomped through the door.

"Taylor, stop!" Layne shouted, holding his hand out. "Stay there!"

Taylor stopped and took a step back. Her voice cracked when she spoke. "Layne, what's going on?"

Layne checked for a pulse on Jordan's wrist with no luck and tried again on her neck with the same results. He sighed and looked at Taylor, who was crying. Stepping over the broken glass, Layne caught Taylor as she collapsed. He fought back tears as he held her and tried to silence her sobbing long enough to call for help. Layne managed to stay calm long enough to answer the dispatcher's questions and provide the address.

"Maybe it's not too late," Taylor said as she tried to stand up. "This has happened before."

Layne dragged Taylor into the living room by her wrists with her fighting him the whole way. "Stop it! You're going to hurt yourself."

"Let me go!"

Layne picked up Taylor and put her the couch, pinning her legs down. "We can't contaminate the scene any more than I already have," he said.

"I have to try to save her," Taylor said through her sobs. "Please help me."

"Taylor, stop." Layne grabbed Taylor's head and held it so he could see her eyes.

"I can't."

"Baby, look at me. She's already gone. There's no pulse, and her body is already stiff. She's been dead for hours."

"You're sure?"

"I'm sure," he said. "There's nothing we can do. I'm so sorry, baby." He pulled Taylor back into his arms and held her while she cried. He soon reaffirmed that her body's response to severe emotional trauma was vomiting. Layne took care of Taylor and waited for the police to arrive.

An officer took Layne into the kitchen to question him after several other officers had secured the scene.

"Mr. Stallings, did you touch the body or move it in any way?" the officer asked.

"Yes, sir," Layne said. "I moved her hair, and I touched her wrist and neck to check for a pulse."

"And what time was that?"

"Seconds before I called 911."

"Did you touch anything else?"

Layne described everything that had happened from the moment he entered the house. He told the officer all about Jordan's suspected drug problems and past suicide attempt. The officer seemed surprised by Layne's story about Jordan trying to drug him and what she'd admitted doing to Taylor's ex-boyfriend.

The officer thanked Layne for his time and asked him to wait in the kitchen while another officer finished questioning Taylor. Layne wanted to stop the interrogation because Taylor was pale and trembling beneath the heavy throw blanket he'd wrapped around her earlier.

The voices around her were loud—yet muffled somehow—as Taylor watched the swarm of people invading her sister's house. Nausea crossed her stomach in waves even though it was empty. She pulled the blanket tighter around her shoulders while she answered the officer's questions about Jordan's suicide attempt when she was a teenager.

"Did you have reason to be concerned about her?" the officer asked.

"I was worried when I found out she didn't respond to Chase. She's always been hung up on him, so it was unusual for her not to talk to him. Not so much for her not to answer my calls. She knew I was still mad at her."

"Why?"

Taylor explained the situation involving her sister and their estrangement, sparing no details.

"She behaved erratically?" The officer made some notes in a small notebook.

"She always behaved erratically, but yeah, more than usual. It's my fault I didn't check my phone. I should have gotten here sooner!" Taylor started sobbing again. "I'm...I'm sorry." She stumbled down the hall to the bathroom. After some painful dry-retching, she collapsed on the floor as darkness surrounded her.

chapter 37

A t the hospital, Layne sat in the private waiting room alone, holding his phone and Taylor's in his hands. He knew the police were notifying Taylor's father but thought Taylor would need her real family when she woke up. He used her phone to call Willow.

"Hey, Taylor," Willow answered. "Happy New Year."

Everything about the whole morning hit Layne all at once, and he choked on his own voice, finally allowing himself to cry for a moment. "Willow…"

"Oh God, Layne? What's wrong? Is Taylor okay?"

He regained his composure long enough to tell Willow what had happened and where he was.

Finding Taylor collapsed on the bathroom floor had scared the hell out of him. He vaguely recalled carrying her out to the paramedics before they whisked her away to the hospital due to Taylor's inability to regain consciousness.

Layne called his sister next and told her what was going on since he and Taylor had planned to eat dinner at Christina's house later that evening. It was supposed to have been a big evening for Taylor, but only Layne knew why.

Christina arrived at the hospital soon and joined Layne in the waiting room, holding his hands. No one would tell them anything since they weren't family members. After Willow and Mr. Cosney arrived, they all sat in silence, waiting for news about Taylor. An hour after their arrival, a hospital volunteer brought into the room a tall dark-haired man who had been crying.

"Just wait here, Mr. Hoffman, and I'll get the doctor to come talk to you," the volunteer said.

"Please hurry," Mr. Hoffman said. "I need to make some calls and arrange funeral services."

Layne stood before Mr. Hoffman could sit. "Mr. Hoffman," he said. "Have they told you anything about Taylor?"

Taken aback, Mr. Hoffman remained standing. "Who are you?" he asked. "How do you know Taylor? Did you know Jordan too?"

Layne stood only inches from his face. "I'm Taylor's boyfriend, something you'd know if you actually wanted to be part of her life."

"Layne..." Christina said.

"Shut up, Chris!" Layne snapped before turning back to Mr. Hoffman. "You only called her a couple of times last year, the day her mother died, and couldn't even remember her birthday. Do you know how much it hurt her? You never return her calls, and I know she's called you at least once a month to check in! You've been a lousy father, and now you show up here like you give a shit."

"I know, I'm not...I get so busy—" Mr. Hoffman began.

"Save it!" Layne yelled. "You've had your head so far up your ass chasing other musical talent or lack of it, you couldn't see what was right in front of you with Taylor the whole fucking time!"

Mr. Cosney stood up and got between them, using his strong arms to push Layne away. "Back off, son," he said. "The man just lost his daughter, and his other one is in the hospital. Cut him some slack."

"Slack? He's going to end up losing both if he doesn't start caring about Taylor. We're her family." Layne wrestled out of Mr. Cosney's grip and left the room, bumping Mr. Hoffman's shoulder as he left.

Layne stood outside the hospital, pacing near the side wall. His first impulse was to punch the bricks. He hesitated, bracing for the pain, but stopped when Christina grabbed his arm.

"You really showed your ass in there, little brother," she said.

Layne didn't turn around. "Give me a minute," he said, clearing his throat and wiping his face. He didn't want to look like a blubbering fool, crying and yelling at everyone.

Christina walked in front of Layne and looked up at him. "She's going to be okay," she said. "Are you? And don't give me some bullshit answer Mom and Dad would expect out of you."

Layne shook his head and tried to keep from falling apart but couldn't hold everything inside any longer when his sister forced him into a hug and pulled his head to her shoulder. Letting go and just losing it for a moment under the safety of his sister's watch allowed Layne to get his emotions under control quickly. "I can't lose her, Chris," he said. "We just moved into my house together. This could break her. I. Can't. Lose. Her. She's everything to me. God, I'm such a selfish asshole. This isn't about me. She just lost her sister and her mom before that…"

"Layne, we all know how much you love her."

It was more than that, and Layne had to tell someone, or he might shatter under the pressure. "I bought a ring."

"What?" Christina's mouth gaped open. "An engagement ring? When?"

Layne nodded. "A while ago. I've been too nervous to ask. I was planning to ask her tonight. You know, ask her to be part of our family forever, at dinner with all of you."

"And you will ask—when her grief is less consuming. Everything you've told me about her—she's strong. Come back inside. The doctor's in there."

"They won't tell me anything. You have to be family."

"Taylor's dad told them we're all family and sent me to find you. Come on, let's go check on my future sister-in-law."

When Layne went back into the room with his sister, the doctor told them Taylor was sedated and stable but would be kept overnight for observation and treated for dehydration. Only one family member would be allowed to sit with her until she woke up. The doctor asked Mr. Hoffman if he wanted to sit with Taylor.

"He's my daughter's fiancé," Mr. Hoffman said, pointing to Layne. "Take him to sit with her. I have arrangements and paperwork to deal with for my other daughter."

Layne was surprised by the unexpected lie and thanked Taylor's father.

"Please send for me when she wakes up," Mr. Hoffman said as he grabbed Layne's shoulder.

"I will," Layne said.

When Taylor woke up, her whole body ached, and she opened her eyes to a sterile hospital room. She tried to sit up and scratched at the itchy tape holding down her IV.

Layne jumped up from the chair beside her bed. "Oh, Taylor, you scared me," he said as he kissed her forehead.

Taylor leaned against him. "I feel like I've been hit by a truck," she said. "What happened?"

"You collapsed. The doctor said you were in shock and dehydrated. You've been asleep for a few hours. Willow and Mr. Cosney are here too. I called them. And Christina's here. And your dad."

"My dad's here?"

"I promised I would get him when you woke up."

Taylor closed her eyes. She hadn't seen her father in almost a year and had only spoken with him once on the phone since moving out of his house. She'd given up calling him altogether after leaving a message with her change of address, not that he would visit her. What did he expect now after so much time?

Her father appeared sullen as he stepped into Taylor's room. He hugged her, which felt more awkward than anyone else's touch. "How are you holding up?" he asked, his eyes bloodshot and glassy. "It's just us now."

But it wasn't just them, not anymore. Taylor had a whole family now that didn't include him at all. Layne and his family, Willow and hers, Kayla and Marcus Cosney—they were her true family. Miles Hoffman was a stranger who happened to share blood but lacked a bond. "Dad, are you going to be okay?"

"I can't believe she did it," he said. "I tried to give you both everything, and she just threw it all away."

Of course, Jordan had inherited selfishness from their father. "Dad, this isn't about you. It was about her. And you know what? It's about me too. I've had to deal with her all these years, and you just threw money at problems instead of facing them. It wasn't my responsibility."

The pain in her father's voice seemed genuine. "Taylor, I know you hate me. Jordan did too. I've been a lousy father, but I do love you. Just tell me what you need. I'll do anything. You're all I have left."

Taylor looked past her father at Layne standing in the doorway. He was already a bigger influence in her life than her father had ever been. "Dad, just stop," she pleaded. "Stop being a lousy father and actually care about me, and we'll be fine. I don't want your money or your PR connections; I just want you to be my dad and do normal things like meet my boyfriend. Layne, come officially meet my dad."

"We've met," Mr. Hoffman said. "In the waiting room. I got the impression he cares about you very much."

Layne shook his hand. "Mr. Hoffman," he said. "I'm sorry for the way I spoke to you earlier."

"You can call me Miles. You were upset. It's understandable. And you were right about everything you said. Thank you for taking care of my little girl. She's precious to me."

"That's one thing we agree on, Miles," Layne said. He turned to Taylor. "Are you up for Willow coming in to see you? She's wearing a hole in the floor out there."

"Sure," Taylor said.

Willow gave a half-hearted smile and hugged Taylor. "Sweetheart, I am so sorry," she said. "Kayla wanted to be here, too, but she's stuck at the hospital back home."

"It's alright," Taylor said. "I understand."

"I don't know what to say."

"There's nothing else to say."

"How are you feeling?"

"Exhausted. Numb, I guess. She *is* gone, right? Layne wouldn't let me see her."

Willow nodded. "He was trying to protect you. He said the coroner pronounced her on the scene after you passed out. They brought her to the morgue here if you want to see her. Your dad said they'll do an autopsy."

A knot formed in Taylor's stomach again. "I think I need to. I didn't see my mom, and I probably should have."

"Don't be mad at Layne. He cried when he told me what happened. He said you needed me. That you needed your family and asked me to come here. He loves you so much, Taylor."

"I'm not mad at him." Taylor never doubted Layne truly loved her from the moment he'd spoken the words. "Hey, what did he say to my dad? Were you there?"

Willow pressed her lips together, and Taylor urged her to speak. "Layne called him out on being a douchebag for not remembering your birthday and being a shitty father in general. Something along the lines of him spending too much time recruiting other talent and not seeing what was right in front of him."

"Layne said all that?"

"Well, I might have embellished a bit, but Layne got in his face and used some language."

"What did my dad say?"

"He didn't say much at all except acknowledge that he knows how talented you are. That's when Marcus pulled Layne away and told him to back off because the man had just lost his daughter."

"Mr. Cosney got involved?"

"Yeah," Willow said. "Then Layne said your dad should pay attention to the daughter he has left before he loses her too. After that, Layne went outside to cool off."

Taylor lay back in bed and covered her face with her arms. "Everything's all messed up," she said. "I told my dad we'd be okay, but how can I fix things with him when I'm not sure he'll ever change?"

"Things are going to be fine with him, but you can't expect him to change his whole relationship with you overnight. But, you should know, your dad's the reason Layne was back here with you when you woke up. He told the doctor you and Layne were engaged so he'd be considered family."

"I find it hard to believe Dad would care enough to do that."

"I think he figured Layne would be the person you'd want to see most when you woke up. We told him about you and Layne while we were in the waiting room. I showed him the videos I took of your original songs at the Mocking Bird. He was impressed. I think it helped distract him some from…"

"I can't believe she's gone."

"I can't imagine what you must be feeling right now."

"I'm not even sure. The last few days have been…I don't even know. Layne and I are just getting settled in his house. I think it will be good to hide out and be away from the Mocking Bird and all the press."

Willow wiped away a tear and squeezed Taylor's hand. "I miss you, girl," she said. "The place isn't the same without you."

Taylor brought Willow's hand to her lips, kissing the back of it. "I'm not gone, Willow," she said. "You're family. You're my chosen sister."

Later that evening, a hospital volunteer took Taylor in a wheelchair to the hospital morgue. The morgue attendant had Jordan's body out and draped with a sheet.

"Would you mind leaving me alone for a moment?" Taylor asked the attendant. After the attendant had left, Taylor looked down at her sister's body. Jordan's hair was messy, and her skin had taken on an ashen tone, but she appeared peaceful. Taylor tried to figure out how she ever lived with her and how she would live without her. As she looked at Jordan, Taylor felt the full weight of her loss and then felt it drift away like an unwelcome visitor.

Layne was sitting in a convertible recliner when Taylor returned to her room. He watched the nurse help Taylor back into bed and rehang her IV bag. "Apparently, I can stay the night," he said after the nurse had left the room. "That is, if you want me to. I don't want to leave you here alone."

Taylor gave a weak smile as though her whole face might shatter under the weight of it. "Layne, please hold me," she said, barely speaking above a whisper. She was pale, fragile, and broken, yet stronger than Layne had ever seen her.

"I don't want to hurt you."

"You won't. I'll turn away so you won't pinch the tubes, and it'll be fine. Please?"

Layne carefully lowered the side of the hospital bed and crawled in with Taylor, wrapping his arm around her. She nuzzled her back into him and took his hand in hers.

"You did everything right today, and I love you so much," she said before falling asleep.

Layne lay awake for hours listening to Taylor's gentle breathing while he watched the glow of the heart monitor in the otherwise darkened room. She had been through so much, and it still hadn't diminished her beauty. He caressed her left ring finger, imagining what the rose-engraved ring would look like on her delicate hand. Maybe seven months together was too soon to ask Taylor to marry him, especially now with the loss of her sister. He could postpone asking until the timing felt right. Forever with Taylor was worth the wait. He had never been so sure of a decision in his entire life. Layne buried his nose in Taylor's hair and fell asleep dreaming of their future together.

chapter 38

Saturday, January 7, 2017

The rest of the week after Jordan's death passed by in a blur for Taylor. She and her dad awaited the results of the autopsy before having Jordan's body cremated. Based on the text message Jordan had sent Taylor and Chase, her death from a drug overdose was officially ruled a suicide. Taylor wondered if Jordan had truly meant to kill herself. The tabloids and more respectable magazines ran similar headlines about Jordan's tragic death, and she was more famous than ever.

Taylor had helped plan a private memorial service for Jordan's closest friends. During the service, the whole thing felt phony, especially the tears from the talented actors and actresses. Blake had shown up with his new girlfriend, who cried more than he did. Taylor couldn't cry at all; she'd exhausted her tears throughout the previous week. She sat in the front row, silent, with Layne on one side and her dad on the other.

Having declined her father's request for her to sing at Jordan's memorial, Taylor watched as Chase and Layne went to the front of the small chapel. Chase stood at the microphone reserved for remarks and signaled to Layne when he was ready to sing. Layne strummed the opening notes to "Fire and Rain" on his guitar, and Chase managed to get through the first verse and chorus before his voice cracked through his tears, leaving him unable to sing. Layne took over at the microphone and sang until Chase had regained his composure to sing the last verse.

Taylor's heart broke for Chase. His tears and her father's tears were the only ones that seemed sincere during the entire service. Mr. Hoffman remained seated with Taylor as the guests filed past

Jordan's photo and urn at the front of the chapel. He gripped Taylor's hand and sighed.

Layne led Chase outside the chapel into the hallway, careful to stay away from the windows to avoid the paparazzi gathered outside. "Will you be okay, man?" he asked. "Have you talked to your sponsor?"

"I've talked to him every day since Jordan died," Chase said. "Thanks for saving me in there. I'm out of practice and lost it for a minute."

"No one cared about that."

"It was Jordan's favorite song we covered with Backdraft. I used to sing it to her all the time."

"Chase, I'm sorry. I know you loved her."

"There was a time when I thought I would spend the rest of my life with her. I know she had her problems and could be mean, but she was different with me. I loved her. If she could have given all this up—the fame—we probably could've had a great life together. I can't come back here, man, it'll kill me. How do you do it?"

"It's about the music, not the fame. I guess that's the way it should be. It's just different with Taylor. She's not into the stuff Jordan was. She doesn't drink, and she's never touched drugs. She never will. I won't touch them, and I don't want you ever touching that shit again, either."

"I won't," Chase said. "It's a struggle every day, but I haven't forgotten you guys saved my life. I don't take it for granted, especially now, since I'm going to be a dad."

"Congratulations," Layne said. "I didn't know you were seeing someone."

Chase leaned against the wall. "Well, you wouldn't, Brandon. *Layne.* I can't even remember the last time we talked before all this."

Layne acknowledged he'd been a shitty friend. "I know I haven't been good about keeping in touch. It's not because I don't care. I just didn't know what to say to you, man. It scared the hell out of me when I found you that night. You and the other guys are like brothers to me."

"I've kept my relationship quiet. We've been together a year. Sara wants to stay out of the spotlight and run our ranch. We already planned to get married in the fall. The baby wasn't planned so soon, but we're happy about it. We just found out we're having a boy."

"Well, I'm really happy for you. I promise I'll do better about keeping in touch."

"Maybe you and Taylor can come visit us at the ranch for the wedding. That just leaves you and Noah now that Kyle's married, and I'm engaged. I seriously thought it'd be you first—to get married."

"Yeah, Noah said the same thing. I'm not in a hurry to beat you guys to the altar. I'm good where I am with Taylor."

"Is she the one, though, man?"

Layne nodded. "All this is making me think a lot about how we shouldn't wait too long to start forever. I think I knew from the start it was forever with her. I measured her finger while she was sleeping right before we moved in together. I bought a ring and had it engraved with something special. I'll wait awhile to ask her now with everything that's happened, but I'd planned to New Year's Day."

"Who's the guy with her?" Chase pointed to Taylor, who was talking to Michael outside the chapel door.

Layne looked over at them. "Her ex from high school."

Taylor walked outside with Michael to say goodbye to him privately. Layne was speaking with Chase farther down the hallway, but they were far enough away she still had privacy. "Thank you for coming," she said. "I appreciate it."

"I'm so sorry, Taylor, for everything," Michael said. He looked down at the floor and touched Taylor's shoulder. "I have to tell you something, and I know now's not the best time, but the guilt…"

"Guilt? What are you talking about?"

He sighed. "The night she died, I sent her a message calling her a liar and told her to tell the truth. I was just so mad about what she'd done to me and how she'd destroyed our relationship. I know she attempted suicide when you were still in high school. I was there that night."

"What?" Had he failed to get help for Jordan? Had he seen her make the attempt?

"I saw you drunk at the party. When your friend took you home, I followed her to make sure you got there safely. I waited outside trying to get the courage to try one more time to get you to forgive me. I saw the paramedics take Jordan away in an ambulance. She attempted suicide, not you."

"I didn't know you were there."

"I might have pushed Jordan over the edge with my comment this time," he said. "Taylor, I never meant for anyone to get hurt."

"Michael…" Taylor looked at the broken, vulnerable man in front of her. He looked exactly like the boy she'd fallen in love with as a teenager, but the years that had passed since then made him a stranger—a stranger she still felt the need to comfort. "Jordan's death isn't your fault."

"Can you ever forgive me for hurting you?"

"I already have."

"Can we ever be friends again?" Michael asked. Tears formed in his eyes again as Taylor shook her head. "Why not?"

"Because you told me you're still in love with me, Michael. It brings up too many feelings from the past, all the pain I've tried so hard to leave behind. I'm sorry I have to be selfish, but I don't think I can heal from this if I still see you and talk to you. It's not fair, but the past is the past for a reason."

Michael wiped his eyes. "You're not selfish," he said. "I get it, and you're right. It's painful for me, too, and us being friends would probably make it worse."

"You have to see that we would never have worked out because we want different things. Things we didn't consider when we were too young and talked about forever. It doesn't mean I didn't love you. Part of me always will. I know you can move on and give someone else your whole heart even if it has to be stitched together like mine. It'll be worth it, I promise, but you have to let me go."

He nodded. "So maybe we were meant to be each other's first love but not the last."

"Yes." A tear trickled from the corner of Taylor's eye, and she tasted the salt as it rolled past her lips. She hugged Michael as hard as she could before letting go. "I love you, Michael. I always will, and I truly wish you all the happiness in the world. Goodbye."

Michael took one last look at her and walked away, wiping tears from his face as he left without uttering another word, taking with him the closure he needed. Taylor closed her eyes and drew her remaining tears inward, reveling in the relief she felt as her first love walked away.

Layne watched Taylor hug Michael and turned back to Chase.

"Does it bother you she still talks to her ex?" Chase asked. "And that she hugs him?"

"It does a little, but I trust her. They have a lot of history."

"Don't wait too long to tell her you want forever. Life's too damn short."

Layne hugged Chase and watched him walk away. When he turned around, Taylor was walking toward him. She bit her lip and walked into his outstretched arms.

"Will you please take me home?" she asked through her tears.

"You're done here?"

"It's over. There's nothing left for me to do and no one else I want to see but you."

Layne cooked dinner while Taylor sat at the bar. He watched her as she scrolled through comments on her phone. She paused to read some and skipped past others.

"Some people are so mean," she said. "And others are wonderful."

"You still looking at Jordan's pages?"

Taylor put her hair into a bun with the hair tie from her wrist and continued staring at her phone. "Yeah. I should just let it go and delete the accounts. Her last publicist gave me all the passwords."

"I can see how it would be hard to let go, like with Michael."

She looked up. "I told him goodbye today and asked him not to contact me again."

Layne tensed up. *I'm such an asshole,* he thought. "You didn't have to do that over me being jealous."

Taylor put down her phone and walked up behind Layne. She wrapped her arms around his waist and leaned her head against his back. "It's what's best for him and me. I want him to move on.

He reminds me too much of all the shit I need to leave behind to be happy. I can't be his friend, not really."

Layne turned to face her. "I understand. We all have to seal off some painful parts of our past so they don't poison us for the future. It's the same reason why Amanda and I couldn't be friends."

"Are you sure you want to be with me? You're putting up with so much."

"I've never been more sure of anything." He pulled the food off the stove and led Taylor to the couch. "I'm not putting up with anything. I love you." He cupped her face in his hands. "You're allowed to feel however you need to. I just hate to see you hurting when I can't do anything to help."

"You are helping, just being here." She hugged Layne.

It was the first night since Jordan's death that Taylor seemed like herself again and even more so while lying in Layne's arms after they had finished dinner and made love. He closed his eyes and enjoyed the warmth of Taylor's body against his as they fell asleep.

Jordan's voice woke Taylor from a deep sleep. "I can tell you're really broken up about my death," she said. "My whore sister, naked in bed with her boyfriend on the night of my memorial."

Taylor opened her eyes to find Jordan sitting on the side of the bed, decked out in red and glowing from within. Jordan wrapped her hands around Layne's throat. "No!" Taylor screamed, grabbing her arms. "Leave him alone!"

"Maybe it's you I need." Jordan released Layne and grabbed Taylor's throat. "Now he'll really see you're crazy."

Desperate for air, Taylor closed her eyes and struggled to free herself from Jordan's grasp. The pressure on her throat dissipated, and her eyes popped open as hands grabbed her face. The lamp beside the bed was on, and she was now looking into Layne's panic-stricken eyes. She told Layne about her nightmare.

"Baby," Layne said as he held Taylor. "It's okay. You're safe."

But she wasn't safe. Even death couldn't stop Jordan from hurting her. "You deserve someone who isn't so damaged. Someone so much better than me who's not so fucked-up." She tried to pull away from Layne's grip, but he wouldn't let go.

"Stop it. Don't say shit like that. There's no one else for me and no one better." Layne's eyes filled with tears as he pressed his forehead against hers. "You're it for me. I want every part of you, even all the scary ones. I can't promise my own shit won't make things difficult, too, but I can promise I'll never stop loving you. Just let me do that. Please…just let me love you."

"You're sure you don't want to run away?" She started crying at the thought of him leaving.

Layne wiped his eyes and Taylor's cheeks. "You're making me all weepy," he said. "I'll never go away unless you want to end things. I love you. We're going to get help for you to make things better, okay?"

Taylor nodded and kissed Layne. "I love you so much it scares me," she said, closing her eyes.

"Losing you is the only thing that scares me. What I feel for you, Taylor, is the forever kind of love."

"I didn't think I could believe in forever…but you're making me feel like it's possible." She kissed the remaining tears off Layne's face and lay awake in his arms until morning.

chapter 39

Wednesday, February 1, 2017

A petite woman in her early 40s, Dr. Clearaby sat with a tablet computer and a stylus poised in her hand. She'd seen Taylor at the hospital the evening of Jordan's death and suggested therapy to help with her grief. "Who are you, Taylor?" she asked.

"I'm not sure how to answer."

"As your therapist, I will ask you a lot of questions. Humor me."

Taylor had asked herself so many times, but she knew the most obvious answer probably wasn't what the therapist wanted. "Growing up I was always Jordan's sister—the Jordan Hoffman. It was pretty much the only identity I had then. I was an actress, but I wanted to be a singer—a songwriter, a musician. I took care of my mother, like a babysitter, because she was an alcoholic and drug addict. Then I was Michael's girlfriend, and then I wasn't anymore. I moved in with my dad and tried to be a good daughter, but I didn't feel close to him. Next, I was an online college student. That's when I started using the last name 'Lee' so no one would know me. I did some voice-over work for Jordan using the same name, so I got to be a singer again but without any recognition until now. After college, I became a bartender at the Mocking Bird and started singing karaoke and writing my own songs. I became Willow's friend and Layne's girlfriend—though I put up a fight about that because I was scared."

As she finished her first round of notes, the therapist looked up. "Why are you here?"

"I can't sleep, and I'm having nightmares when I try."

"How long have you been experiencing the nightmares?"

"For the last month or so."

"Why do you think you're having nightmares?"

Taylor laughed. "Dr. Clearaby, I'm paying you to help me figure it out."

"You're paying me for therapy. In my initial evaluation of you in the hospital, I didn't believe you had a mental illness. I still don't. In my professional opinion, your episode was an extreme reaction to grief and unresolved trauma from your childhood. My plan for our sessions is to help you analyze your feelings and find healthy ways to deal with your grief and past trauma. You'll ask yourself difficult questions and delve deep to find the answers you seek. Are you prepared to do that during the next several weeks?"

Taylor nodded and locked her hands together. "I want you to fix me."

"I'll help you fix yourself. Why are you here?"

"Because I can't seem to let Jordan go. She's still hurting me, even though she's dead."

"Tell me about Jordan. What was it like to be Jordan's sister?"

Taylor told her therapist all about her problems with Jordan, including the drugs, the rape of Michael, and the attempted drugging of Layne.

"Why do you think Jordan did that?"

"To hurt me."

"Why?"

"Jealousy, I guess. A lot of people started saying I was more talented than her. It upset her, and she wanted to get back at me."

Dr. Clearaby put down her tablet. "I'll ask again. Why do you think Jordan raped your boyfriend? Was it really just to hurt you?"

"Maybe."

"What does jealousy mean?"

"Being envious of what someone else has...holy shit...she was trying to have what I had. She tried to sing, too, but couldn't..."

"I am going to give a list of characteristics. Tell me which ones were typical of Jordan. Lacking empathy."

"Yes."

"Manipulative."

"Yes."

"Arrogant."

"Yes."

"Sense of entitlement."

"God, yes."

"Need for constant admiration. Thoughts of superiority. Willingness to exploit others for personal gain."

"Yes, all of those. What does it mean?"

"Those are characteristics and traits of someone with Narcissistic Personality Disorder, which generally manifests in adolescence. That paired with your sister's drug abuse…"

"She was fucked-up."

"Well, for lack of better terms—in less colorful language— yes."

"I'm sorry…for the language."

"There's not much I haven't heard," Dr. Clearaby said. "You're safe here, Taylor. Use whatever language you need to express yourself, profane or not."

They spent the rest of the session discussing the many ways Jordan's personality fit with the disorder the doctor suspected, and Taylor left with homework. She was to make a list of the ways— both healthy and unhealthy—she had dealt with the abuse from Jordan in the past. Taylor left the session feeling hopeful. Having a name for what might have contributed to Jordan's behavior made her think about everything differently.

Layne stood up as Taylor walked into the waiting room. "You okay, babe?" he asked. "Do you like the doctor?"

"I do. I actually feel a little better. She gave me a lot of things to think about."

"Good." Layne kissed her on the temple and grabbed her hand to walk her out.

The next session dealt with Taylor's homework. She told Dr. Clearaby about her avoidance of Jordan that began after the breakup with Michael. With tears in her eyes, Taylor recounted every detail she could remember about the evening Jordan attempted suicide when they were teens. Telling her therapist about the emotions she'd felt that night made Taylor calmer through the rest of their session.

"So, you dealt with the abuse by staying out of her way, then you tried drinking. What happened with Jordan after her suicide attempt?"

"My father sent her to rehab and used his money to make everything go away. She apologized to me after she got out and told me the drugs were responsible for everything she'd done."

"Did you believe her?"

"I wanted to. But no, I didn't believe her. She was hateful to me long before the drugs. During the sitcom, she was upset when the producers wouldn't let her sing with me. They made her audition and told her to stick with acting and dancing because she couldn't carry a tune. She blamed me for her inability to sing."

"But you tried to forgive her?"

"I said I did, but I felt indifferent about the whole thing. After rehab, she didn't live with me. I changed my appearance to not look like Jordan anymore. I got some tattoos to make myself feel better and some piercings. I earned a degree online. I hung out at dance clubs and started hooking up with some guys—a lot of guys."

"You were promiscuous?" Dr. Clearaby pressed her stylus against her pursed lips.

Taylor looked down at her hands and nodded.

"I'm not asking to chastise you. I am asking you to own it. Own your past so you can move on."

"Yes," Taylor said. "I was slutty. I hooked up with different guys several times while I was in college and then progressed to a few times a week for a couple of months after I moved into my apartment above the bar. Drunk guys were the easiest to deal with."

Dr. Clearaby stared at Taylor. "Why did you do it?"

Taylor leaned her forehead against her hands. "I was trying to get over Michael. I know now he and I weren't meant to be together. I missed him but didn't want to risk getting my heart broken again by taking him back or trying a relationship with someone else. I just shut out the possibility of love and had sex instead. We'd have sex, then I'd kick the guy out and not see him again."

"How did that make you feel?"

"I don't know."

"Yes, you do know. When you were having sex with those different men, how did you feel?"

Taylor stretched out in the chaise lounge and felt cliché doing so. To benefit from therapy and get her money's worth, she'd have to spill her darkest, scariest secrets. "In control, I guess. No one could hurt me if I had no expectations. It was fun at first."

"Fun *at first*. What changed?"

"It stopped feeling good. Maybe it never did. Afterward, I felt lonely, but I still didn't think I could handle a relationship. Then a guy hit me." Taylor told the doctor everything about it, how scared she had been, and what Willow had said to her. Talking to the doctor was the first time she cried about the whole experience.

Even the pain of having been hit that night hadn't caused any tears. She was too shocked because she'd never thought about the possibility of one of the guys hurting her physically.

"How did your friend's insights help change your perspective?" Dr. Clearaby asked.

Taylor sighed. "She was right. I was using sex as a distraction from the pain of everything. Like a drug. An addiction. It wasn't healthy, but it was better than the actual drugs Jordan did. She stayed sober for a couple of years. Still a diva and a bitch, but sober during the first two *Awake* movies. I started talking to her again when she begged me to help her do the voice-over work so she wouldn't get fired. Part of me wanted to repair our relationship, but another part just wanted the money to pay for college so I wouldn't have to ask my dad."

"What did Jordan mean to you, Taylor?"

Taylor thought about her answer for a moment. "My sister is a song I can't get out of my head. A song I've only heard once and can't remember the words. The melody haunts me because I'll never hear it again or learn the words. I'm afraid the song will always be there in the background, like an unwanted soundtrack for the rest of my life."

"You are a true poet, Taylor," Dr. Clearaby said, smiling as she closed the cover on her tablet. "And I'm confident you can heal and have a new soundtrack for the rest of your life."

During another session, Taylor talked about Layne.

"Why did you invite him to your apartment?" Dr. Clearaby asked. "Did you plan to have sex with him that evening as you had with the other men?"

"I'd be lying if I said I wasn't thinking about hooking up with him. He was attractive and had just sung one of my favorite songs on the karaoke stage. We talked for hours and did end up having sex. Afterward, I felt cold and shaky, and then I kicked him out."

"You panicked?"

"I guess so…"

"Why?"

"I was afraid he'd hurt me."

"Did he hurt you?"

"No, but I knew he could," Taylor said. "Because I felt something, something more than physical. Something I hadn't felt since Michael, only stronger. I didn't want to feel anything."

"You must have wanted to feel something even if it was only physical. And you must have known you couldn't avoid Layne completely since he was your new neighbor, right?"

"So, you're saying part of me knew I'd see him again, and it could be more than just a one-time thing?"

"Is that what I'm saying?

Taylor nodded, her head aching with thoughts Dr. Clearaby had uncovered.

"Taylor, did you do any reflection or self-analysis during the lapse between the last guy and Layne?" Dr. Clearaby pressed her stylus against her lips, a habit Taylor had observed during their sessions.

"That guy hitting me shook me up. I started thinking about what it would mean to stop being casual. I didn't think I could fall in love again or have a serious boyfriend. I worried about being lonely, but I was already lonely."

"Are you in love with Layne?"

"Yes."

"Do you think he is in love with you?"

"Yes. He tells me all the time. He encourages me and respects me. He supports my dreams and builds me up when I'm feeling self-conscious. He never treats me like I'm his property."

"You would classify it as a healthy relationship?"

"Yes. We moved in together two months ago. It made sense."

"In what way?"

"I knew it was a big step since we'd only been together six months at the time, but we already spent every night together in one of our apartments. We can record our music at the house since it has a studio and not disturb our neighbors like we would in the apartments."

"Then it sounds like part of your life is already getting better since you're confident about your decision to move."

"Tell me about your relationship with your parents," Dr. Clearaby asked at another session.

During Taylor's story, Dr. Clearaby listened intently and took notes on her tablet, starring a few points as Taylor went on to talk about her mother's drug abuse and stroke.

"So, the roles reversed for you when your mother was taking drugs—you cared for her when she should have been caring for you, is that correct?"

"Yes," Taylor said. "I had to. Jordan had her own issues, and Dad was with his new girlfriend. Dad let me live with him after Mom's stroke, but I still didn't feel like I could talk to him."

"Taylor, do you blame yourself for your mother's stroke?"

Taylor nodded. "Everything rational tells me I shouldn't, but I do. I should have done something. I should have stopped being afraid of Jordan and called the police or something to get out of that place. I should have made Dad listen to me and get help for Mom, but I didn't."

"You mentioned in another session you thought Jordan might have done something to your mother at the rehab center because of something she said while she was drunk. Do you blame Jordan for your mother's death?"

"Some, I guess. But, really, Mom had the type of personality that if she hadn't gotten the drugs from Jordan, she would have found her own connections. Jordan was at the rehab center the night of the fatal stroke. She'd bitched for months about the cost of Mom's care. We were each paying half, but I had the final say since I was power of attorney upon turning twenty-one. It was something Dad arranged with the courts while Jordan was in rehab, and he'd paid for everything up until then.

"It was a lot to deal with—too much—but she was my mother, and I loved her. I think what I feel most guilty about is the relief I felt when Mom finally died. It felt like the longest death in history. It wasn't about the money as much as it was the exhaustion of seeing no progress and wondering how much longer she would linger there, not dead but not alive. I learned Jordan had financial problems at the time she died. If I had known, I would have covered the whole cost of Mom's care."

"Taylor, you have a lot more insight into your feelings than you think," Dr. Clearaby said. "Before our next session, I want you to work on forgiveness. Start with forgiving yourself, and then we can work on forgiving the other people who've hurt you."

Dr. Clearaby dismissed Taylor from therapy after almost four months of weekly sessions. "Taylor, you have made remarkable progress since I met you. You now have the insight and self-awareness to move forward and work on being happy—for yourself. You also have positive coping skills to deal with your guilt over the deaths of your mother and your sister."

"But what about our discussion last week about me legally changing my last name?" Taylor asked. "Do you still think it's a good step to take in my journey to happiness?"

"Yes, I do. If it's the only thing holding you back, then, by all means, change your name. But keep in mind, changing your name won't change who you've become. It's something to help in the journey you've already started to move forward to the next great things in your life, which you've identified as songwriting, releasing an album, and continuing your relationship with Layne."

Taylor stood and shook her doctor's hand. "Thank you, Dr. Clearaby."

As she closed the door to Dr. Clearaby's office for the last time, Taylor thought of it as closing the door on her painful past. She chose happiness. She chose to leave her guilt behind that door.

chapter 40

Saturday, May 27, 2017

In her scarlet bridesmaid dress, Taylor stood beside Willow and Kayla while they recited their vows in a park full of their friends and families. They had picked "I Choose You" for their wedding song. When Willow had asked Taylor to sing it during the ceremony, she happily agreed. She had never seen two people more in love with each other or more committed to uniting their families. Taylor scanned the crowd and found Layne. He looked up and smiled at her. *Well, maybe there is one other couple,* she thought. She could imagine marrying Layne someday. He was the most beautiful person she had ever met. Her soulmate—a realization both comforting and exhilarating.

Later, as they danced during the reception, Layne held Taylor close and tried to overcome his nerves, certain she could feel him trembling. He'd checked his jacket pocket at least a half-dozen times. While holding the ring box in his hands during the ceremony, he'd imagined sending positive energy into the small gold band. The week before, during a secret phone call, Layne had told Willow about his plans to propose soon, and she insisted her wedding reception would be the perfect place. How she'd managed to keep it secret from Taylor, Layne would never know.

"Can you imagine being happier than we are right now?" Layne asked Taylor as they finished their dance to Lifehouse's "You and Me." Willow and Kayla motioned to him from the head table to get on with it.

"No," Taylor said. "Almost everything feels perfect. The last step for me is to finish the paperwork to legally change my last name. What do you think?"

"I think it's a good idea to change your last name," Layne said. He fumbled with the ring box in his pocket as he led Taylor back to their table.

"Should I stick with Taylor Lee?"

Layne kissed her on the forehead. "I had another idea in mind," he said as he pulled out Taylor's chair for her and motioned for her to sit down.

"Like what?" she asked before she took a sip of her water.

"We'll figure something out." Layne sat down and placed the small velvet ring box in front of her. "I got you something."

Taylor held her breath for a moment and stared at Layne. "What's this?" she asked with a slight grin. "My birthday's not until tomorrow."

"It's not a birthday present. Open it."

Inside the box, a white gold ring engraved with a diamond-embellished rose rested on the green velvet lining. Taylor picked it up and looked at the engraving inside. "I'll love you always," she read.

"I had this made to show you that you were never a wilted rose, Taylor. I hope you like it."

"I love it," Taylor whispered, barely finding her voice. "It's beautiful."

Layne dropped to one knee beside Taylor and took her hands. Everyone around them went silent and stopped to watch. "I hope you'll consider the name Taylor Lee-Stallings."

Taylor gasped. "What are you saying?" she asked.

"Taylor, I adore you. I love you more than I ever have or ever will love anyone else, and I hope…" Layne took a deep breath and exhaled slowly, his pulse pounding in his ears. *Don't pass out. Don't mess this up.* "Taylor, will you marry me?" Every memory he had with her flashed through his mind in rapid succession as he waited, praying for her to answer the way he hoped.

After what felt like several minutes but was likely only a few notes of a song Layne could feel thumping in his chest, Taylor spoke in a soft melody while everyone in the room focused on them. "Yes. I will."

Epilogue

June 9, 2018

The studio audience roared with applause. "It's great to have you here with us, Taylor," the TV host said, once the thunderous noise settled down.

"Thank you," Taylor said, looking out at the audience. Her heart pounded, and her palms felt clammy.

"You've been on tour for the last three months promoting your new album. Are you glad to be home for a break?"

"Touring was amazing. The fans have been incredible and so supportive of the music. I am glad to be home to rest and start writing some new material."

"What was it like touring with your husband since you're both promoting solo albums?"

"Layne's been my biggest inspiration, watching him grow as an artist. We both have a love for music, so being there to support each other during the recording of the albums and the tour has been a wonderful way to spend more time together during our first year of marriage. Our first anniversary is next month."

"You sang duet covers during the tours," the host said. "Can fans expect to see original duets in the future from you and Layne?

"Absolutely. Layne's actually collaborating with some other artists now, so I'm anxious to see what they come up with."

"You've each had break-out internet hits with songs you performed at the Mocking Bird, but the song you debuted on tour has been tearing up the charts. Tell us a little about your latest single."

"I wrote 'With Love' after the death of my sister, actress Jordan Hoffman. It's not something I've spoken about much. My sister struggled with mental health issues and substance abuse for years. I saved her life when she attempted suicide at nineteen, and she went to rehab, but unfortunately, she couldn't overcome her problems and reverted back to abusing drugs before her death from an overdose."

"I'm so sorry for your loss."

"Thank you. It's been a long process to heal from the trauma of that experience. At first, I blamed myself for not getting to her in time to save her. She was a talented actress and a force to be reckoned with, and I admired her commitment to her career. We grew up together on the set of *The Spectacular Smiths,* which was recently syndicated, and I cherish the memories of that time in my life. Jordan had a lot of problems before she died, and our relationship was strained. None of us knew the depths of the demons she hid, but I loved her, and I'll always miss what could have been."

"Thank you," the host said. "Ladies and gentlemen, join us after the commercial break for Taylor Stallings performing her new single, 'With Love.'"

Taylor took the stage while the commercials aired. She quickly tuned her guitar and glanced at a text from Layne.

Layne: **Love you, baby. You're the classiest, most beautiful woman I know.**

Taylor: **I love you too. I couldn't have done any of this without you.**

Layne: **Not true. You're amazing all on your own.**

Taylor: **So are you.**

She smiled and waited for her cue to perform the song that was painful to write but therapeutic to share with the world.

She wouldn't give up the life
Or all of the lies
She couldn't give up her vice
And she paid the price

She didn't know what to do
She was so high over you

The lies left me jaded
And memories have faded
It's so complicated—with love
From the sister she hated

I could take all the blame
And hide from the shame
But the scars will remain
'Cause you only knew her name

She didn't think twice
Before she said goodbye
And she changed my life
The day she died

She realized too late
To let go of the hate

The lies left me jaded
And memories have faded
It's so complicated—with love
From the sister she hated

JORDAN'S SISTER

I could take all the blame
And hide from the shame
But the scars will remain
'Cause you only knew her name

I could take all the blame
And hide from the pain
But her scars will remain
'Cause you only knew her name
It was all just part of the game
The price she paid for fame

ABOUT THE AUTHOR:

Brandi Easterling Collins grew up in Arkansas where she still resides with her husband, two children, and two dogs. When she's not writing or reading, she enjoys spending time with her family, thrift store shopping, painting, drawing, and leisurely walks outside.

Jordan's Sister is her second novel. Her other novels are *Caroline's Lighthouse*, *What I Learned That Summer*, and *One Shot*.

For more information, about future publications, visit caniscareyou.com.